UNTIL
ALISON

A NOVEL

KATE RUSSO

G. P. PUTNAM'S SONS

NEW YORK

PUTNAM
— EST. 1838 —

G. P. PUTNAM'S SONS
Publishers Since 1838
1745 Broadway, New York, NY 10019
An imprint of Penguin Random House LLC
penguinrandomhouse.com

Book design by Kristin del Rosario

Library of Congress Cataloging-in-Publication Data

Names: Russo, Kate, 1982– author.
Title: Until Alison: a novel / Kate Russo.
Description: New York: G. P. Putnam's Sons, 2025.
Identifiers: LCCN 2024040184 (print) | LCCN 2024040185 (ebook) |
ISBN 9780593850688 (hardcover) | ISBN 9780593850701 (epub)
Subjects: LCGFT: Thrillers (Fiction) | Novels.
Classification: LCC PS3618.U7743 U58 2025 (print) |
LCC PS3618.U7743 (ebook) | DDC 813/.6—dc23/eng/20240927
LC record available at https://lccn.loc.gov/2024040184
LC ebook record available at https://lccn.loc.gov/2024040185

Printed in the United States of America
1st Printing

The authorized representative in the EU for product safety and compliance is
Penguin Random House Ireland, Morrison Chambers, 32 Nassau Street,
Dublin D02 YH68, Ireland, https://eu-contact.penguin.ie.

For my parents

UNTIL ALISON

1.

Nobody deserves anything. I can promise you that. Maybe you think you earned what you've got, but I can guarantee you someone else has worked just as hard for the same thing and they don't have it. They probably think they deserve better. And then there are those who've been served a real shit sandwich, wondering to themselves *What the fuck have I done to deserve this?* They don't deserve *that* either. Nobody gets get what they deserve, because nobody deserves anything. Nothing happens for a reason. Good shit, bad shit, it all just happens. Justification is nothing more than counting sheep, a way to get to sleep at night.

Alison didn't deserve to die.

I don't deserve to be sitting here typing this sentence. And yet.

The night Alison was murdered, I could have stopped it. But retrospect is as useless as justification. That night, there wasn't a tab in my brain that suddenly opened up to inform me that *in one hour someone will drive Alison to a remote pond and hit her head on a rock. Would you like to stop what you're doing right now and save her?* For the record, I would have. If I had known someone was going to kill her, I would have saved her. I mention that because, at some points while you're reading this, it'll probably seem like the opposite is true.

On the night in question, in the fall of 2016, I saw her leaving a campus party. It was a Saturday night and there were dozens of people around, so why do I feel like I was the only one who watched her leave? But it was always this way. She was always in the corner of my eye, like one of those fucking floaters, trapped in my vision. I couldn't help it—whenever she was around, it was like I didn't know who I was anymore. I'd only ever known myself in relation to Alison.

The party was hosted by my boyfriend, Cam. Alison wasn't supposed to be there. As far as I knew, the two of them had never met. Most of the girls at Cam's parties were either the girlfriends of his friends or freshman girls who didn't know any better; they hadn't yet been invited to more exclusive parties or learned to be wary of Cam's antics. Alison didn't fit into either of these categories, plus she lived in the chem-free dorm, but there she was, nonetheless, drinking a hard seltzer and talking with some guy with heavily shellacked helmet hair whom I didn't recognize. But I never knew who anyone was. The two of them were leaning into each other because "American Girl" was blaring, even though I'd told Cam a thousand times that Tom Petty wasn't party music. Perched alone on a windowsill, I wasn't talking to anyone, so I watched Alison and the guy flirt. What was she doing in my world? Why had she infiltrated it? I spitefully pondered these very questions while swigging Bacardí Limón from the bottle.

Once again, I'd allowed myself to get far too drunk. Not pacing myself was becoming a pattern. Back then, I was one of those people who drank to feel more sociable, but I'd gotten into a routine of drinking past sociability and straight back into introversion. Cam wasn't paying attention to me; he was holding court behind his makeshift bar, pouring marshmallow Smirnoff directly into the mouths of freshman girls. I didn't really know anyone else besides Alison, though we didn't make a habit of talking to each other. I suppose I could have known more people if I'd made any effort at all, but it was senior year and I'd long since told myself it was too late. There were three girls, my colleagues on the newspaper staff, whom I considered friends. I think they considered me a friend, too, but it's no secret they all had closer friends than me. Lindsay and Brie had said they might come to the party, but they'd let me down. I knew they had been secretly hooking up since last semester. And Jen wouldn't be caught dead at one of Cam's parties. She was probably already in her pajamas, reading Audre Lorde.

Alison, at one point, was also my friend. Ages six to twelve. I think she would have considered me her best friend back then, but at Cam's party, she pretended not to see me, even though we could not have been more than ten feet apart. Instead, she laughed performatively, a little drunk, to the musings of this random guy, who'd spilled beer down the bottom of his blue shirt. I barely noticed him, only scoffed when his eyes stayed glued to her tits, large milky mounds, still a little tan from her summer in Rome, peering over the soft cotton of her flowery dress. When she started talking about life after college, I squinted, hoping that impairing my vision would improve my hearing. *Harvard*, I heard. And *Fulbright*. She'd have her pick. Her life was charmed like that. The short, flowery dress swayed as her head bobbed in explanation. I watched it caress the tops of her thighs, remembering how she used to dress when we were girls: wide denim shorts and oversize Disney-themed T-shirts to hide her big boobs from the ridicule of all the boys in our class. Just then, the guy leaned in and whispered something in her ear. She laughed again, both timid and flirtatious.

The intimacy of this scene was so grotesque I dropped my gaze down to the dark gray carpet tiles, but then the tiles started spinning, so I closed my eyes. When I opened them, the room started to tip and tilt like a fun house. I closed them again and rested my head on the window, instructing myself to breathe. A few deep breaths and I'd probably, just about, be able to get myself back to Cam's room and into his bed. I inhaled, counted to four, then exhaled and counted to eight, just like the school therapist had taught me to do.

My eyes opened when the song ended and I heard the front door unlatch. Alison and her guy were leaving. Suddenly I was up from the windowsill and feigning sobriety. Several people stopped what they were doing to witness my sudden movement. As straight as I could, I walked past Cam's bar, where now the freshman girls were pouring the Smirnoff into his mouth, to the front door. I didn't think Cam had seen me, until I heard him shout out, "Babe, where are you going?"

I ignored him. I flung open the door of his suite and let it slam behind me. Down the end of the hallway, Alison and the guy spun around.

"Woo-hoo, Alison!" I shouted, waiting for her to engage. She turned away from me, just shook her head.

When the guy put his arm around her waist, they continued walking away.

"Be nice to her!" I shouted even louder, addressing him, but determined it was she who should acknowledge me. "Don't be like Brad Hutchins!"

She didn't turn around, but I swear I could detect a chill emanating from her body. That's when Alison's stranger glanced over his shoulder and grinned at me. Did he wink, too? Or was I just making that up? He pulled her down the hall and they disappeared around the corner.

When they were out of sight, I let my back hit the corridor wall and I slumped down to the floor. I closed my eyes and let all the colorful dots spin. The suite door opened again, and Cam came out. "Nardelli, you're fuckin' hammered." He laughed. "Get in here."

2.

I found out Alison was dead when Brie came running into my dorm room on Monday afternoon. I'd just returned from Physics for Poets—the study of the physical world for the metaphysically minded—the last of my two required science credits needed to graduate. But who was I kidding? I didn't understand poetry either, so I was barely passing. I hadn't even set my books down, when Brie came barging in. "Did you know Alison Petrucci's roommate reported her missing?"

I wasn't sure I heard her right. It was one of those moments where my brain couldn't compute the question. But my body understood immediately. I froze, dropped my notebook and my copy of Galileo's *Sidereus Nuncius* on the floor. "No."

"They're pretty sure they just found her body at some nearby pond."

I sat down on the edge of my bed. A million Alisons paraded in front of my eyes, from first grade all the way to Saturday night. "What pond?" was all I could manage.

Brie shrugged. She was from New York City and, like most students, had seen little of Maine beyond campus. "Pleasant? Do you know it?"

Yes. I'd only been there once, on the final day of eighth grade. I remembered the sun was shining that day. We kids all smelled of tropical sunscreen. Alison was lying on her towel far away from all the rest of us, wearing a black one-piece and a large straw hat that shaded her face. She was reading her dog-eared copy of *The Hunger Games.*

I winced, then nodded to Brie, hoping to block the lingering memories from that horrible day. I thought I was over it, then last year at Cotillion it all came flooding back. That was the night when Brie and Lindsay found me passed out drunk in a bathroom stall. They'd shaken me until I woke up, then I'd proceeded to vomit all over both of them. According to Brie, I put my head in her lap and kept saying, "I wish it never happened." When she asked me what happened, I kept saying, "Everything." And it was washing over me again, all because Brie said "Pleasant." Why not the ocean or a lake or any other pond, Alison? What was she doing *there*?

"Some of my crew teammates went there this morning to row," she said, stuffing her hands in the front pouch of her Denman hoodie, where the string of a navy blue Denman lanyard hung out. Brie was the kind of person who wore all her loyalties right out in the open. Her corkscrew blond curls were tied in a tight bun and tucked into her Yankees cap. Like the words that came out of her mouth, her clothes said what they needed to say and nothing more. "The cops were there. I guess a dog walker found her body?" When I flinched again, at the word *body*, she intuited that I needed her to stop. "You alright?"

"I'm fine."

"Rach, your eyes are bloodshot. What's up?"

I was hungover. Badly hungover. Two days in a row. I'd barely made it to my one p.m. class. The night before, I'd hung out at Cam's and drunk what was left from Saturday's party. I'd spent all day wondering what Alison was doing at Cam's party. Had I imagined her? Had I shouted something at her? I'd only intended to have one hard seltzer and to ask Cam what she was doing there, but he was in a mood so I didn't. I drank by myself on his sofa.

"Nothing," I said to Brie. "Stayed up late finishing a paper. Do Lindsay and Jen know?"

"Not yet. I'm on my way to the newsroom."

Me, Lindsay, Brie, and Jen comprised the senior editorial team of our campus newspaper, *The Denman Weekly Review.* Freshman year, we started as lowly reporters, but by junior year we all held assistant editorships. Now, senior year, it was ours. For most reporters, the newspaper was just a club, an extracurricular activity, but juniors and seniors with positions on the editorial board were eligible for academic credits, and for English majors with a concentration in journalism, like me and Lindsay, these credits were necessary to graduate. This made it difficult for us to publish stories that criticized the administration. "Let's not bite the hand that feeds us" was Lindsay's constant refrain. She was our editor in chief, voted to that position by a committee of her peers the previous spring, ahead of me, the only other applicant. I'd been crushed, but secretly, I understood why I didn't get the job: I lacked big-picture vision and was far too easily overwhelmed and discouraged. Lindsay, on the other hand, was patient and methodical, not easily defeated like me. Plus, under pressure, she had these epic giggling fits that endeared her to everyone. Like me, Lindsay had also been the editor of her junior high and high school newspapers. But growing up in an affluent Boston suburb, she'd had a lot more competition for these achievements. Where I grew up, in Waterbury, Maine, there was no such passion for anything that didn't involve a ball. When we arrived at Denman freshman year, these differences were immediately evident. She was the daughter of a brain surgeon and psychiatric-nurse-turned-full-time-mom. I was the daughter of a special-ed teacher and a seamstress. Her parents were friends with the editor in chief of *The Boston Globe*. Lindsay had had internships at *The Vineyard Gazette*, where her family summered. I had once, in seventh grade, taken a tour of the newsroom at *The Waterbury Sentinel* with my advisor, Mr. Beal, and ten other students who only came because they'd been promised Applebee's after.

By senior year at Denman College, I'd landed as the news editor, the supposedly fearless scoop-getter, though I was far from fearless. Given how long I'd been at it, I should have been more intrepid, but if anything, I'd become more fearful over time. With each passing year, I'd found myself growing more skeptical of my journalistic impact. Did anyone read my stories? Did anyone care at all about what happened on campus? Did I? I could barely summon the courage or the necessary hunger to chase down any story. If something wanted to remain unseen, I was happy to let it. I'd found myself passing the buck, giving tough article assignments to younger, more eager reporters. The big problem being, of course, that this was my major, my supposed passion: English with a concentration in journalism. And given that it was my senior year, I couldn't change my mind unless I wanted to delay graduation by another year or two. But I didn't have the money for nor the interest in doing that. Being a reporter had become my fate.

As managing editor of the paper, Brie was queen of the details. She set deadlines, chased down reporters, and frequently asked the paper's other editors: *Did you leave your beer-soaked brain in the bottom of a Solo cup over the weekend, because what the fuck is this?* Her no-nonsense approach to journalism was perfectly complemented by her no-nonsense approach to fashion. Her athletic build and jock-ish persona meant that people often forgot she was affiliated with the paper. For this reason, she was our biggest asset. People who would never confide in me or Lindsay would confide in Brie. That she knew Alison was dead before I did hadn't surprised me in the least.

I didn't want to be alone, so I went along with Brie to Prescott, where our basement newsroom was located and where Lindsay was likely holed up. It was on the other side of campus from my dorm, a twenty-minute walk past endless brick buildings that were blazing red against the cerulean sky of autumn. We walked most of the way in silence. I appreciated this about Brie; she never spoke unless she had something to say. Sometimes I thought she was my favorite friend at Denman. I would never have said best; we didn't know each other well enough for that. She just seemed to accept me as I was. She didn't prod, nor did she judge me, though it had crossed my mind on occasion that maybe what I'd perceived as acceptance might have actually been apathy. She always let me off the hook, just as she had done back in my room when she noticed my bloodshot eyes. She'd accepted my first answer. My lie. In the same situation, Lindsay and Jen would have narrowed their eyes at me, tossed out their penetrating questions: *Really? Are you sure? Does this have anything to do with Cam?*

In lieu of conversation, Brie jangled the lanyard in her hoodie pouch. The sound was just distracting enough to keep me from forming succinct memories of Saturday night. What happened that night wasn't entirely clear to me. It never would be. All that Bacardí, the hard seltzer. Was I the last person to see Alison alive? Had I seen her leave with some guy? There was also the freshman plastered on marshmallow Smirnoff who fell off the coffee table while dancing to Drake and sprained her ankle. Did that happen before or after Alison left?

"Did you know about this?"

"Huh? What?"

I must have looked panic-stricken because Brie scrunched her face and smiled the way someone would at a skittish dog. "Dude." She pointed down to the long stretch of pathway in front of the library, covered in thick chalk-scrawled proclamations. *Future Dictator* was just ahead of me. I was standing on *Hail Twitler.*

"Oh, yeah. Jen texted me about this last night. I was just about to come here and take pictures when you showed up." Another lie. Jen *had* texted me, but I had completely forgotten. The route to my physics class didn't involve going past the library.

"Think Jen wrote them herself?"

"Probably," I scoffed. The Democratic Socialists, the Feminist Society, the Anti-Racism League, and the Queer-Straight Alliance were all regular sidewalk poets and Jen was a member of all these groups.

I pulled my phone from the pocket of my denim jacket and took a photo of *Love Trumps Hate*, written in blue chalk inside a red heart.

"Just in case Lindsay still wants a story," I said. "Though it doesn't seem important now."

"Maybe it is," Brie suggested. "Maybe one of these people saw her."

"Alison?"

"Yeah."

At the suggestion, I felt a wave of relief. Here I was worrying I was one of the last people to see her alive, but maybe she was here last night with the Feminist Society and a giant stick of blue chalk in her hand scrawling the word *Love*.

"I'll ask Jen who was here." And suddenly I felt like I had a job, a real journalistic pursuit, not just a mind littered with drunken, shameful half memories.

A couple minutes later, we wove our way down the stairwell into the basement of Prescott, an administrative building that also housed our newsroom and a dining hall most students avoided. In the newsroom, Lindsay was lounging comfortably on our ancient, gray sectional sofa, reading the recent issue of *InStyle*, her pale pink fingernails wrapped around a cover image of Michelle Obama. In bold letters, it read: *Powerful*. Tucked into the sofa's corner, the always serene-looking Lindsay was only moments from falling asleep.

Lindsay smiled sleepily at the sight of us. "This fucking sofa," she said, pulling herself into an upright, seated position. On layout nights we had a ritual of shouting "NO!" to stop each other from falling asleep on it before the paper was finished. When Lindsay read the looks on our faces, her smile dropped.

Brie explained. I still couldn't.

"Suicide?" she assumed.

The same thought had crossed my mind, but then I remembered Alison's smile on Saturday night. The smile of someone happy to be alive.

When neither Brie nor I answered, Lindsay asked, "Did anyone know her? The name isn't familiar."

The obvious answer to this question was yes. *Yes, I knew her.* And yet that felt so complicated. How much did I really know Alison anymore, except for the fact that she hated me?

The conveyor belt of Alisons-past once again paraded in front of me: frizzy-haired Alison with the high-waisted jeans, the Alison whom the boys in junior high called a "dog," the Alison who had the biggest boobs and the first visible period stain on her jeans, the one all the girls referred to as tragic, the Alison who always started every sentence with "Did you know . . . ?" The Alison who kept a plastic unicorn named Guinevere peeking out from the front pocket of her backpack "so she could breathe." The Alison who was the heir to Maine's eponymous camping brand and Central Maine's largest construction company. (The girl who grew up around so much wealth her parents bought her two of every Barbie: one to stay pristine in the box and one to play with. Back when we were friends, she'd play with her favorite All That Glitters Barbie, but she would always let my Basic Bitch Barbie with hand-me-down clothes drive her pink Corvette.) Later, the Alison I told—around the end of seventh grade—that I would be sitting with Callie Hamel at lunch, and there wasn't enough space at the table for Alison to join us. She'd smiled back, pained, and said it would "give her a chance to catch up on her reading." The same Alison, a day later, offered me a piece of gum that I rejected for fear that it would infect me with her inherent uncoolness. And last in the parade, Saturday night Alison, who I'd pretended to ignore until I'd practically chased her out Cam's door.

I wasn't going to say any of that out loud. Instead, I said the one thing I knew would explain why Lindsay didn't know her: "She lived in chem-free."

"Right. Huh." Lindsay shivered and added, "Is it cold in here?" She pulled her strawberry blonde hair down from its ponytail and let it fall over her shoulders, as though her thick mane could double as a blanket.

Brie rubbed both of Lindsay's arms, vigorously, up and down, to warm her. The two suitemates and best friends were an odd couple, so odd, in fact, that they hadn't actually come right out and admitted to any of us that a bona fide couple was what they were, but everyone knew. "We need to get someone down to the pond," Brie prompted. "I bet all the other news outlets are already there."

Lindsay regarded me. "Can you get there?"

"I don't drive."

"Right. Shit. Well, you and Jen can go together."

"No," I said. "Give her something else to do. I'll ask Cam for a ride."

"He's not on the paper, Rachel." She scrutinized me and added, "He'll make it worse." Then, because she'd had to pull rank, she started giggling.

I wanted to strangle her.

"Jen and I going together is a waste of resources."

Jen was the features editor, promoted last year from arts and entertainment editor. She should have been writing longer pieces about campus life, stories that gave the bigger headlines some context, but despite the promotion she still only wanted to write about music and poetry.

Lindsay sucked her cheeks to stop the giggles from undermining her authority. She narrowed her eyes at me.

Until the spring of sophomore year, I had considered my former roommate, Jen—a sulky, speculative, Goth-adjacent introvert with a temper—my best friend on campus. She was a Chicago native and I was a local Maine girl, but we both felt like outsiders on a campus where everyone else seemed to know each other from the twenty-minutes-outside-of-Boston high school sports leagues. We were both curious and judgmental in equal measure. And we enjoyed making fun of our classmates, whom we found to be shallow. For two years, we'd been inseparable, but things changed at the end of sophomore year, when Jen told me she wanted to get a single room. She'd claimed it wasn't personal, but it wounded me deeply. That was the year she'd joined the Feminist Society, the Queer-Straight Alliance, and the Anti-Racism League. I'd tried to tag along, but I never really felt like I fit in with those clubs. They didn't like that I was a "journalist" (Jen writing about music and poetry was okay), and whenever I hung out with her new friends I felt so stupid for not knowing about historic events like Stonewall or the Tulsa race massacre. But I *didn't* know, and I was too ashamed to ask. I tried once. It was at lunch with Jen and her friend Chantal from the Anti-Racism League. They were talking about Juneteenth. "June what?" I'd asked. I'll never forget the look Jen gave me: *I'm embarrassed to know you.* This, I was certain, was the reason she didn't want to be my roommate anymore. Ultimately, I hid behind the paper, gave Jen's new friends a wide berth, claiming journalistic neutrality. Of course, this blew up in my face spectacularly when, in the fall of junior year, I started dating Cam, poster boy for the Denman Conservatives. *This* is what Jen would point to as the demise of our friendship. Cam was her mortal enemy, but also a guy who never made me feel ashamed of not knowing, mainly because he was eager to explain everything.

"Can't she stay here? Get the mood of how students are feeling?" I suggested to Lindsay.

She appeared to be mulling this over when Brie's phone dinged. "They're going to hold a press conference in the gym in an hour. Press conference first? Then divide and conquer? Where is Jen anyway?"

"Poetry class," I said. "Until four."

Lindsay looked at her pink-strapped Apple Watch. "We'll pick her up on the way."

Her poetry class was sitting in a circle on the freshly mown grass of the Humanities Quad. Staring down at their notebooks, the class was reading along as one kid recited the end of his poem:

> And so it goes, it seems to me.
> The thing you already knew that night

And so it goes, and so it goes
That Billy Joel is always right.

The young man looked up, trying to gauge the reaction of his classmates. Most of them nodded in quiet contemplation. A few offered a light round of applause. Jen was gazing at him, his curly dark brown hair, his small, serious eyes. She was pining. As I knew well from having been her roommate, Jen had a long-standing crush on a *young* Billy Joel. She was very clear about this. She had no attraction to him in his present form. Still, I always found her love of Billy Joel bizarre, given her otherwise sulky and anarchist demeanor, but she insisted it was because of her dad, who'd raised her on a steady diet of "Only the Good Die Young."

The professor, a gray-haired man in stonewashed jeans, noticed the three of us standing behind Jen. "Sorry," Lindsay said, "we need to borrow Jen. It's an emergency."

"The fuck?" Jen mumbled, startled. Quickly getting to her feet, she glared at me. Everything was my fault.

We pulled her away from the circle, not wanting to alarm her classmates. Jen busied herself swiping the grass off her black jeans, but she spun around when Brie said, "Alison Petrucci's body was just found at Pleasant Pond," with the tone of a local news reporter.

Jen started to say *Who?* but something about Alison's name must have registered. I'd complained to her about Alison early in our freshman year, the rich girl from my town who was too good for everyone. Jen squinted like she was trying to recall this, then her dark brown eyes met mine, causing me to look down at my feet. When Jen looked at you, it was never just a look of concern. She mined your soul through your eyeballs. Instead, she asked, "Where's Pleasant Pond?"

"About twenty minutes away," I answered, remembering the long dirt path, then the stone steps that led into the pond. I thought about teenage Alison, wading into the water, then, just as quickly as someone flicking a switch, I imagined her body floating there, lapping up against the stones.

"Fuck. What do you need me to do?" Jen asked Lindsay.

Lindsay regarded me and I stared back at her, hard, until she relented. "We're all going to the news conference, then I want you talking to students. What do they know? Let's gauge the general level of fear on campus. That kind of thing. Rachel's heading to the crime scene. Brie, you need to work on layout. The entire paper will need to be restructured. The two of us can work on what to cut, and I'll call the printer and see if we can get an extension on tonight's deadline. We'll need every minute we can get."

We all nodded at our instructions, then something struck Jen and she grabbed my arm and asked the one question I'd hoped she wouldn't: "Wait, didn't you know her?"

It was just a matter of time until she twigged. The only things about Alison that I'd ever shared with Jen were unkind. I couldn't say, *Yeah, I hated her.* I shoved my hands deep into the pockets of my jacket. "When we were kids."

"Rach! Why didn't you say that earlier when I asked?" Lindsay said.

"Sorry. Just shock, I guess. I mean, we didn't hang out here or anything. Barely talked."

All three girls were suspicious of why I'd neglected to mention something so obviously important. They did this thing they'd been doing a lot recently, sharing glances, as though I were blind.

"Are you okay to do this?" Brie asked. "You can sit this out."

"I'm fine," I said. My gut told me that if they could do this article without me, then they could do *any* article without me. There would be no point to me. I suspected they'd already come to this conclusion.

"Was she at the chalking last night?" I asked Jen.

"I don't know what she looks like, don't think so. Why?"

My heart sank. "Just thought maybe we could place where she was last seen."

"I can go with you to the pond?" Jen suggested. "You need someone to drive you." The fact that I didn't have a driver's license was usually something Jen would tease me about, but not then.

"Cam's taking me." I'd texted him on the way to meet Jen. He'd responded, Bring money for gas.

"Christ. Seriously?"

I knew what Jen was thinking: *He'll distract you. He'll fuck everything up.* But in truth, there was nothing for Cam to fuck up because Jen and I both knew I didn't have a clue what I was doing. This wasn't the usual *Denman Weekly Review* news story. The lead article the week before was "Students Rate Chapman as Their Favorite Dining Hall."

This was some serious CNN shit going on right now. And *fuck.* It was *Alison.*

It dawned on me then that everything from this point on would be defined as before or after the moment I learned Alison had died. Before Alison. After Alison. Not only would everything be tinged by the knowledge that she was dead but also, maybe, the awful possibility that I could have done something to stop it.

"Rachel, maybe you should call Fishman?" Lindsay prompted. "Get a quote."

I had a standing, weekly meeting with the dean of students, Dr. Lorraine Fishman, so this should have already occurred to me. The dean and I hadn't really gotten off on the right foot that semester. Our meetings had become a stalemate. Most weeks, I'd arrive in her office armed with the most recent campus security blotter, and I'd unsuccessfully press her for more information on each of the logged incidents: simple assault, simple assault, sexual assault, theft, theft, theft, sexual assault, simple assault, simple assault. It was a roster of crimes that no one took seriously, including me and Lorraine. It was my job to ask and her job to dodge the questions. I knew she could tell my heart wasn't in it and she was relieved. If anything, I attended the meetings to keep up appearances and to safeguard my academic credits. I'd become complacent about Fishman's evasive answers. Once, when I asked her to explain the prevalence of harassment complaints made by female students, the dean responded that female students often "perceived threat" where there was none. "Off the record," she'd said, "some young women go as far as to harass themselves." I should have published the quotes. But I was thinking about my credits.

"She's probably too busy to talk to me now. I bet she's getting panicked calls from parents all over the country."

"I'm sure she is, but we still need a quote. It's a place to start." A giggle crept out before she composed herself. "Do you need *me* to do it?"

"No, I got it." Taking out my cell phone, I moved away from the group and located the dean's number in my list of Recents. In the last two weeks, I'd only called four numbers: Cam, my mom and dad, and Dean Fishman's office. It was Fishman's assistant, Debbie, who answered. "Hi. This is Rachel Nardelli. Would it be possible to talk to Dr. Fishman?"

"Hi, Rachel, honey," Debbie said in her syrupy voice. It was Jen's belief that Debbie had been directed to talk this way by Fishman to lull callers into a false sense of security. "Can I have her call you back? She's inundated right now."

"Yeah, that's fine."

I looked back at the other three, huddled fifteen feet away, staring at me. Briefly, I considered telling them I thought I'd watched Alison leave with some strange guy on Saturday night, but they'd have too many questions. They were already suspicious about my neglecting to mention I knew her. I'd have to tell them I'd blacked out.

Snippets of that night were coming back to me in cloudy bursts. *Did I follow them into the hallway? Did I shout something at her?*

"Great, honey. How you holding up? This is all pretty scary, huh?"

A quick flash: a guy's arm around Alison's waist, him looking over his shoulder at me, smiling. I shouldn't have been asking Fishman for a quote, I should have been telling her what I'd seen. I tried again to conjure the image of Alison that had comforted me earlier, the vision on her writing *Love* in blue chalk. "Yeah, thanks, Debbie, I'm hanging in there."

Lindsay raised her hands in the air as if to say, *Any news?*

"Sorry, when can I expect her call?"

"I'll make sure your message is top of her pile, sweetie."

Rejoining the others, I said, "My request is *top of the pile*."

"You should have stayed on the line until Fishman picked up," Brie said. "That's what I would have done."

Angry, I offered her my phone. "Knock yourself out."

"Guys, let's not fight," Lindsay said. "We need to stick together today. Otherwise, we don't stand a chance."

Don't stand a chance of getting the story, that's what Lindsay meant, but we all looked at each other, each wondering if the others had also heard the other meaning—that no woman was safe.

3.

Positioned in front of the gathering crowd of students and local reporters, I readied myself for the news conference, pen in hand and notepad open. Lindsay had her phone, ready to record. Brie and Jen flanked the two of us like bodyguards. In front of us, a podium stood at the free-throw line of Denman's basketball court.

The folks filing in and taking up the bleachers at the side of the gymnasium were the Denman locals. I'd have recognized them anywhere. The local men, in their unironic, fleece-lined flannel shirts, their Carhartt's, steel-toed boots, and buzz cuts. With them were their wives in flare-cut Lee Riders jeans and pink sweatshirts with OLD NAVY written across the front, straight from the sale bin in Augusta—I'd riffled through it myself a million times. We were only thirty minutes down the road from Waterbury, where I grew up. Their presence among the Denman student body made me uneasy, like my past life was encroaching on my current reality. The locals didn't flood the gym floor as the Denman students did. Rather, they clumped together on the bleachers, reminding me of what my dad used to say about bees: "They're more afraid of us than we are of them." Still, they all looked so familiar to me, like I knew each of their names. Some of them were probably employed by Petrucci Construction. For these local residents, this wasn't just the murder of Denman student; it was the murder of a Maine girl, a Waterbury girl. Except, *would* they have considered Alison one of their own? After all, she'd had things many Waterbury girls didn't: opportunities, money.

It was hard to imagine why she'd even stayed in Maine for college. If I were her, I'd have gone as far away as I could. I recalled seeing her in the student union during freshman orientation. I knew full well she'd be at Denman; I'd seen it on her Instagram. I didn't follow her, but her feed wasn't private either. (She had 638 followers to my meager 182.) In the spring of 2012, she'd posted a photo of her acceptance letter to Denman, then one month later, she'd posted a photo of herself in a Denman College sweatshirt with the caption *Denman, here I come!*

We hadn't even been on campus forty-eight hours when she'd come up to me in the student mailroom during freshman orientation and said, "I bet you weren't expecting to see me again."

She looked just the same, but different. I guess that's what happens when you spy on someone over social media for several years. She still had perfect posture and long curly brown hair, though by now, she'd figured out de-frizzing conditioner.

I played dumb. "Alison. Hey!" I tried to sound enthusiastic. "You're here."

"My parents went to Denman, so . . ." She leaned casually against the mailboxes. I thought she was going to let the sentence drop, but then she continued, "They really wanted me to continue the tradition. I guess Harvard will have to wait until grad school."

She shrugged, then finally smiled at me. It had just a hint of malice behind it. "But I knew you'd be here."

"You did?" *Was she spying on my Instagram, too?*

"You got a Mitchell scholarship."

I nodded and looked around for Jen. We'd come to the student union together and I wasn't sure I wanted my new roommate, the daughter of two high-powered Chicago attorneys, to know I was a scholarship student.

"My dad was on the committee," Alison explained.

I wondered how big the committee was, pictured her dad's dissenting vote when my name came up.

"Oh. Maybe I should send him a thank-you?"

Alison brushed that off. "What classes do you have?" She leaned in like it was gossip.

"Composition." I shrugged; every freshman had to take that. "Intro to Philosophy. Intro to everything, basically . . ."

"Are you in Intro to Canine Fiction?"

"Wait, what? Is that a thing?"

Alison threw her head back, laughing. "Of course, not! But if it was, you and I could teach it, right?" She gave me a knowing nudge. She was referring to our eighth-grade English teacher, who assigned only books about dogs. *White Fang, Old Yeller, Marley & Me, Where the Red Fern Grows.* "I told everyone at Exeter about Mrs. Morgan's dog obsession. What a waste of space that junior high was."

Everyone at Exeter. Despite all her Instagram followers, everything about that statement rang false. According to social media, in high school she'd participated in theatre (a club for the perennially uncool) and cross-country (a solitary sport). On her page, there were team photos, cast photos, all heavily staged, nothing candid or intimate. Photos of her cat. Home for the holidays. I felt ashamed thinking it: *Alison is still a weirdo.* I mean, if she had so many friends at Exeter, why was she being so nice to me? A person who, after junior high, she had every reason to hate.

"Ha! Right," I said, hoping it didn't sound too fake. Spotting Jen out of the corner of my eye, I waved. "I guess I'll see you around, Alison."

It was weeks before I saw her again in the flesh, also in the student union, where she was hanging out with a large group of friends. She hadn't even noticed me walking by, alone.

That first semester of freshman year, I must have checked her social media pages probably fifty times a day. Was she at the library? Was she making friends? Met a guy? Every day was pretty much the same: photos of Alison and her crew from the chem-free dorm. There was the girl in the hijab, the redheaded girl, the guy in really wide-wale, mustard cords. Every day a new photo of a dozen freshmen, crowded around the same ugly brown common-room sofa, smiling, smiling, always fucking smiling. I should have been happy for her. I should have been relieved. But instead, I wondered why. *Why? Why? Why? What is so fucking great, Alison? What is so great about now that could make you forget about then?*

In the predominantly middle-class Waterbury, Alison's cardinal sin was that she was rich. In our town, it was possible to be too rich, and because the Petruccis were far wealthier than anyone else, Alison was born with a target on her back. Growing up, I'd heard countless rumors about the way the Petruccis lived: *Everything in their house has gold trim. They have a five-thousand-dollar-a-week grocery budget. They have servants who wear French maid outfits. Each bedroom in the house has its own hot tub. The house is so large that everyone needs walkie-talkies to communicate.* My favorite was the rumor that every room had a secret passage to another room on the opposite end of the house, like in Clue. None of those rumors were true, of course, but everyone believed them. I'd been to the house countless times. Yes, the outside was stately, set back from the road with a crescent driveway. Yes, it had columns and a wraparound porch. It was probably six times the size of the house where I grew up. But once you were inside, it was just a house. The people in it, a family. But I never said that, I never debunked the rumors. I laughed right along with everyone else. In our eyes, she was a princess born to an heiress and a self-made millionaire. She'd never know hardship. And that, I suspected, was why the locals were crowding the Denman gymnasium: If the Petruccis couldn't keep Alison safe, what chance did they have of keeping their own daughters safe?

Lindsay, Brie, and Jen didn't notice the locals gathering. Instead, they looked around, surveying their fellow students and faculty who had come together on the basketball court, pointing out, "Look there's Professor So-and-So," and "Over there, look, Abby Wallace. Did you hear Mac Turner broke up with her?" Before Alison, I probably would have pretended not to notice the locals either, but I felt their eyes on me then, wondering what I was playing at down on the basketball court with all the rich Boston kids. *Who does she think she is? Has she forgotten she's a Waterbury girl?*

I didn't have any questions written on my notepad, though I knew I'd need to ask at least one. Dennis Mackey, the college president, would almost certainly call on me first. He liked to encourage me, but his helpfulness always felt patronizing, his optimism insincere. Did he really think I was going to become some important journalist? How would I even do that without getting another degree that would require both grades and money I didn't have? Even if I had both, I couldn't picture myself asking the tough questions or a scenario in which my reporting would make any difference. I was certain that whatever developed in the Alison story over the next twelve hours, my reporting wouldn't matter in the slightest. *So why bother asking questions?* If there was a story to break open, I didn't believe I was the person to do it.

This article was yet another opportunity for me to let everybody down. Until Alison, my biggest story had been "Female Professors Paid Thirty Percent Less Than Their Male Counterparts." But it wasn't *news*, just confirmation of what everyone already knew. Had any female professors gotten a raise on the back of my reporting? If they did, they hadn't thanked me.

I faced forward, just focusing on the empty podium. As I waited for someone to step up, my mind rewound eight years and suddenly I was waiting for fourteen-year-old Alison herself to take the podium, to read from one of her short stories like she'd always done in junior high.

I pictured her as she'd been at the front of our eighth-grade English class and my stomach tightened the way it always had back then. I imagined her in her baggy T-shirt with Hannah Montana on the front, holding a microphone, though you could only see the top half of the TV character because so much of the T-shirt was tucked into Alison's high-waisted, fire-engine-red jeans. Her hair was pulled back in two bushy pigtails that hung over her shoulders. Standing in the dead center of the room, as if there was an *X* marking her spot, Alison would clear her throat, then glance down at the story in her hands.

. . .

Guinevere, the Faithful Unicorn," Alison read out loud, and there was a smattering of groans. This wasn't the first time she'd written about her backpack unicorn. The one that Brad Hutchins had stolen from her bag in seventh grade. He'd pushed on Guinevere's horn until it snapped, then handed her back, damaged. Now, Alison looked up and surveyed the room, her eyes falling on Ethan Monroe, the eighth-grade heartthrob, who was sitting right in front of me, keeping his head down.

Since kindergarten, thanks to the alphabet, Ethan was the boy who sat in front of me in every class. Monroe, Nardelli. Over the years, I'd developed a major crush on the back of his head. He was also the only boy who was nice to Alison. They were neighbors on Allerton Heights. But given his many attributes, he could afford to be kind to her. When I still used to go around to Alison's house, we'd watch him from her bedroom window, across the street, kicking a soccer ball around his front yard. "I'm going to marry him," she would say, like she could just go buy him at a store, like a Barbie Corvette. But unlike the car, Ethan was the only thing she wouldn't share with me. "Which boy will you marry, Rachel? We can't both marry Ethan."

In English class, Alison stayed focused on him, like a teacher would, the eyes-on-me stare, determined not to read until Ethan was watching. When he finally looked up, she continued, "'There once was a hornless unicorn living among properly horned unicorns.'"

That was all it took for the giggles to become laughter. Normally, I was too uncomfortable to find humor in these situations, but even I laughed at that opening line.

"'Her mane was lush and long, her fur a shimmering pale pink, her eyes the deepest blue, like sapphires glinting in moonlight.'"

"Isn't a hornless unicorn just a horse?"

Everyone spun around to see who'd raised this objection. It was David Bullock, class jokester, in the back row. He looked around the room like, *Am I right?*

Our teacher, Mrs. Morgan, didn't like David. She didn't really like any of us. She was a dog person. She actually wore a button on her winter coat that read: "Dog person." But who could blame her for not liking us when we all whispered and giggled about the seams of the wide-coverage panties—visible through her cheap chinos—whenever she turned to write on the whiteboard. "Seeing as how unicorns are fictional in the first place, there's really no point arguing whether or not you can breed a hornless one." She returned her attention to Alison. "Please continue."

Alison went on with her story about Guinevere, who'd been banished to a swamp for her hornless-ness. "'"You're nothing but a mule!" the other unicorns shouted!'" Alison shouted it, too. She liked acting out the parts.

"See!" David Bullock said, vindicated.

"'Guinevere walked in the swamps for days and days, lost and alone, until one day she came upon a handsome centaur,'" she continued. "'He looked like Zac Efron with a horse's body.'"

The most popular girl in school, the mousy Misty Everett, gasped. The rest of the room burst out laughing, again. Next to me, Lizzie "Shorty" Simpson—Misty's best friend and real-life teen-movie villain—had her face in her hands, she was laughing so hard. Only Ethan and I weren't laughing. He had his head down again. He only looked up when Alison, once again, stopped reading, her eyes on him, waiting for his full attention.

She read on, "'The centaur told Guinevere that if she wanted to grow a horn, she had to believe. "In what?" she asked. "In faith," the centaur added.'"

By this point, David Bullock was apoplectic, interrupting Alison again. "Hold up. You can't believe *in* faith. Belief and faith are the same thing."

"Let Alison finish," Mrs. Morgan scolded. David Bullock's reputation as the class bullhorn was so toxic that teachers often told him he was wrong even when he was right.

Shorty had tears streaming down her cheeks from laughter. When I regarded her, she rolled her eyes in a grand gesture as if to say *Alison is so tragic*. Surprised by her brief extension of camaraderie, I rolled my eyes back. But immediately, I felt guilty.

"'And so, Guinevere believed in her faith,'" Alison continued. "'She believed it as hard as she could. And her horn grew and grew until it was the most spectacular horn there ever was—hard as a rock, sharp as an arrow.'"

Stunned silence. Erect penises were a fairly new concept for most everyone in the room. It was an altogether awkward time for Alison to unknowingly bring them up, especially in a story about a *female* unicorn.

David Bullock had barely opened his mouth, before Mrs. Morgan shushed him.

Ethan had his face in his hands now. He wasn't going to look up no matter how long Alison waited for him. The rest of us stared at the clock.

· · ·

Earth to Rachel?" Jen grabbed my elbow and shook it. "You okay?"

All three girls were staring at me now.

"Yeah. Fine."

"So, Rach," Lindsay chimed in. "Her dad is the guy with all the trucks?"

I nodded. The white pickup trucks that had "Positively Petrucci!" written along their sides were all over Denman, Augusta, and Waterbury.

"And her mom is the heiress to Hammerton Outfitters?"

I knew where Lindsay was going with this and I didn't particularly want to follow. "Yup."

"How did we not know about this girl before?" she wondered

out loud, forgetting that I *did*. Lindsay was fascinated by the ultra-rich, particularly America's dynasties, those who were ridiculously wealthy by inheritance, even if that inheritance was from a middle-of-the-road camping gear brand that Lindsay herself would never buy. Being the daughter of a brain surgeon was, to Lindsay, dull by comparison. You couldn't be the heiress to brain surgery.

Brie gave her suitemate a knowing look before tucking a loose strand of Lindsay's hair behind her ear. "Alison's parents aren't going to adopt you, Linds. Get that idea out of your head."

I grimaced at Brie's tactless attempt at a lighthearted joke. To my surprise, Jen noticed and put a hand on my shoulder. I couldn't remember the last time she'd done something like that. Probably before I'd become a complete embarrassment to her. I felt a nice tingle up my neck. Maybe this was how I'd get my best friend back. *Pity.* Ashamed, I reminded myself that Alison's life for my friendship with Jen wasn't a fair trade.

Again, Saturday night flashed before my eyes. The strange guy looking over his shoulder and smiling at me. I couldn't really picture him beyond the back of his blue shirt walking away, a sly smile and eyes so nondescript they could have been anyone's. There was only one question on my mind when the police chief took the podium, and it was the question I couldn't ask.

Was I the last to see her?

The chief started with the facts: "The body of a young woman . . . We believe the body is Alison Petrucci . . . reported missing on Sunday morning by her roommate. We suspect foul play. Officers are following leads at this time . . ."

Lindsay was recording it all on her phone. She stretched it so far in front of her she nearly toppled over.

In a flurry, I wrote it all down. My heart was thumping so loud it was difficult to hear. *Found this morning at Pleasant Pond, Water-*

bury, Maine. My vision of Alison with chalk in her hand the night before morphed into fourteen-year-old Alison in her black swimsuit, her full figure stretched out on a towel, somewhere between sunbathing and dead.

"... Any students who have information about Alison's whereabouts between Saturday evening and this morning should talk to an officer."

My brow felt hot, damp. Suddenly, I imagined myself under the harsh glare of police station lights, me on one side of the table, the police on the other. *I didn't know him. He was just some guy. I'd been drinking. She looked like she was having fun.*

I swallowed it all down, every word I couldn't say. So what if I *did* see Alison leaving Cam's party? It was a *party*; I saw lots of people coming and going. More than likely, one of the other partygoers would have already reported the same thing, right? Why waste their time? I could barely remember what the guy looked like—any description on my part, surely, would have been irresponsible, possibly even point the finger at the wrong man.

"Why aren't you writing?" Jen nudged me. She was always watching. It used to feel good, like having a guardian angel, but just then her diligence felt more like that of a prison guard sniffing for guilt. I wished she would go back to putting a hand on my shoulder.

"Sorry, just thinking."

"I'll take questions now," the police chief said, his buzz cut glistening with sweat. He looked right at me and I froze.

Lindsay was looking at me, too. All of the professional reporters were shouting questions from behind me.

I took a deep breath and raised my hand high in the air—without a question in mind—seeking permission to speak. The chief nodded at me. Suddenly I knew what I wanted to ask. "Is there any useful footage on the school's security cameras?" If there was footage of him, then there was nothing I knew that they didn't.

Out of the corner of my eye, I saw Professor Michaela Stannard standing to the left of the podium. More than six feet tall, she towered over those around her. Smiling, she nodded approvingly at me. This fall I was in her intermediate fiction workshop. Last year, I'd started in her creative nonfiction course, thinking it would add another layer to my reporting, but we got along so well, she'd encouraged me to take a beginner's fiction workshop in the spring. A couple weeks ago, after I'd handed in my short story about a girl who was bullied in junior high, she'd told me I was a writer. "A *writer*," she'd said, not a *journalist*. It felt like flying, a break from a future of relentless fact-checking and the deadlines of journalism, until reality set back in: I needed a career, not a fantasy.

The chief looked me in the eyes and said, "We are viewing the relevant security tapes," then quickly turned to the other reporters.

I glanced over at Stannard again and she gave me another encouraging nod.

"Sorry!" I interrupted, my voice cracking. "So, nothing yet?"

"We're still going through footage," he reiterated, irritated.

Jen put her hand on my shoulder again. Briefly, I thought I might turn into her chest and just start bawling. Instead, I turned to President Mackey, a short, stout man, who, according to my September article, "Five Things You Didn't Know About Denman's President," idolized Larry Bird and had seen Tom Waits in concert four times. "President Mackey, should students be concerned for their safety?"

"We are confident the perpetrator will be apprehended. However, until then, we are encouraging students to travel in groups and not leave their dorms in the evening unless it's absolutely necessary. Thank you, Rachel."

Professor Stannard was shaking her head at Mackey's response. I don't think she even realized she was doing it.

"They've got nothing," Lindsay whispered in my ear, and a giggle crept out.

"Yep," I said.

I busied myself paraphrasing on my notepad, when someone shouted, "Was she raped?"

I looked up to see it was Jen.

"There will be a formal autopsy report in forty-eight hours."

Lindsay leaned into me again. "That's a 'yes.'" No giggle this time.

4.

As it became apparent that the police had no real information to share, students and locals started to filter out of the gymnasium, leaving behind only a couple local reporters and news crews packing up equipment. Lindsay was still holding out her phone, hopeful for a new nugget of detail, but I'd closed my notebook, capped my pen.

"I guess we should get to the newsroom," Lindsay said to Brie and Jen. "I need to make some calls." She turned to me. "When are you heading out?"

I looked at the time on my phone. Four-thirty. "Half an hour."

"Do you have a camera?"

I shook my phone at her.

She looked unconvinced. "Check the photos are good before you leave the scene."

I knew Alison's body wouldn't still be there, but I imagined that's what I'd be photographing. Alison in the water. Alison laid out on the shore.

"Come straight to the newsroom when you're done."

When Jen and Brie left with Lindsay, I hung back, contemplating how a packed room could suddenly empty, how people could just move on to the next thing.

"Good questions," I heard a voice say from behind me. One I recognized.

"Thanks, Professor," I said. More than once she'd encouraged me to call her Michaela, but she was a *New York Times* bestselling author and one of the smartest and funniest people I'd ever met. I couldn't bring myself to do it. We were on different planes. In a couple months, she'd publish an essay collection on the influence of seventies television on her young life. Once I'd read it, I didn't know if I'd be able to talk to her at all.

"How you holding up?"

"I've been better," I admitted. "I wish they knew more. You?"

"Wrecked," she said. "Absolutely wrecked."

I could only nod, so she did the same. One writing student, one writing professor, both at a total loss for words.

She motioned for me to join her on the now-empty bleachers. "That news conference was a whole lot of nothing, wasn't it? I should have remembered that would be the case after my days as a reporter. I kept wishing I'd stayed home with my kid and watched *SpongeBob SquarePants*."

"I didn't realize you were a journalist," I said, taking the seat next to her.

"I wouldn't go that far. I was a stringer at a local paper for a while."

"You didn't like it?"

"I prefer to lie," she said with a smile.

I nodded, thankful for the shift in subject matter. I shifted it further. "How old is your son now?"

"Six. At some point, I'm going to have to figure out how to raise him not to be a bastard." She sighed. "Being born a boy yields surprisingly little insight." She chuckled, parting her hair over her shoulders, a nervous habit I recognized from being in her class, one she performed particularly when mentioning being transgender.

"You've got time," I said. "*SpongeBob SquarePants* doesn't strike me as the apex of toxic masculinity."

Stannard offered her signature chuckle again. "I like you, Nardelli. Keep that up."

I wanted to laugh, too, but I couldn't. Instead, I regarded her, glassy-eyed, and said, "I'm not sure I can do this."

Stannard, never afraid of eye contact, stared back intently. "You've got this. You'll be fine." She pulled an old receipt from her bag and wrote her number on it. "Call me if you need anything. No big deal."

"Thank you." I gripped the receipt, but I was shaking my head, knowing she didn't understand fully.

• • •

Stannard's intermediate fiction workshop took place around a large, oval-shaped, wooden table in an annex on the top floor of the main library.

"The job of a novelist is to suspend reality," she told us on the first day. "What better metaphor than climbing to these lofty heights. You have the whole ascent to clear your mind and the descent to reacquaint yourselves with the mundane."

Eleven of us took a seat around the table, cheeks red with exertion. Someone was late. Three of us were nervous, eyes darting, because we'd already handed in our first stories at the end of the summer and knew our fellow classmates were trying to work out how much was autobiographical, how much was fiction.

The professor was nervous, too. She took a moment to sit,

pushing her Harry Potter glasses up her nose and parting her long auburn hair over her shoulders. She laughed to herself as she looked up at the low, suspended ceiling and added, "Also, if you want to be a writer, you'd better get used to some really shit spaces."

"You do know that people have sex on this table?" Tristan McInerney spoke from under his low Denman baseball cap, the visor of which he'd curled so aggressively it could be a scoop. Tristan believed the only author worth emulating was Hemingway, though he never did say it out loud; you could just tell. He took the seat directly across the long end from Professor Stannard and waited for her to react to his question.

The rest of us, about to put our notebooks on the table, let them hover in our hands just above. I was already aware of this rumor. All last spring Cam had tried to convince to me to have sex on the table that was nicknamed "the good wood." There was, apparently, a sign-up board in the men's second-floor bathroom. Cam eventually got sick of hearing me say no and stopped asking, but I knew if I told him I now had a class around it, he would most certainly renew his campaign. I planned to keep my mouth shut.

Stannard, who had already dropped a stack of papers on the table, now stared down at them, then across the table's twelve-foot length, eventually making eye contact with Tristan at the other end. "Well, I suppose the dimensions are too irresistible not to. Next time, I'll bring Lysol."

I positioned myself centrally on the long side that was closest to the far wall, so I could see the door, a compulsion I had. I didn't necessarily need to be close to a door, but I needed to be able to see it.

"We'll give our straggler another minute and then we'll begin. Rachel, I thought we might start with you." She smiled in my direction.

I smiled back nervously and said, "Uh-oh."

"Nonsense and you know it," she said.

Stannard checked her watch, then gave the open door another long stare.

I reread the first line of my story: "There's one in every year. In our year, she was Alice."

"I have the power to summon with my eyes!" Stannard said to a chorus of laughs.

I looked up from my story and there she was.

Alison took the empty seat next to Stannard. "I had an appointment that ran late." She tucked her brown curls behind her ears and looked around the table. "I'm sorry to keep everyone waiting." Her eyes fell on me last. I smiled, but she didn't smile back.

"Who wants to get the ball rolling?" Stannard asked. "What did we all think about Rachel's story?"

"I like the title, 'Tragic,'" said the girl sitting next to me, Chelsea, I think her name was. "I like the double meaning, because, like, kids use that word to be mean, but also, like, the story itself is pretty tragic."

While Chelsea spoke, Alison kept her head down, flipping through her stapled, blue-inked pages of the story.

Stannard nodded. "I agree. Rachel has a great instinct for honing in on the meaty word and letting it do the work."

"Is it manipulative?"

Everyone looked at Alison, stunned. No *likes*. No *maybes*. Just a simple question.

"Interesting," Stannard said to Alison. "Expand."

"Is it leading? Is the author, is *Rachel*, telling us what to think before we've even read the opening sentence?" When she said my name, it was with no familiarity whatsoever. Her eyes passed over me, a stranger in her midst.

Stannard nodded. "You don't consider this part of the author's role? To guide the reader?"

"I think the story's narrator pities Alice, but she doesn't necessarily understand her. The narrator *thinks* she's telling Alice's story, but actually she's telling her own." She looked me dead in the eyes. "Whose story is it?"

Stannard regarded me, too. She had a rule in her classes: The author could only speak when asked a direct question. "Interesting point, particularly because the narrator is never given a name. Your thoughts, Rachel?"

I swallowed and looked down at my own words, now jumbling in front of me. "I think the narrator is conflicted. I don't know that she necessarily wants the reader to pity Alice." Just then, I locked eyes with Alison again. "It's more like she wants the reader to understand the nature of cruelty."

For a moment, nobody said anything, they just stared at me.

Tristan finally lifted both hands and shrugged his shoulders. "And what's that, exactly?"

When I answered, I didn't bother looking at him. I held Alison's gaze. "That we're all capable of it."

.   .   .

With all the courage I could muster, I turned my glazed eyes toward my professor. "Did you know that I knew Alison before your class? Before Denman?"

"No," she said. "I didn't."

I waited while her mind silently worked its way backward. If I tried to articulate any further, I would surely cry, so I just sat next to Stannard and waited for the penny to drop.

"Oh, Jesus. *Alice.*"

5.

I'd agreed to meet Cam at the library after his econ class. On the way, I listened to a voicemail from my mom. Her voice was shaky. "Rachel, honey, we've just heard. How horrible," she said, followed by a long silence and garbled weeping. I felt my own throat tighten. "I can't imagine what this is like for her parents." I deleted the message.

I stopped in front of the library, where on the exterior wall, scrawled in bright pink chalk, was PUSSY GRABS BACK in big bubble letters. I could picture Jen with the chalk in her hand. How clever we all thought that meme was when it had come out a few weeks prior. Now it rang hollow.

"I wish pussy would grab back." Cam put his arm around me and smiled. "If only." He laughed his hissing little laugh, the one he reserved for finding himself funny.

He'd just summed up so effortlessly why I'd gone off the meme. Anyone could interpret anything however they wanted to. No one better than Cam.

I frowned, letting him know I wasn't in the mood for his jokes.

"How was the press conference?"

"Not very helpful."

"Not surprised. I bumped into Fishman earlier."

"Seriously? I'm still waiting for her to call me back."

"I think she's more concerned with reassuring donors than talking to the campus newspaper."

I could feel myself frowning again.

He turned me, by the shoulders, away from the library to face him. He was about eight inches taller than I was, so he had to crane his neck a little to meet my brown eyes with his bright blue ones. "I bet you twenty bucks that when you do get a quote, she uses the word 'vigilance.'"

Cam had always been competitive, but recently his rivalrous streak was getting worse.

"I'm not betting anything, Cam. Someone is dead."

"I know that, Rachel." He never called me Rachel unless I was getting on his nerves.

I offered a weak smile as an apology.

It felt strange that neither one of us had said *her* name. Cam didn't know any more about my history with Alison than Jen, Brie, and Lindsay. He'd only learned Alison and I grew up in the same town when, over the summer, he'd spotted her across the street, on his lone visit to Waterbury. We'd been to an organic food shop, buying corncobs, and Alison was sitting outside, across the street at Drip-Drop, Waterbury's first pour-over coffee place, drinking a cold brew.

"Doesn't she go to Denman?" he'd asked.

"Yep."

"Wait. I'm confused," he'd said, grabbing my arm. "Remember at Cotillion last spring? She kept looking at you and I asked you if you knew her and you said no."

"I probably thought you were talking about someone else." I kept walking.

"Let's get a coffee. Say hi."

"I don't want a coffee. We had one an hour ago."

Cam was transfixed. "I don't get it. Why don't you want to say hi?"

"I don't really know her. She went to private school."

"Yeah, but she's from the same town. Get to know her."

"Cam, please."

"Sorry, it's just, you're not exactly the most social person. Maybe it's time to make some friends besides the newspaper girls."

"I'll be in the car. If you want another coffee, go get one."

N ow, in front of the library, Cam kept staring at me.

"You know I sort of knew her."

I thought of asking him if he knew that Alison was at his party on Saturday night, but he pulled me in for a hug and kissed the top of my head. This was the first day in a long while that both Cam and Jen had wrapped an arm around me. I fought back the tears again, just as I had with Jen. "Let's get some food before we head out," he said.

"What? No. We need to go." I looked up at the sky. It was just past five p.m., the sun wasn't due to set for an hour, but during the news briefing, it had become cloudy and already it felt dark. "I'm on a deadline."

"When's the deadline?" This was classic Cam. Whatever I answered to this question, he would challenge.

"ASAP."

"That's not a deadline, that's impatience. Let's eat something, Lindsay can't deny you sustenance, can she?" Another one of his clever tricks, suggesting that my friends couldn't possibly be so cruel. Either way he got what he wanted—food or an admission that my friends were the worst. Win-win. He smiled and started walking toward his dorm and I followed.

While we walked, Cam looked down at the chalk, sighing at all of it. "What's the point of this?"

I couldn't admit that the chalk seemed like the stupidest fucking waste of time. I told him what I would have said if he'd asked me before Alison. "They're spreading awareness, I guess."

"I'm sorry, but if spreading awareness requires a visit to the coloring aisle at Walmart, maybe you need to rethink your message."

I smiled and took his hand; sometimes he really could cheer me up without even realizing he was doing it.

"Don't tell me you have an article about this?"

"We probably would have. Now I don't know."

Cam was still reading as he walked, amused. "'Future Dicktator'?! Yeah, that'll teach him . . . such brilliant political minds at work here . . ." Then he stopped cold. "'Silence is violence'?! Fuck off." His amusement had turned quickly to anger. "Silence is silence. Morons."

The phrase troubled me, too, but maybe not for the same reasons as Cam. For him, it was clear: A bystander was neither victim nor perpetrator. Any other definition created chaos. I wasn't so sure. Did silence lead to violence? Was I myself a bystander when I'd witnessed Alison leaving the party with that guy? By not speaking to the cops, did that make me complicit?

"Come on," Cam said. "All this ridiculousness is just making me hungrier."

Back at his suite, I flopped myself on the couch in the common room he shared with three other guys—Asa, Mitch, and Brandon. Like Cam, Asa and Brandon were also members of the Denman Republicans. Brandon, as president of the club, was a stalwart Texas conservative, but Asa, as he put it, "joined for the dope red pocket square" they all wore every time a political speaker came to campus. Mostly, Asa's life was running track and apologizing to his girlfriend, Kimmy, who hated everything about him except his muscular thighs and trust fund. Mitch, their fourth roommate, like most students at Denman, was an apathetic Democrat who preferred not to discuss politics at all. Only a sophomore, he was two years below the other three. Few sophomores were lucky enough to get a single room in a suite, so when the rest of them got talking about politics, he'd just shut his bedroom door.

The door was shut when I was lying on the sofa. It was quiet. Brandon and Asa must have been out. I looked at the time on my phone. Five-forty. "Eat fast. I need to get going."

I could imagine the scowls on the other girls' faces if they saw me lounging at Cam's while they were hard at work in the newsroom. I knew I had to get this article right. I was already on thin ice with Lindsay and Jen in particular. They knew I was slacking. The week prior, at an editorial meeting, Jen had taken a swig of my coffee and tasted the whisky in it. It was the same day I'd read Alison's short story for Stannard's class and I was feeling a little edgy, so I'd poured a shot of Cam's whisky into my dining hall coffee before the meeting. Lindsay had told me I was disrespecting the paper. Jen told me I was turning into Cam. I'd apologized, but it was weak and defensive.

"What exactly are we looking for at this pond?"

I glanced over the arm of the sofa to the back of the common room, where Cam had set up a large fridge and a bar. He had bread laid out on the counter. Next to it, a pack of roast beef. He was squirting mustard on the bread.

"*We're* not looking for anything. You're just driving me there."

"I know what I'd ask the cops," he said. "I'd ask if they're putting their focus where they should be. On the townies."

"What?" I sat up. "Why do you say that?"

"Think about it." He took a giant bite of his sandwich and made his way to the couch with it and a banana. He threw the banana in my lap. "Only a local would know that pond was there."

"That's not true. Brie said some of her crewmates went there to row this morning."

Cam smiled. "Come on. You think someone on the crew team killed her? Beat her with an oar?" He looked at me and saw that his sarcasm had gone too far. Still, it wasn't in his nature to apologize. But it was in his nature to provide. He eyed the banana on my leg. "Eat that."

I peeled it and took a begrudging bite.

"I'd have made you a sandwich, but . . ." But I was a vegetarian, and according to Cam, there was no such thing as a vegetarian sandwich.

While I chewed, I thought about Alison in the water, not dead this time, but as she'd looked wading into the pond on that last day of eighth grade, slowly, her fingers delicately skimming the surface while she watched Ethan Monroe cannonball off the diving platform.

"All I'm saying is, I think they should check the local dive bars, bet there's some guy in there bragging." He stuffed the last of his sandwich into his mouth, and out of the corner of his lips he said, "Let's do this."

6.

Take the next left," I said to Cam, glancing at the map on my phone, even though I didn't really need it. When I looked up, I spotted the road sign alerting us we were two miles from Waterbury and hoped Cam wouldn't notice it.

"Should we drop in on your parents? Have a beer and a game of cards?" Cam cracked his neck. He always did that when he wasn't being serious. It was his tell.

I pictured his mammoth white Land Rover in my parents' driveway next to their new—well, new to them—2011 red Honda Element and shuddered.

I hadn't seen my parents since returning to Denman for fall semester. The proximity of college to home meant that I was extra careful to keep my independence at Denman. I tried to imagine myself someplace completely different, Pennsylvania or something.

Besides, my parents were not fans of Cam. "You're twenty-one, you're allowed to date whomever you like," was their shared response after they met him, delivered by my mom, like the fucking White House press secretary.

"How are Ray and Michelle anyway?" Cam asked, chewing a piece of gum. I could see the blue blob between his teeth when he turned to smile at me.

I glared back. "Turn."

He did so, then turned up the music and mumbled along. Nineties and classic rock power ballads were his preferred genres. He liked to sing along, loudly and flamboyantly, to Chicago and Foreigner *because it's funny*, but I suspected he really loved the music. Just then, the REO Speedwagon guy sang that he was going to love me forever. The lyrics hung there strangely between Cam and me. We used to say we loved each other, but we hadn't said it since he'd visited me in Waterbury over the summer.

"So, how far away is this pond from your house?"

"Ten minutes."

He nodded distantly, and I wondered if he was going to ask me something about Alison. Instead, he said, "You're pretty hungover."

"I'm fine."

"You're doing it again."

"Doing what again?"

"Getting blackout drunk like you did at Cotillion last year. You passed out on the couch last night." He looked over at me. "I had to take you by the arms and Asa took you by the legs and we tossed you on my bed."

"That didn't happen."

"It did."

It could have. I didn't remember going to bed the night before.

"Same thing on Saturday night," he said, his eyes on the road this time. He sped up and passed the driver in front of him without indicating.

I pretended to concentrate on the map.

"Why?"

I looked up. "Huh?"

"Why do you keep getting blackout drunk?"

"I don't mean to. It just happens. Next right."

"Maybe you should stop for a bit."

"I'm sorry, but you're the one who encouraged me to have a drink last night when I was still feeling hungover."

"I didn't mean you should drink a whole case of hard seltzer in one sitting."

"Turn."

"I got it."

"It's just not fun for me when you get that drunk."

"I'm sorry I'm ruining your good time."

"You wouldn't like it either if the shoe were on the other foot."

"I said I'm sorry."

We drove a little longer saying nothing. REO Speedwagon morphed into something very familiar. It started softly, just Celine Dion's voice and some keyboard or synth thing. *The whispers in the morning* . . . I yanked down the volume knob.

"The fuck?" He cranked it back up. "What's your beef with Celine?"

He sang along, full-throated. He knew all the words, about holding on to bodies, not forsaking love. He even belted he was my lady and I was his man, while he laughed.

I couldn't keep up with him. One minute he was indignant, the next he was goofing around. I tried smiling; it seemed the better option than bursting into tears. I let him continue, even though I worried his commitment to his performance would drive us off the road.

"Do the drums, Rach! Now!"

I knew where to do the drums, but I didn't.

He hit his falsetto and his voice cracked out the word *love*. He wasn't looking at me. I told myself it was because he was paying attention to the road. "Tune!" he shouted, then nudged me. "Come on. I just sang my heart out. I don't need a round of applause, but a smile—"

I didn't offer one. Instead I said, "Turn. Up here on the right."

"Damn. You're cold. I'm not the enemy, Rachel," he said, pulling into the parking lot. "The enemy's out there," he added, pointing in the direction of the pond as though Alison's murderer was still hiding in the bushes.

7.

From the parking lot, we couldn't see the pond. We couldn't see anything. The dark, eerie gravel lot was unlit. Cam pulled in next to the police SUV. It had a decal running along the side that read *Help Solve a Crime*, followed by *Text HANDSUP and your tip to 55555*. I wondered briefly if I should text what I saw on Saturday night but then remembered my phone was registered to my parents' address. An officer would probably show up there to question me.

Cam laughed at the decal. "Hands up, Rach! God, I love Maine. Weirdos." He turned off the ignition and suddenly it was dark.

When he opened his door, I said, "If you're coming with me, give me space to do my job, okay?"

I knew I wouldn't be able to get him to stay in the car, and by some measure, I was relieved. Had I managed to go to the pond on my own, I think I would have felt compelled to tell the officers what I knew. Would they have taken me back to the station for questioning? Would they have taken him, too?

"Of course I'm coming with you. Someone was murdered here." He still hadn't said her name.

When I stepped out of the car, it smelled of cold air and dead leaves, nothing like it had on that June day eight years ago. *Freshly mown grass and hot dogs.* Shirtless boys and bikini-clad girls. *Sunscreen and—*

When I last stood there, age fourteen, the sun had been the brightest I'd ever felt on my face. My teacher, Mr. Beal, was leaning on a nearby tree. He smiled at me and asked me if I wanted to join a Super Soaker battle back by the pond. I'd barely wiped away my tears and shook my head, no. That's when I heard tires coming down the gravel path to the parking lot, a white BMW SUV. There was only one of those in Waterbury. Alison, in her coverall and floppy hat, stepped out from behind a shady tree to open the passenger door. Following closely behind her was Ethan Monroe. He swung open the back door and climbed straight in without looking at me. But Alison's eyes narrowed in my direction. We held each other's gaze for a moment, then she climbed into the car and they drove off. It would be freshman year at Denman before I would see her again.

Cam slammed his car door and it sounded like a clap of thunder, causing me to look up at the night sky, now clear again, and full of stars I'd never be able to identify. Stupidly, I wondered if one of them was Alison.

Cam lit the flashlight on his phone and started toward the dirt path only just visible through the trees. I knew it led to the water, but how did he?

Once we were among the trees, Cam asked, "Why did she come here?" But he wasn't looking at me. He seemed to be asking himself. Then he looked at me. "Do you think she was already dead in the back of his car, or do you think he killed her here?"

The question jarred me. Not because of its bluntness; I was thinking the same thing. That was the problem. The question struck me as familiar. Were we both thinking of the same guy?

"Here," I said. I could imagine it easily, the two of them walking down this path. It wasn't so different from the way they'd appeared in the corridor outside Cam's. But now I was picturing the darkness, the remoteness, the awful powerlessness of the moment when it dawned on Alison that she was going to die and there was nothing she could do to prevent it.

I felt Cam's eyes on me. When I said nothing, he offered his own theory. "Agreed. This is a long way to carry a body. He probably made her walk."

Did he know she was there on Saturday night? Surely, if he'd seen her, he would mention it. Or was it possible that everything I was remembering, all the little fragments of Saturday night were nothing more than dreams? I'd done this kind of thing before, gotten far too drunk and woken up with a deep sense of dread. One time, I woke up convinced that I'd stolen Asa's girlfriend's watch from her dorm room at a party the night before. I ransacked my own room looking for it, spent the whole day planning how to get it back into her room without her noticing. After hours of looking, I burst into tears and confessed to Cam and Asa what I believed I'd done. They both looked at me, puzzled, and said we'd never been to Kimmy's the night before. For days, I wondered whose watch I stole. But I never found any watch. Maybe Alison was never at Cam's party? Maybe it was all a dream?

Cam was now giving me the same puzzled expression he had the night I'd confessed about the watch. But I wasn't ready to ask him. For the moment, I was breathing a little easier thinking maybe none of it was real. After all, Alison had always loomed larger in my imagination than in my reality.

"Do you think this guy knew he was going to do it? Like, when they were walking down this path together. Did he know he was going to kill her or was it an accident?"

Cam sighed. "He probably knew."

My gut sank, but I deserved it after asking a question for the sole purpose of wanting a reassuring answer. *Tell me it was an accident. Tell me she probably slipped.*

Cam put his arm around me. "Why else would you come here? This place is creepy."

I wanted to tell him that maybe Alison had fond memories here, the pond where she spent her final day as Waterbury Junior High's most tortured student. The place where she bid farewell to her bullies. Except I knew it wasn't a good day. It couldn't have been her choice to come here.

"There's real bad apples out there," he said, pulling me in tighter. "No matter what the newspaper girls tell you, there's worse guys than Republicans."

He stopped in the middle of the path and kissed me, his way of dotting that particular *i*, crossing that *t*. His tongue tasted like stale gum. I could feel the cold rubbery lump in the corner of his cheek. When he pulled away, he took the gum out of his mouth and chucked it among the trees. "Treat for the birds."

. . .

Junior high was in the rearview mirror that day at the pond, but I was still a twig, flat-chested and bony. I'd been obsessing about what to wear. Callie had informed me all the field hockey girls ordered J.Crew bikinis, but I knew my mom wasn't going to go for that. She took me to the Old Navy in Augusta and told me that given it was a school event, I should pick something more conservative. We compromised on a teal-striped blue tankini. Callie showed up in a bikini she'd ordered from Hot Topic that made her look like a sexy, iridescent Ariel from *The Little Mermaid*. Needless to say, she had the boys' attention, her shape bursting from every seam. The only girl with a more curvaceous figure was Alison and she kept on her coverall for most of the time. Despite his athleticism, Ethan was still a boy in his navy-blue board shorts, not yet a whisper of hair on his chest, and his arms still lacking the definition they'd later gain.

Mrs. Morgan, one of the chaperones, told us all to be careful not to swallow the pond water. "There's bacteria in there," she said. "It'll give you diarrhea." But that didn't stop David Bullock from leaping off the wooden platform in the center of the pond and taking in a mouthful. He spent the rest of the day in the bathroom stall.

Callie suggested we set up our towels right by the steps into the pond. Given our mortal terror of getting diarrhea, neither one of us wanted to get in, but Callie wanted the boys to see us when they got out of the water. "Check their trunks for erections," she said. "They can't hide them in wet trunks."

Later, when Ethan came out of the water, I was careful not to look. I didn't want to know. Instead, I glanced at Alison, who was over on the grass. She was staring right at him.

· · ·

Cam and I finally reached a clearing, where we could see past a large stretch of dirt and patchy grass to the water. At six-thirty, it was a vast blackness with glistening ripples of light. The trees on the other side were barely visible. Just on the shoreline, the water was cordoned off by yellow crime scene tape. We stopped on the grass by the picnic tables and looked around for the cop who belonged to that SUV.

Closer to the water, he spotted us with his flashlight before we spotted him. "You can't be here," he said. "This is a crime scene."

Cam walked over to the cop without hesitation. I followed.

A good two inches taller than the officer, Cam sized him up and reached out his hand. The cop couldn't have been much older than us. He still had a full head of light brown hair. You could see the pores on his skin and five-o'clock shadow, even in the dark.

"Hi, Officer, Cameron Parker. This is Rachel Nardelli. She writes for the *Denman Weekly Review.*"

The officer remained unimpressed.

"Would it be possible for me to ask you some questions?" I suggested.

He kept his hands on his gun holster, as he was trained to do. I looked at his gun, because guns terrified me. Cam, on the other hand, kept eye contact.

"I can't tell you anything. You'll need to go to one of the press conferences."

Cam leaned into the cop's uniform. "Officer Kimball?"

He regarded Cam, deadpan.

"We wouldn't expect you to tell us anything on the record," Cam said.

The officer then looked at me. "Is he the reporter or are you?"

"Me?"

"You need a bodyguard, do you?"

Cam was quick off the mark. "Considering there's a guy out there killing girls, I'd say she does."

"Cam, shut up."

The officer smiled at me. "I'm only here to protect the scene from tampering. You need to talk to an investigator."

"Were you here?" I asked. "When the body was found?"

He sighed, looking beyond the crime scene tape to the water while he weighed my question. "I was."

My eyes followed his. "She was in the water?" I didn't know why I asked. I absolutely did not want to know. I was *trying* to picture Alison alive, standing on the edge of the water, looking out to the glistening surface, her head on her killer's shoulder—happy.

"She was," he said. Then, for some reason, "It's shallow there, so . . ."

"Right," I said and swallowed hard, because I already knew the water's depth and I sensed that he was recounting his own horror at having witnessed her body there, easily visible from the shore, water lapping over her. If I could picture it so easily, it must have been burned into his brain.

"How do you think he killed her? Rock?" Cam asked. "Off the record, of course."

The officer threw his hands up in the air and said, "Nope. Sorry. I'm not the man for that question."

I took my phone from the pocket of my denim jacket. "May I take a couple photos?"

"Go ahead." He sighed. "Every other newspaper has."

From where I stood, I pointed my phone horizontally at the crime scene tape, figuring that was the most important element of the photo. Without it, it was just a pond in the dark. "How do I turn the flash on?"

Cam took the phone from my hand, did something and handed it back to me.

"You could have shown me," I griped. "Then I'd know. Teach a man to fish. Isn't that your thing?"

The officer, walking away, shook his head. I detected what I thought was another little smile.

Cam clocked the smile and motioned at Kimball, *What's so funny?*

The cop was wise enough not to engage, instead making his way back to his post in front of the tape, where he continued pacing its length, bored.

I thought this would make a decent photo, *officer at the scene*, so I snapped him mid-stride. He looked over when the flash went off. I checked my phone to see if it had come out. The light from the flash bounced off the water and blended with the crime scene tape, washed out the officer. I was a terrible photographer.

"Get closer," Cam said.

"That won't make it any less dark, Cam."

He was growing impatient. "What are you trying to photograph?"

"The crime scene," I said, knowing he meant something more specific but wanting him to fuck off.

"Give me your phone." He reached out and I handed it to him.

He walked closer to the crime scene tape and Officer Kimball kept a close eye on him.

"Where in the water?" Cam asked Kimball. "There?"

The officer didn't confirm or deny, he just said, "One photo, then get out of here."

Cam squatted in front of the tape. The flash went off and he pulled himself up. He lingered for a moment, said nothing to Kimball, then walked back to me. "Let's get out of here," he said, handing me my phone. "That guy is a dick."

"I thought he was nice." I looked back at the scene. The water behind Officer Kimball looked black and slick as oil. Had it been this dark when Alison went into the water? Had she gone in alive? Was she dressed? All questions I should have asked.

The yellow tape was flapping in the light breeze. That was the only sound, anywhere. I thought about a song my mom loved. *Nightswimming deserves a quiet night.* Did Alison know it? Before our trip to Pleasant Pond in eighth grade, I would listen to it on repeat and imagine going night swimming with Ethan. One night over the summer, Cam and I actually had gone skinny-dipping in the sea by his parents' beach house, but I wasn't recalling that memory, only my fantasy of me and Ethan, jumping off the platform in the center, naked, into the black water, a low moon lighting us.

Did Ethan know?

Cam nudged my arm. He wanted to go.

I shouted back to Officer Kimball, "Thank you!" But he didn't answer, just stared out at the water.

8.

W hat's going on with you?" Cam asked when we got back to his car.

I ignored him, got in the car, and shut the door.

"Your mood lately is really irritating," he added from the driver's seat.

I just stared at him, contemplating, as I sometimes did, what he stood to gain from picking a fight with me. All day, his behavior had been erratic. At times goofy, sometimes angry. What was he hiding?

And then there she was. Alison, clear as day in my mind, wearing her flowery dress on Saturday night. Not a dream. She'd looked at me when she leaned into her date and said, *Fulbright.* "She was at your party."

"Who? The dead girl?"

"Alison! Yes!"

"At the party? There were lots of people there."

"There were *some* people there, and one of them was Alison." I was surprised by my own conviction, given that less than an hour ago, I'd convinced myself I dreamed her presence, but my fantasies only lingered when they implied guilt. Their validity vanished quickly when they suggested my innocence.

Cam reached back to grab his seat belt, an excuse to look the other way, but when he turned around and saw I was still staring at him, he released it. "I didn't notice her."

"Seriously? When you came to Waterbury this summer, you were completely obsessed with her. Now you don't notice her when she's at *your* party?"

He shrugged, confounded, as though I'd made it up.

My phone vibrated. A text from my mom. **Let us know you're okay, Rachel.** I sighed. "Jesus, Mom."

Cam looked at my phone. "Why can't you just tell her you're fine?"

"If I text back, she'll call. It's not a good time." With my mom, it was never a good time to talk about Alison. All I ever did was let Alison down. All my mom ever did was remind me.

Cam shook his head and took the phone from my hand. "I'm fine," he said while texting the same. "Busy with paper stuff. Talk soon." He pressed Send. "There. Easy. Now she knows you're not dead." He tossed the phone back in my lap.

"I can't believe you just did that."

"Yeah, and do I have to do everything for you?"

"I'm sorry?"

"I had to drive you here. I had to convince the cop to talk to you, I had to take the photo for you. Twice I've had to toss you into bed when you were blackout drunk."

"I told you to let me do my job!" I could hear my voice rising. "You wouldn't!"

He ignored me and turned on the ignition. And after a long

pause, he said, "If we're going to be together, I need you to take more initiative."

There it was. The reason for the fight: an ultimatum. It wasn't a surprise. What were we even doing together?

. . .

When we first met it was in the student union, late September of our junior year. I'd been reading alone at a table set up for recruiting writers to the newspaper. Brie and Lindsay had been around earlier, but they'd run off somewhere, saying they'd be back soon.

"Who'd want to write, voluntarily?"

I looked up from my book to find Cameron Parker smiling at me. He came around the table, taking one of the seats Brie and Lindsay had left vacant. He didn't introduce himself, but he didn't need to. Everyone knew Cam. He was the guy who, according to Jen, liked to pick fights with the Denman Feminist Society. He had shaggy, sun-bleached hair, parted to the side, a fresh-off-the-boat look. And not the immigration boat, more like the one-hundred-foot yacht in the other boat's way.

"People who like to write?" I ventured, squinting at him. Thinking, *What the fuck are you doing on my side of the table?*

He lifted his hands like he didn't mean to offend. "To each their own," he said, but his smile betrayed his sentiment.

I ignored him, returning to *Bad Feminist*. Professor Stannard had assigned the book for my creative nonfiction workshop and I was enjoying it so much I was having fantasies about dropping out of journalism and becoming an entirely different kind of writer.

"Of course," Cam said, like I was doing something he'd predicted.

I looked up again.

"I'm curious, is she really a bad feminist?" he asked, pointing to the cover. "Or is she an angry one?"

I considered saying that it was possible to be both. Instead, I said, "Read it and find out."

He smirked and raised a skeptical eyebrow.

"It's actually pretty funny."

He nodded, frowning a little, the way people do when they're impressed by or reconsidering something. "Alright. How about we start a book club?"

I surveyed the room for anyone else to include in this *we*. "You and me?"

"Yeah." He shrugged. "I'll read that book this month. Next month, you read David Brooks's *Bobos in Paradise*."

I made a sour face. That guy wrote for *The New York Times*. Jen hated him, too.

"It's actually pretty funny," he said, smiling smugly, pulling his chair closer to me. He knew he had me.

"Maybe," I said, and returned my nose to my book.

I could feel him studying me while I chewed on my pen cap. "This could be a meet-cute and you're missing it."

I gave in. I turned down the corner of the page I was reading and closed the book. How did this guy even know the term *meet-cute*? He seemed to me to be far too goofy to alarm anyone at the Feminist Society. He awaited my response, but I just stared at him.

"Okay, now you're being a little intense." He stood up. "Hinkley, 308," he said. "Stop by and I'll loan you *Bobos*."

Brie was Hinkley, 302. I wondered what she would think if she saw me walking past her room and going into Cameron Parker's.

"We can have a drink."

"You're joking."

"No."

"You don't even know my name."

He picked up an issue of the *Denman Weekly Review*. My article "Student Council Debates Blocking Pornography in Campus Computer Labs" was front page, above the fold. "Some people can't afford a computer. Where are they supposed to jerk off?" He looked at me. "You can quote me on that, Rachel Nardelli."

A week later, he was waiting for me outside the dining hall, holding a copy of *Bobos in Paradise*. "I'll admit the competitive Scrabble essay was funny," he said.

"Oh, we're doing this book club now?" I said. I was in a hurry. Just then I was on my way to Professor Stannard's class, which I'd been excited for all day. *Bad Feminist* had inspired me to write an autobiographical essay about my first year as a reporter on the *Waterbury Junior Gazette*, and once I started, I couldn't stop. The words just poured out.

"You're right," he continued. "Some of the book was pretty funny."

"You should tell Roxane Gay," I said over my shoulder and kept walking. "I'm sure she'll be relieved to know you approve."

Cam laughed and fell in step beside me. "Good story about Whitman, by the way," he said. My most recent story was about the quiet dorm's shoddy plumbing, which made the whole place smell like shit. "I've always thought that dorm smelled rancid. Not that I go in there much. I've been banned."

Against my better judgment, I asked, "Banned for what?"

"Apparently, I'm TOO LOUD," he said. His laugh was the hyper one of a teenage boy. Did I make him nervous?

I already knew he'd been banned from Whitman. Jen, who lived there, had been instrumental in his removal, but I decided to play dumb given how nervous he seemed. "I didn't know you could be banned."

"I'm the only one. They had some dorm meeting and they voted. Deep state, if you ask me. Lots of the Feminist Society in there. When they're not shouting angrily from their soapboxes"—here he switched to a whisper—"they like it quiet."

I couldn't help but laugh. What he was saying did describe Jen perfectly.

We reached Osborne, the English building. "Later," I said. I could see Professor Stannard in the hallway and I wanted to catch her before class.

But Cam was not easily dismissed. Raising his voice, he said, "Seriously, come over for a drink sometime or you'll hurt my feelings." He held out the *Bobos* book. I wondered if all the people walking past us were wondering, *Who is that girl who's talking to Cam? Doesn't she know he's a Republican?*

It was my turn to raise a skeptical eyebrow, but I reached out and took the book. Something about him looked vulnerable as he backed away. Was it possible Jen had him all wrong?

A week later, I found myself on Hinkley's third floor, walking past Brie's room—thankfully, the door was closed. I wasn't even sure I was going to go into Cam's, but the door to his single was open. He spotted me immediately and grinned.

His mini-fridge was stocked with sweet, malty beverages— Mike's Hard Lemonade, White Claw Hard Seltzer—and when he offered me one, I accepted, though I rarely drank at that point.

From his rolling desk chair, he motioned for me to take a seat on the edge of his bed, then grabbed his copy of *Bad Feminist.* "Angry," he said. "*Angry Feminist.*"

I hadn't even cracked the hard seltzer. I started to stand up. This was a bad idea.

"Hold on," he said. "Seriously? You only hang out with people who agree with you?"

I didn't know what to say to that. Truthfully, I didn't really hang out with anybody much my junior year. That was my problem. That's why I was in his room. I wasn't going to say it, but I sensed he already knew.

I sat back down and crossed my legs tight at the knees and ankles, looking at the open door.

"You don't seem like your friends," he said. He must have sensed I was offended, so he qualified it. "Your articles. You seem like you really try to get both sides of the story."

I shrugged. "It's the job."

"Tell that to Rachel Maddow," he said.

I motioned to get up again. "You're joking, right?! Tell that to Tucker Carlson."

He smiled, took the can of hard seltzer out of my hand, cracked it open, and handed it back to me.

This is how it went, roughly three nights a week, that fall. I'd show up at his room and we'd taunt each other for an hour or so. I'd go back to my room buzzed on hard seltzer and the excitement of having argued with him. I'd win some arguments, lose others, but I also understood they were completely pointless. They were becoming more flirtatious, and each night Cam's rolling chair rolled just a little bit closer to the bed I was sitting on, until one night in early November, our knees finally touched. "You never come to any of my parties," he said.

I knew he liked to cram lots of people into his little room for poker games, karaoke, or flip-cup, a game that involved chugging a beer and then flipping the cup. I also knew that most people attended out of pure curiosity. What was the argumentative Republican like with a drink in his hand? Other than Brandon and Asa,

Cam didn't have close friends, but he had plenty of witnesses, those who hung around him just to see what he'd do or say next.

"Not really my thing."

"That's your uptight newspaper friend talking, not you. What's her name? Jen?"

He was already driving a wedge between Jen and me, and he knew it. I hadn't told her or anyone I'd been seeing him. After that first visit, I'd started entering and leaving his dorm from the far entrance, so Brie wouldn't see me coming and going. Cam liked to keep his door open. I think he liked the people walking by to know he had female company. Though I was worried about Brie walking by, I preferred the door open myself, fearing everything he'd want to do if we closed it.

"You should come." He tapped my thigh lightly with his fist, and his fingers lingered there. My whole body tingled. "I read *Bad Feminist* for you." This would become part of a running gripe for Cam: I never read *Bobos in Paradise*.

"Fine, I'll read the damn book."

"Come on, Rachel." He pushed back on his chair. "We both know what's going on here."

We did, though I was still far too afraid to act on it. I hadn't hooked up with a single guy in college. I suspected everyone I knew would tell me that Cam was the wrong place to start. But here he was, the only guy who'd expressed even the slightest interest in me. And we were having fun. I needed to grow up, get on with it. Before I met him, I was considering spending the semester holed up in my room, trying to write like Roxane Gay. But Cam offered another possibility, a chance at a more stereotypical college experience: drinking and sex, loud music and games. All the stuff I'd spent my whole life fearing, but also craving. I felt stupid for wanting it, but I was so sick of being scared all the time, so I told myself that, at the very least, it would give me something to write about one day. I think I truly believed this, even though I knew perfectly well that the stories we write are never quite like the stories we tell ourselves. Anyway, I went to his next party and stayed all night.

. . .

Cam stared at me intensely, the engine running, waiting for an explanation. When I couldn't find one, he said, "Why are we even together, Rachel? You're not even trying."

"This isn't about you, Cam." That wasn't entirely true. What he said was right. I wasn't sure why we were together. I'd been cagey for a year, wondering how it was possible that I could both love and be embarrassed by him. Was he right? Was I even trying? Even still, right then, it wasn't about him. Not at all. I glanced back at the path that led to the water. "When we were kids. We went on a school field trip to this pond. Alison, too."

"I thought you said she went to private school."

"Not at first." I regarded him. "Sorry. I think maybe it's hitting me kind of hard."

He sighed and turned off the ignition. For a moment, he tapped the steering wheel, thinking. "So, you lied to me this summer. You did know her?"

"Yes. I'm sorry. I just didn't feel like talking to her. I feel shitty saying that now."

He shook his head before leaning over the emergency brake to kiss me. "You should have said." I kissed him back, thankful we weren't at the end of our relationship just yet. Even if it felt inevitable, that was far too much to handle right then. He ran his fingers through my ponytail. I exhaled and let my shoulders drop. I put my hand to his cheek and let our eyes meet. He looked like he might want to say something else, something that let me know he was vulnerable, too. Instead, our lips locked with a tenderness I hadn't felt in a long time. And then I felt his hand moving up from my torso to my breast. "You know, it's pretty empty here."

"Come on, Cam. Not here."

He kept kissing me, but all I could think about was us kids in our bathing suits in eighth grade, so much young teenage flesh on display: Callie's boobs peeking out of iridescent spandex, my barely there breasts failing to fill that tankini. *The boys won't be able to hide their erections . . .*

Cam took my hand and put it on his own erection. "Please?" he said, keeping my hand there. He regarded me earnestly, maybe even a little desperate. "It won't take long, Rach. You kinda owe me."

I put my hand in his pants and started to stoke him. It felt easier than arguing.

He leaned back and groaned, pushing my head toward his groin.

I felt sick. I willed Officer Kimball's flashlight to come ambling. Nothing.

He smiled and whispered, "Swallow, okay? The last thing I want is my semen at the crime scene."

9.

Campus had an eerie feeling when we returned. It was only seven-thirty, but female students were walking together, huddled and guarded. When we drove past the dining hall, the floor-to-ceiling windows were all lit up. Some students stared outside nervously, but I could also see a group of guys in Ultimate Frisbee sweatshirts, laughing and eating. They weren't questioning whether they'd be alive tomorrow.

The mood in the car was no better. Cam didn't seem any happier for the supposed favor I'd done him. We'd driven back in silence. I'd chickened out of asking him about the guy at his party. Had he seen him? I doubted whether this mattered as much to Cam as it did to me. He'd only reiterate that being a bystander wasn't a crime. He was so *certain* about that: *Silence isn't violence. It just rhymes with violence.*

"You coming back to mine after?" he asked.

I'd barely slept in my own room all semester. "I don't know. Depends how long this takes."

"Do me a favor and sleep in your own room. I want to go to bed early."

"Alright."

He pulled up outside Prescott. All the lights were off but for a faint glow emanating from the basement, where I was headed.

I unbuckled my seat belt. "Thanks," I said. "See you tomorrow?"

He didn't respond at first, just stared at me, hands stroking the steering wheel. "Don't walk home alone. It's not safe."

"I won't." I felt like I was appeasing one of my parents. Did he think I was a child? That I couldn't possibly know I was in danger until *he* told me I was? Was any woman's fear real until a man validated it?

When I hesitated, he looked at me like *What now?*

Did you invite her? Did you invite him*? Did you see them leave? Is all this my fault?*

But I couldn't ask him any of this. His answers were written all over his blank face. In order for Cam to be so certain that silence wasn't violence, he'd have to have kept silent about plenty. I felt it in the pit of my stomach.

"I think she was with a guy at your party."

Cam shrugged his shoulders. "If you say so."

"I just..." I hesitated. "I didn't know who he was." I didn't know what I was hoping for, but I wanted Cam to give me something—acknowledgment, at least, that we were at the same party.

"I didn't see him." He looked right at me then, daring me to refute his account.

I looked down at my lap. "They were flirting."

Cam gripped the steering wheel tight. "Flirting's not a crime, Rachel. All the stuff in your head. It's just guilt. Because she's dead and you're not. You can't bring her back."

I'd had enough. I got out of the car and before I could properly slam the door, Cam was pulling out. The door flung back at me and his tires were screeching from the sudden reversal. He slammed on the brakes and glared at me as if it was all my fault. After I clicked the door into place, he sped off.

I watched his headlights disappear and I was alone.

10.

The newsroom was quiet when I walked in, but it was that sudden kind of quiet, like all the noise and words that had previously filled the space hadn't yet settled on the ground. Everyone was concentrating too hard on whatever they were doing: typing, writing, reading. They'd been talking about me.

"Hey," I said.

Lindsay spun around in her swivel chair. "How was the pond?"

"Awful."

Brie reached out her hand to me, but she was still focused on her computer screen, on the blank space saved for the story I needed to write. "Let me see the photos. I'm hoping there's one that'll work. I need a horizontal."

I handed her my phone.

"Have you eaten?" Jen asked, sitting at the large chipboard table we used for editorial meetings. She had a slice of pizza in her hand, and was flipping through a notebook full of quotes with the other. Two picked-over pies were laid out in front of her on the table.

"Not really, but I'm not hungry. Where is everyone?"

"Sports, Opinion, and Arts are all done. Sent them home," Lindsay said. "It's just news."

"Right. I'll get on it." I squeezed myself past Lindsay and Brie and took the computer on the far end. When I put my hand on the mouse, the screen came to life with a desktop photo of the four of us holding up copies of the newspaper. It had been taken freshman year, all of us with our first *Denman Weekly Review* articles printed inside.

"This one is perfect," Brie said, holding my phone screen out for Lindsay and Jen to see. I knew which photo it was.

"You'll have to give Cam photo credit. He took it."

The other three groaned.

"Can't we just lie?" Jen asked. In her mind, assholes were not capable of taking good photographs. She wouldn't have lasted one week in an art history class.

"Sorry. I was having trouble with the flash."

Lindsay took hold of my phone. "You really get a feel for how remote it is."

"Every place looks remote in the dark," I said, snatching back my phone. I opened my notebook to a nearly blank page. I could feel them all looking at me, like I owed them something. "They found her in the water." That was all I had to offer. "That's all the cop would tell me. He wants to remain anonymous."

"That's it?" Lindsay asked.

"He was just there to make sure no one tampered with the scene. I didn't get the sense that he was the investigating kind of cop." I'd watched just enough crime dramas with my parents to know there was a difference.

Lindsay put her face in her hands. "We don't have a story. The news conference was worthless. What are we going to print?"

It was silent again. I stared at my blank computer screen and tapped my pen on my notebook. It was another few seconds before I realized they were all looking to me for the answer.

"Did she have any enemies growing up?" Lindsay asked.

"Seriously?" Brie said. "That's your angle?"

Lindsay shrugged.

"She was bullied a lot," I said, stabbing the open page with my pen. I drove it in, piercing the paper. "But I'm not writing that."

"Maybe you shouldn't be writing the article at all."

I spun around and glared at Jen.

"Chill, Rachel. I just mean, if it were me, I wouldn't want to write it."

Jen, Lindsay, and Brie all exchanged a look. Whatever it was, it was an extension of the silence that greeted me earlier. How effortlessly they could exchange looks like I wasn't even there. It made me wonder how often they talked about me, how harshly.

"Could you call her parents?" Brie suggested.

"No," I said emphatically. "I can't do that."

"It might be better talking to you, rather than a stranger."

"Trust me, it won't."

Suddenly, I was back in Alison's house. She's crying, I'm crying. Her parents are staring at me. *Rachel, do you want to tell us what happened?*

The three girls shared another one of their looks.

"Did you hear from Fishman?" Lindsay wanted to know.

After Cam had dropped me off, I'd stood outside and listened to a voicemail from the dean. I also had another two from my mom, but I skipped over those, knowing she'd likely been offended by the terse text Cam sent on my behalf. She'd want to talk about Alison, what a wonderful girl she was, how nobody on earth deserved this fate less than Alison. I couldn't. I went straight to the dean's: "Hi,

Rachel, sorry to get back to you so late. We're working around the clock as you can imagine. President Mackey and I want to urge students to be vigilant while the police do their work. We're continuing to encourage students not to walk around campus alone for the time being. We're in the process of setting up a helpline for students who are experiencing anxiety and grief. We hope to have it up and running by tomorrow evening. And, Rachel, newspaper aside, you should call your mother, she's already called my office." I'd hung up on the rest of the message.

She'd used the word *vigilant*. I sighed, wishing Cam and I were in a good enough place that I could tell him he was right.

"She left me a voicemail," I said. "There was no reception out by the crime scene. She gave a usable quote about setting up a helpline and student vigilance."

Lindsay rolled her eyes. "Fine, better than nothing."

At the top of my screen, I typed "Denman Student Dies at Pleasant Pond" and tried to pretend that it was just any Denman student, not Alison, a random death. Shock and confusion consumed the Denman community Monday as news of the recovered body of

Only a few weeks ago, I'd seen Alison in the dining hall with a large group of friends. As was often the case, I was there by myself. While my bagel made its way through the toaster oven, I watched how happy they all were. When Alison said something funny, everyone at her table laughed. One girl laughed so hard she had to rest her head on Alison's shoulder. I stared at them until my bagel went *thud* in the metal tray, then I took a seat by the window and gazed at the students walking by outside. To and from classes they went, chatting away in their sweaters and canvas jackets. It was only fifty-eight degrees, and the leaves were turning. When I was younger, desperate to be out of the Waterbury school system, this is what I'd imagined college would be like—camaraderie, intellectual debate, and thick cable-knit sweaters. Except I'd imagined I'd be part of it. I'd hoped dating Cam would turn me into someone else, but I still felt like an outsider. Across the room, Alison and her friends stood up, piling all their napkins and cups onto their trays. I had a flicker of recognition, the past flashing before my eyes, only different. Alison spotted me, but she neither smiled nor waved. Had she experienced the same flicker? *How does it feel, Rachel, to be all alone?* And then they were gone.

Now my fingers were still hovering over the keyboard. In my mind, Alison and the guy were standing there by the pond. He had his arm around her. She had her head on his shoulder. I imagined them laughing, then, suddenly, her hand on his erection, he tells her to swallow. I shut my eyes tight, but now her body is in the water.

"Linds?"

I opened my eyes.

Lindsay turned to look at Jen. "What?"

"This is probably going to take a while, right? Can I go back to my dorm until you need me? I have a poem due Wednesday."

Lindsay regarded her sternly. "We have to stay together."

"Write a poem about this," Brie suggested. "This is a once-in-a-lifetime kind of thing."

Sensing a chance to lighten the mood and snuff out the horrible image burned on my brain, I smiled at Jen, the kind of smile we would have shared a year ago, when our friendship was strong. "Anything would be better than that god-awful Billy Joel poem."

Brie and Lindsay both burst out laughing.

"We totally caught you swooning over that guy," Brie said.

"I wasn't swooning. That shit is the last thing on my mind right now."

"Maybe it's the last thing on your mind *now*, but it wasn't then," I said.

Now it was Jen who didn't want to make eye contact.

"It's cool," I added. "We're just teasing you, he's probably a nice guy."

Jen shook her head. "How the hell are we supposed to know anymore?"

We all fell silent.

I still couldn't finish typing my sentence.

My mind wandered back to the pond. There they were again, cuddling by the water. The guy was squeezing Alison's hip while she laughed at the joke she probably imagined would be theirs for the rest of their lives. Then he looked over his shoulder at me with his broad smile and winked.

I went back to the headline and deleted it. After a deep breath, I started typing again. Alison Petrucci Murdered at Pleasant Pond.

11.

"Maybe he didn't mean to kill her?" We'd been working silently for twenty minutes or so when Lindsay offered this out of nowhere. "Maybe it was an accident."

I pretended I wasn't listening. My brain was playing similar tricks on me. What we didn't know was still filling me with unrealistic possibilities. Maybe the guy I'd seen her with was her boyfriend from some other school. He could have nothing to do with her death. Or maybe they'd broken up and she was upset. She went to the pond to be alone, to think, and she slipped. Maybe she wasn't dead at all. Maybe her parents had gone to the morgue and said, *No, that's not Alison.*

"Like, maybe she accidentally hit her head on a rock? I mean, we're not even totally sure there was a *he*. Right?" Lindsay kept going. She was desperate for an angle, but also, I suspect, desperate for any explanation that meant she wouldn't suffer the same fate.

Brie regarded her like a parent who was about to disappoint her child. "The way the cop was talking at the press conference, it didn't sound like it. Remember the way he answered Jen's question? She was raped."

I wanted to scream STOP SPECULATING!

Lindsay shrugged. "Maybe he meant to rape her, but he didn't mean to kill her."

Silence again as we considered whether that would make this guy any less of a monster. I made a fist and lightly punched my thigh.

"Lots of men think they're owed sex, right?" Lindsay looked to me for confirmation of this theory, as though I'd be the most likely to agree, the most likely to have firsthand experience.

I thought back to all the warnings my mom used to give me about boys when I was in junior high. *They'll manipulate you to get what they want.* At only thirteen, I was already worried about trying to be the perfect girl: attractive, but not too slutty. I remembered how boys at WJH used to examine girls' straws for evidence of their blow job technique. (*Stay away from her, she chews her straw!*) Already, it was about giving boys what they wanted, but not too much. *At thirteen.* At some point, every girl messed up. She gave too much or not enough. Which scenario had got Alison killed?

It won't take long, Rach. You kinda owe me.

"Can we please stop talking about this."

They shut up.

The four of us were still entrenched in this uncomfortable, festering silence, when a box of Munchkins appeared from around the door. "Come out, come out, wherever you are," Stannard sang, peering in at us and gliding into the room like a dancer, "and meet the young lady who fell from a star."

We all watched her perplexed. What on earth was she doing here?

"*The Wizard of Oz*? Munchkin parade?" I knew the song, but I was so surprised to see her that I didn't react. When the other three showed little recognition, she said, "Tough crowd," and set the donuts and a box of coffee on the central table, next to the leftover pizza. From under her arm, she pulled out brown paper cups with Dunkin' written on them.

Lindsay leaned in and helped herself to a cup. "Oh my God, you're my savior," she said, turning the valve on the coffee that released the steaming brown liquid.

Stannard took a seat across from Jen, who'd been trying to scribble a poem, but in the presence of an accomplished writer had flipped over her notebook. "How's it going, team?"

I continued to stare at her, completely thrown. Why weren't the other three surprised to see her?

"You look like you need a donut," she said to me. She opened the box of Munchkins and pushed it in my direction. I took one, bit into it while she was watching me, then set the rest on my notebook when Lindsay grabbed her attention.

"We're nowhere," Lindsay said to Stannard. "We've got nothing."

The professor nodded, thoughtfully. "Here's the thing. Tonight's article isn't the most important one you're going to write. I know it probably feels like you've got nothing. Believe me, I bet the police feel the same. But for you all, it's about how you report on it in the coming weeks and months that is really going to count. You're not a daily paper, nobody is expecting the hard facts from you. It's your job over the coming year to give your classmates context for what's happened. You can't print what you don't know. This isn't intermediate fiction." She looked at me and smiled. "If only." Satisfied with her advice, she grabbed a chocolate Munchkin.

. . .

Three weeks after intermediate fiction workshopped my story, it was Alison's turn.

Stannard had emailed Alison's story and two others on a Thursday. We had until the next Tuesday to read them, but you better believe I dove into Alison's right then and there. I wondered if it would be like the stories she wrote in junior high, complete with a fictional unicorn.

Let me tell you, that would have been preferable to the story she'd produced.

Take Back the Night. By Alison Petrucci.

The highlights: Two young women who haven't seen each other for five years run into each other at a Take Back the Night march. At the beginning of the story, they make eye contact in a crowd. Told from the perspective of both women, each one tries to recall what she can about the other's dating history and speculates about what and who brought her to the march. Each girl compares her own trauma to what she thinks happened to the other girl. They contemplate whether the other girl "deserves" to march. At the end of the story, only one of them starts marching, leaving the other one behind.

I remembered the night Alison was using as inspiration. It was freshman year, about a month after I saw her in the student union, at the campus's annual Take Back the Night march. The event started at the library with a vigil, then by candlelight, students marched to the dean's office with a list of demands. Covering the march was my first above-the-fold assignment for the Denman paper.

Earlier that day I'd already met with the event's organizers. I knew their list of demands: better lighting in the parking lots, more female officers to be hired for campus security, and the cancellation of the elective sexual health seminar: Waxed or Not Waxed? According the organizer I'd spoken to, every year there were three demands, two difficult or expensive ones to execute, and the low-hanging fruit. That seminar was toast.

I stood on the sidelines of the candlelight vigil with a notepad and paper. I didn't think anyone would want to talk to me, so I tried to write what I saw. *Young women embracing, classmates coming together in solidarity, candles flickering in the darkness.*

When I looked up, I saw Alison with this other girl. They had their arms around each other.

She spotted me and smiled sympathetically.

I waved back with a half smile.

She and her friend approached me.

"Rachel, this is my roommate, Natalie." She regarded Natalie. "Rachel and I know each other from Waterbury."

"You're not marching?" Natalie asked.

Alison watched my eyes dart around. "Not as such. Technically reporting," I said, waving my notepad and pen, then shrugging, "but supportive, obviously."

"Right," Natalie said, stuffing her hands in her pockets. She put all her weight on her toes and looked down while she teetered.

"Would you be willing to tell me why it's important to you to be here tonight?"

Natalie hunched her shoulders. "I'm not sure I do want to be here, actually," she said, then her eyes widened. "Don't write that," she said. "Sorry, it's just I don't want my name in the paper."

I felt terrible for her; she was obviously still suffering.

Alison ran her fingers through her roommate's hair, then she looked at me. "I'll answer."

"Oh, of course," I said, swallowing my anxiety about what she might say.

"I'm here because assault isn't always physical." She stopped while I wrote. Even when I'd finished writing, she stayed silent, then I remembered eighth grade, Alison reading her story at the front of the class, her eyes-on-me face. I looked up and she continued, "There are men out there that try to make us feel small, make us feel alone. When we march tonight we let them know we're not alone. We're many and we're strong."

I gulped, then clenched my jaw, tears welling up in my eyes. It was a good quote. "Great," I said. "Thank you for that, Alison."

Our eyes lingered on each other, until the crowd started moving down the hill and Alison and her roommate moved with it.

The class had had mixed feelings about Alison's story.

As was becoming routine, Tristan was the first to express his opinion. "I find multiple perspectives in the short story to be daunting. I didn't feel I learned enough about either character."

"What did you want to know?" Alison asked him right out of the gate. "What's not there that should be?"

Stannard lifted a finger. Alison wasn't supposed to talk.

Tristan tapped his pen on the table. "That's a little defensive."

"Bra size?" Alison asked, undeterred.

Everyone chuckled, even me.

"Well, you joke, but actually I think it would have been helpful to know a little more about each woman's physical appearance."

Lydia, sitting on the other side of Alison, disagreed. "I like the way Alison handles the descriptions. I mean, it's not like the characters can describe themselves." Lydia flips through the story, quoting, "Amanda sees Rose as 'still mousy. Her small, dark eyes always darting, always looking for a safer corner.' And Rose sees Amanda as 'the girl whose wingspan stretched farther than anyone else's.' Whether this was true by measurement or delusion was immaterial. To everyone else, Amanda's presence was larger than life, larger than it should have been. If Rose had to describe her, she would say she's 'too much.'"

"Yeah, but that confuses me," Tristan said. "Am I to take that to mean Amanda's fat? Or, like, zany?" He lifted his hands and gave them a jazzy shake.

"I think the story proves she's eccentric. What does it matter whether she's fat?" Lydia asked.

Tristan scoffed. "It adds context."

"How?"

"To know whether or not to believe Rose. In the story, Rose thinks Amanda hasn't had many sexual partners. If we had more information about Amanda's appearance, we'd be better able to understand whether or not Rose is a reliable narrator."

"But!" Stannard interjected. "Any physical description of Amanda would likely be given by Rose and therefore would be subject to Rose's tastes and prejudices. Would it not?"

"Are you saying if Amanda *is* fat then Rose is probably right about her not having sexual partners?" Lydia stared Tristan down.

"Not necessarily," Tristan said, unconvincingly. "I'd just like to have a better picture of her."

"I think, in a roundabout way, Tristan brings up an interesting point about narrative and the choices we make as writers." Professor Stannard paused, trained her eyes on Tristan, scrutinizing, just in case he mistakenly thought she was paying him a compliment. "The information an author shares has to serve the story's ending.

In this case, I think Alison was right to be ambiguous with that information."

Alison smiled to herself.

"What does everyone think about the ending?" Stannard asked.

The girl next to me, Chelsea, said she thought it was obvious that "the author of the story hates women."

"That's not obvious to me," Stannard said. "Could you explain?"

Chelsea adjusted her butt in her chair, looking down at the story. "It's not very supportive of women, like, the way the two main characters are judging the other girl's trauma without even knowing it."

Alison rolled her eyes.

"I wonder," Stannard said, "If maybe that was part of *the author's* intention: to highlight that there can be a competitive nature to trauma. Alison, would you like to speak to that?"

Alison was quiet.

I was finding eye contact with both her and Stannard difficult, so I was flipping through the pages of the story like I was searching for a specific quote. When I finally stopped and looked over at Alison, curious why she wasn't talking, she spoke. "Yeah," she said. "I think Professor Stannard's point is true. Unfortunately, I think it's *really* true for young women. There's far more pain out there than there is sympathy. We end up fighting over compassion. I'd like that to be one of the takeaways of the story."

"Sorry," I was surprised to hear myself say. "But if you want that to be one of the takeaways, then why don't both girls march at the end?"

Stannard's head bobbed, like she was trying to decide if this was a good question or not.

I continued, "Do you believe *only* Amanda deserved to march?"

"Not at all, both deserved to march, of course," Alison said.

I shrugged my shoulders at her. "So? Why don't they?"

"I think the story ends with both girls being ashamed of her own judgments. But I think Amanda ultimately comes to understand the march is about solidarity."

I nodded. Fair enough. "And Rose?"

"Rose is a coward."

. . .

A nd don't forget," Stannard added, after swallowing her donut, "you'll soon have a quote from me as her professor."

I looked at her, panicked. The fact that Alison and I were both in her class was one of the many facts I'd still withheld from the others. Maybe if I could get her to write down her quote, I could continue to keep this secret. I held out my notebook to Stannard. "Write it down for me, please?"

"Make it long," Lindsay said. "We've got a lot of space to fill."

Stannard took the notebook with a smile. "I'm known to be loquacious. That said," she continued, "what *do* you all have?"

Lindsay looked at me to answer.

"There was everything we learned at the press conference. And the cop at the scene told me she was found in the water. He wouldn't tell me anything else. We got a picture of the scene taped off."

"What was it like there?" Stannard asked. "Describe the scene."

I thought about pulling into the empty parking lot, about how Cam seemed to know his way to the water. I thought about the drive there. Did he start to turn in to the parking lot before I told him to turn? Maybe, but that's just Cam. You can't tell him anything. He already knows everything.

"It was empty. There's a parking lot, then a half mile or so walk to the pond through the woods. It's completely dark."

"Shit," Jen said. "That's crazy remote."

Stannard nodded. "That's an important detail."

It was stupid of me to think that everyone knew what the pond looked like just because I did. "It's a pretty big pond. There are these stone steps leading into the water. The beach is mostly grass and dirt. I think it's popular in the summer with fishermen."

"Would Alison have known it?" Lindsay asked.

"Yes," I said. "We went there together on an eighth-grade field trip."

Everyone stared at me.

"So, she had a reason to be there?" Brie asked.

"She knew of it. I don't know if that's a reason."

"She could have been meeting someone there?" Lindsay ventured.

"This is all speculation." I regarded Stannard, confused. What was she doing here? I had intended for the short story I wrote about Alison to remain fiction, but now Stannard was here and she knew that it wasn't, not really. How long before Lindsay, Brie, and Jen knew that, too?

"For the moment, it's investigation," Stannard clarified. "You're not going to print anything you don't know. But answers rarely come without asking questions."

Jen turned to me, grabbed my arm. I had no choice but to look at her. "Is there anyone from your school days that she kept in touch with? Someone she would have met there?"

SHE'S GOING TO GET
WHAT'S COMING TO HER

That Alison and I were such good friends was peculiar for Waterbury, a town that, like most towns, was very turfy. Whatever neighborhood you lived in, you tended to stay in. I was an east end kid and Alison was a west ender. I lived on Cherry Street, which was at the top end of the north-to-south-running George Mitchell Drive, the busiest road in town. It was a leafy and residential neighborhood populated mostly by the families of teachers, nurses, bank tellers. It wasn't as nice as the west end neighborhood, known as Allerton Heights, which was only a couple blocks from the attractive end of the east-to-west-running Main Street. There were the few nice restaurants and the fine food store, the Epicurious Farm, which my dad called the Extortionist Farm. Allerton Heights was where the big brick houses were, the ones with sprawling front lawns and two-car garages. Right between the two neighborhoods was the junior high and, across the street, a strategically placed Dunkin' where all us kids hung out after school. But when school was on vacation, the west end kids didn't join us there as much. They already had the good snacks at home: double-stuffed Milano cookies, Ben & Jerry's ice cream, variety packs of Lay's and Kellogg's. Their parents were doctors, or they owned car dealerships, or they worked at Denman College. Or they were the Petruccis.

Regardless of our socioeconomic differences, Alison and I had similarities, like our shared Italian heritage—the only two kids in Waterbury. Because of this we both had frizzy hair and furry arms, though her complexion was darker than mine. Our parents got us together early, because that's what Italians do, despite the obvious power structure: My dad worked for Alison's dad's construction company in the summers, painting houses. After that first summer my dad painted, our parents set up a playdate. Alison and I must have been about six. I remember my mom asking me if I knew her from school. "She's having trouble making friends," my mom said. At the time I didn't think I knew her—she wasn't in my class—but two days later, she was selected as student of the month in school assembly. When she stood up so tall and so proud in front of the whole school, I remember my heart sinking. *Oh no, not her.* Regardless of my misgivings, we got along. She was odd—I thought that right away—but I suspected so was I. She was very ambitious, which inspired me to be the same. When we played Barbie, hers was always a "heart doctor" and mine was an "animal rights lawyer," but at night they were a popstar duo called the Smarty-Panties and they had several chart-topping hits. According to Alison, our Barbies could have it all and so could we.

By junior high, Alison and I were both in all the high-track classes, but this is when I started to notice our stark differences. She was becoming surer of herself. She didn't care what anyone else thought, whereas I cared deeply. She seemed to be increasingly dependent on her imagination, preferring to live in a fantasy world, whereas I was becoming more observant. As much as I would have loved to live in a fantasy, it felt impossible. I could see cliques starting to form without me, mostly by sports teams, academic achievement, and definitely by neighborhood. Waterbury was a Goldilocks kind of town, not too rich, not too poor, your family's money had to be just right. Soon, Alison was being picked on for having too much money and the South Waterbury kids were being ostracized for being too poor. The town's geography—the busy four-lane end of Main Street separated South Waterbury from the rest of the town—allowed ludicrous rumors about South Waterbury kids to spread unchecked, like the rumor that their parents owned guns and didn't keep them locked up. The south end kids would have been just as unpopular as Alison if the rest of us weren't a little afraid of them. Buses took them to and from school, so they never got a chance to hang out at Dunkin' and set the record straight. And with only a KFC, Joey's Discount Liquor, Mainely Smokes, and a sketchy bar called the Low Down, there was really no reason for anyone who didn't live in the south end to be in the neighborhood. The Walmart on the other side of the four lanes was the closest we got.

On the popularity ladder, I was balancing, precariously, one rung up from Alison and the south end kids. Any wrong move could have me making that tumble, albeit short, to the bottom. I understood that as long as the bullies concentrated on Alison, they'd likely leave me alone. When they went for her, all I had to do was pretend I didn't see.

This is when Callie Hamel came into my life. Though she'd always lived down the street from me, I'd never really known her. She had a reputation for being mouthy and she liked to hang out with Micah Saltzman, the one boy from South Waterbury who was popular with everyone because he sold stolen hood ornaments and

Zippos. Callie and I didn't know each other because we'd never been in the same classes. I was the only east end kid who was in all honors classes. Unsurprisingly, there was an undeniable link between a family's means and their child's performance in the classroom, meaning I was in a classroom full of west end kids, none of whom would hang out with me after school, except Alison. That is, until an aptitude test between sixth and seventh grades showed that Callie Hamel's talent for math was far greater than she'd been letting on. On the first day of seventh grade, there she was in my honors algebra class, another east ender and a fish out of water. Our friendship formed slowly over that year, as we tried to feel each other out. Since she hung out mostly with Micah and skater boys, she needed a female friend, and I needed to detach myself from Alison or be bully bait. What Callie wanted more than anything was a captive audience to absorb all her conspiracy theories. I was happy to oblige. Invisibility was better than being a target. Our friendship was based on nothing more than this. By eighth grade we were best friends.

I often considered this one of the bigger junctures in my life. Could events have gone differently if I hadn't ditched Alison for Callie? When I didn't want to take the blame for my own actions, I found myself blaming Waterbury. A town's geography can inadvertently shape the whole course of a kid's life. This wasn't some grand discovery I'd made. History proved this point time and time again, if you were paying attention. The thing is, we kids in Waterbury, we weren't paying attention. We just let it all play out, like it was inevitable, and maybe it was.

In junior high, lunch was a big deal. Where you sat, who you sat with, what you ate was all scrutinized, all part of the web of ridiculous factors that determined your reputation.

Callie picked our table by the railing because it looked over a ramp that led down to the eighth-grade locker bay. She wanted to keep an eye on the comings and goings of our classmates, possibly catch snippets of conversations we wouldn't otherwise be privy to. It was also to keep an eye on her "boyfriend," Micah, Waterbury Junior High's resident rebel—a skinny kid with shaggy hair covering his eyes, who wore either a Che Guevara or Rage Against the Machine T-shirt, depending on the day. He often took trips to his locker to retrieve the merchandise he sold to our classmates: cigarettes, Zippos, regular lighters, car hood ornaments, and hubcaps.

We shared our table with the orchestra girls. It was an amicable agreement. They didn't particularly like us, or we them, but each table seated eight and there were six of them. You didn't want an empty seat at your table. This was an invitation for Brad Hutchins, chief troublemaker, to take a seat and commence torturing you. Or worse, Alison could take it and try to be your friend. Alliances were necessary to preserve whatever meager social standing you had.

The theatre posse, led by David Bullock, took up two tables. At sixteen strong, they could be as weird as they wanted to be. That summer, they'd all been to Boston to see *Wicked* and to the annoyance of everyone else in the cafeteria, they liked to sing the soundtrack with food in their mouths.

Each sports team had their own table, the two most important being the boys' soccer and girls' field hockey teams. The field hockey girls occupied two tables in the corner where the railing met a cinderblock wall, a highly trafficked corner. Always, they had their sticks by their sides, whether they were in season or not. They were led by Misty Everett and Shorty Simpson, west end girls with superiority complexes. Actually, Misty wasn't so bad. She'd never been mean to anyone, more like indifferent. Shorty, on the other hand, was the worst. She was two-faced and aggressive, and spoke in a baby voice whenever a cute boy was in earshot. Everyone knew better than to walk the hallways of WJH alone if Shorty was nearby. "Oops. Sorry!" she'd say, after "accidentally" clobbering your ankle with her stick. Then she'd snicker to whomever she was walking with. Shorty Simpson never walked alone.

The soccer team sat more centrally, along the cinderblock wall, just under the painting of the Purple Puma, the school mascot, standing on its hind legs, one paw thrashing midair, the other dripping blood from its claws. They were sixteen boys who were always together, always laughing, always kicking things or balancing random objects on their heads and then catching them in the crooks of their necks. The beautiful Ethan Monroe, with his lovely wide-set eyes, a tiny nose with a flat bridge, and hair that caressed the tops of his ears, was one of these boys. They were led by their captain, Brad Hutchins. Brad wasn't just the ringleader of the soccer team; he was the eighth-grade despot. He had an equal-opportunity approach to torture. It didn't matter whether you were his teammate, friend, or foe. This is what made him the most revered boy in our school, despite being a lanky, pimply kid from the east end. He could turn on you at any time.

Alison occupied an eight-top table all to herself, right smack-bang in the center of the cafeteria, one table in from the soccer team. Nobody else dared sit that close to Brad Hutchins when he had food to fling. I told myself she sat there by choice. She didn't.

The day she read her unicorn erection story out loud in English class, the cafeteria was buzzing with reenactments. If Alison noticed, she pretended not to. She had her head buried in a copy of *Breaking Dawn,* a Milano cookie in her hand.

"Omigod, Zac Efron on a horse's body? Is it true?" Callie wanted to know when I set my brown bag on our table. Despite it being October, Callie was still dressing for summer. Only the faintest edge of her pink denim shorts was visible under her giant purple hoodie, and only visible because her pasty white thighs were bursting out of those tight shorts, desperate for circulation. The summer had been transformative for Callie's body. The curves had arrived. Some from puberty, some from spending five days a week at Dunkin'. I was still rail thin, all bones and angles. And dressed seasonally appropriate in jeans and a maroon sweater, because my mom would never let me leave the house in shorts in October.

I pulled out my chair, wincing at the recollection of Alison's story. I hoped Callie would let it go, but she didn't.

"What is her deal? Thank God you're not friends with her anymore, can you imagine?"

Yes, the image was crystal clear. There would be two tragic losers at that table for eight, instead of just one.

"Stop staring at the weirdo, weirdo."

Until Callie said that, I hadn't realized I was still standing, watching Alison bite into her cookie with a dainty pinkie in the air. I took my seat and opened my brown paper bag. A cream cheese and red pepper sandwich. An apple. Some pretzels.

Just then, Callie started laughing. "Look."

Behind me, Brad Hutchins, in his well-worn New England Revolution jersey, had two straws up his nose, like a walrus, barking at his teammates. Ethan was sitting across from him, his back to me. Always, his back was to me.

"Earth to Rachel!"

I spun back around and took a bite of my sandwich. "Sorry."

"Come on, I want every detail. Micah says Shorty said Alison doesn't even know what an erection is." Callie took a bite of her ham and Fluff sandwich, a sight that always made my stomach lurch.

"I don't want to talk about penises while I'm eating," I said, recalling the eye roll I had shared with Shorty in English class. Callie would have been so proud of that. She was forever coming up with schemes to boost our popularity.

"You're no fun." This was one of Callie's most popular refrains, one of her long-standing theories for why we weren't more popular. That and what she referred to as my "asexual vibe" because I didn't have a boyfriend or a crush. Of course, I did have a crush. I remember the exact moment I knew I was in love with Ethan. Fifth grade. Sex ed. This would have been 2005, the Bush years, so it was really abstinence education. The video we'd watched that day was called *Hang On to Your Hat!* Sitting on the floor, we kids were uncomfortably craning our necks to stare up at one of those big boxy TVs on a stand. As usual, the alphabet placed me on the carpet next to Ethan, both of us sitting crisscross-applesauce, our kneecaps touching while a cartoon cat wearing a trilby told us our virtue was a gift that we'd one day want to give to someone else, but we'd only be able to gift it once. The cat said sometimes knowing who to choose could be hard, but it was important to get it right. *Stupid cat*, I'd thought. *It's not hard. He's sitting right next to me.* Then I spent the rest of the class staring at Ethan's peach-fuzzed kneecap as it caressed my own. But that information would have been kryptonite in the hands of Callie Hamel. She picked at her Doritos and stared at me like she was cataloging all the things about me she wanted to fix. "Micah says Misty's having people over to hers before the dance next Friday."

Micah says . . . This is how every problem started between me and Callie. Her romantic relationship with Micah Saltzman began over the summer with a kiss that went so wrong he had to tell her to stop midway, when her spit started running down his chin. I wondered if they were really going out. Since that supposed kiss, I'd never seen them together. Her fascination with him was obvious: Despite being from South Waterbury, Micah was one of WJH's most popular boys. The kid defied all barriers. He lived in an apartment block across from the Walmart with his mom, but he had a BMX bike and therefore, he believed, no boundaries. Every day, he rode that thing straight across the four lanes of traffic, plus the Walmart turn lane. He wasn't about to let the constraints of fascist town planners hem him in. That was the other thing about Micah: everything he didn't like was fascist. And because of his many dealings, he had his nose in everyone's business, a one-man gossip mill.

It was no surprise that Misty was having people over before the dance. Since her grandmother had died the year before, Misty and her friends hung out in the vacant in-law apartment above her parents' garage, drinking the endless supply of tiny liquor bottles the old lady had been hoarding. All this, according to Micah, of course. I'd never been invited. Neither had Callie. This bothered her more than it did me. The thought of drinking and making out with boys scared the crap out of me.

"Is Micah going?"

"Maybe. Misty won't let him smoke in the apartment."

"Then go with him." I knew this would shut her up. She wouldn't admit that Micah was keeping his relationship with her secret from all the west end kids.

But she got me back. "You should wear something slutty to the dance. No Disney T-shirts like your buddy Alison over there."

"I don't own any. When have you ever seen me in a Disney T-shirt?"

She ignored this. "You need to act more . . ." She stopped and searched for the right word. "Available."

"No thanks," I said.

Callie said nothing and I was relieved she'd finally dropped it. Then I realized nobody was talking. In the whole cafeteria. I looked behind me and found the reason why.

Brad had just taken a backward seat right next to Alison at her eight-top. He pulled up close to her, their shoulders touching. Another inch and he could have rested his chin on her head. Brad pretended to find Alison repulsive, but that never stopped him from invading her personal space.

Though Brad lived with his mom two streets over from me, his dad lived with his new family in the west end, not far from Ethan and Alison on Allerton Heights. Brad had no contact with them. According to rumor, he skulked around in the woods behind his dad's house most days after soccer practice. Seeing him there once, his stepmom called the cops and Brad had to be taken home to his mom's in a police car.

Despite his proximity, Alison didn't look up, pretending to be deep in her book, even when he tapped his fingers on her table, quietly at first, then louder. Finally, he leaned in close, like he was having trouble reading the title, and started howling like a werewolf, sending the whole cafeteria into fits of laughter. Even then, Alison kept her head down.

Naturally, I watched Ethan. Like me, he seemed paralyzed by what he was witnessing. I could easily imagine the deliberations going on in his head. Their parents were good friends. *If I tell Brad to stop, will people start picking on me, too? If I don't tell him to stop, will I hear about it from my parents later?*

"I heard about your story, princess," Brad said, loud enough for everyone to hear. "Heard your unicorn had a serious boner?"

Alison closed her book and reached for her backpack, which was resting on a nearby chair.

"How many boners have you seen, princess?"

She unzipped her bag and stuffed in the book.

"Probably none, right? I mean, who would get a boner around Princess Alison of Allerton Heights?"

Alison calmly got up from her chair, tossing her bag over her shoulder. She surveyed the cafeteria, cataloging every witness who'd neglected to come to her defense, but she never looked at Brad. Eventually, her eyes landed where I knew they would. On Ethan. My gaze bounced between them. Ethan did nothing. When Brad noticed I was watching Ethan, he scowled at me.

"You're a child, Bradley," Alison said, then walked off, leaving Brad alone at her table.

"Better than being a loser!" he shouted. Then, suddenly, his eyes were on me. "Am, I right, Nerdelli?"

Brad's grudge against Alison kept him pretty busy, but he had a problem with me, too. Back in third grade, he would occasionally come over to my house to kick a soccer ball around in the backyard with my dad, who'd felt sorry for this fatherless boy. This went on for a few weeks, until the day my dad had encouraged me to join them. Five minutes in, Brad got really jealous. When my dad passed the ball to me, Brad started stomping the ground. Sensing his anger, I kicked the ball back to him. When it reached his feet, he didn't hesitate. He kicked it hard, right at my face, then stormed off while I sobbed.

Callie nudged me. "Say *right*," she whispered angrily.

"Right," I mumbled as, through the railing, Alison's backpack streaked past, down the ramp, to the eighth-grade locker bay. I swear she looked up at me. I could feel her eyes burning my cheek, but I didn't look back.

Brad cackled and returned to his table.

"You know she likes it."

I made a face at Callie. "What?"

"When Brad tortures her. She likes it."

"That's twisted. No, she doesn't."

Callie rolled her eyes. "Whatever gets Ethan's attention."

That year, I was editor in chief of the *Waterbury Junior Gazette.* Our advisor, Mr. Beal, had asked me to take the job at the end of seventh grade, after I'd done such a good job covering exhilarating topics like the school flu outbreak—the fault of a clogged ventilation system that hadn't been cleaned in decades. I'd actually called the ventilation company to ask for the service reports and found out that the system had never been serviced. When I'd hung up the phone that afternoon, a smile crept across my face. I'd caught my school district red-handed, and it felt awesome. That was the day I'd declared to my parents I was going to be a reporter.

Unfortunately, Callie was less enthusiastic about my life plans. She believed the school newspaper had zero redeeming qualities besides getting one-on-one time with Mr. Beal. All the girls in my class thought he looked like a nerdy Nick Cannon, but that's just because they didn't know of any other Black guys. Moms loved him, too, because he was a young, enthusiastic feminist. My mom was always saying things like *Thank God for Mr. Beal,* whenever his name came up. Despite his popularity, none of the cool kids were on the paper because *Why would you want to give yourself extra homework?* Only two eighth graders were that dorky. Me and you-know-who. Callie didn't think I'd ever be truly shed of Alison until I gave up journalism.

We had a *Waterbury Junior Gazette* meeting after school on the day Alison stormed out of the cafeteria. Even though I was standing up in the front of the classroom with Mr. Beal, Alison wouldn't look at me.

Mr. Beal began the meeting by asking, "Who wants to cover the boys' soccer team? They're undefeated this season."

Alison's hand shot up in the air.

The rest of us—me and half a dozen other reporters, all seventh graders—stared at her, then each other. *Was she nuts?* Didn't she know that would mean interviewing Brad Hutchins?

"That'll be easy for me," she said. Then she added, "Ethan Monroe is my neighbor," like it was some sort of accomplishment.

"Ethan's not captain," I said.

"An undefeated season from the perspective of the goalie," she said to Mr. Beal instead of me. "It's different. Interesting."

"Could be fun." Mr. Beal shrugged. "I like it." Mr. Beal had a soft spot for Alison. Encouraging her participation in the school paper was the one small thing he could do. He couldn't make anyone be her friend. He'd already tried that.

I forced a smile. "Sure. Alison is on soccer."

When I got home that afternoon, my mom was in the kitchen making a casserole and Dad was sitting at the kitchen table reading something in a manila folder.

"How was school?" Mom asked.

I thought about Alison storming out of the cafeteria and the horrible things Brad had said to her.

"Fine," I said.

My dad looked up from his reading. "Any big stories brewing?"

"Soccer team is undefeated," I said.

He rolled his eyes and adjusted the beat-up old Red Sox cap he always wore. The popularity of soccer among kids my age irked him.

"Is that the lead story?" Mom asked.

"Probably not. They replaced the pizza dough in the cafeteria with whole wheat. Parents are up in arms."

"Parents," Mom scoffed. "God forbid they try to feed kids anything nutritious."

"Can I go on Facebook?"

"Sure," Dad said, nonplussed, but Mom looked up from grating cheese on top of half-cooked ziti, wearing a slight frown. She hated Facebook.

Social media wasn't the only topic where my parents' love for each other was padded with a healthy disregard for the other person's conclusions. Take our house: It was full of mismatched, oversize, or oddly colored furniture because Mom ordered it all from the seventy-five-percent-off section in the back of the Pottery Barn catalog. It was the stuff nobody else wanted, like our oversize sofa, which Dad affectionately called "the whale" because of its strange seafoam-green color. Because it was on sale, the massive sofa was even cheaper than the smaller, more appropriately sized version. Mom always wanted to position it in the middle of the room the way sofas are positioned in magazines. Dad, who understood nothing of furniture staging, would just push the stupid thing back up against the wall. All of our furniture was clunky like this—the items too fat to be deemed elegant by more discerning buyers. Still, it made Mom happy to know she was buying a nice brand at Walmart prices. Dad always said as long as Mom and I were there, he didn't care what else was in the house. This was how he took the high moral ground, *All I need is my girls,* which really pissed off my mom.

Growing up, whenever I asked about our financial situation, my mom would sigh and say, "We're scraping by." My dad would pull me in for a hug and say, "We have all we need." Conversely, if the subject was *someone else's* money . . . if I said something like, "Misty Everett's dad just got a new Mercedes," my mom would say, "Who cares?" My dad would grind his teeth before saying, "Typical. People are starving, but Mr. Everett needs a new car."

While my dad was the more easygoing parent—he had a things-have-a-way-of-working-out philosophy—Mom always had exceedingly high expectations for me. I'm her one kid. *Measure twice, cut once* seemed to be her unspoken parental philosophy.

She set down the grater. "Seriously?" She was a small woman— the kitchen counter came up to her rib cage—but her *seriously?* was ten feet tall, looming over me. "You somehow finished your homework before you even set foot in the house?"

· · ·

I'd joined Facebook over the summer but my membership was highly conditional. Mom and I had a contract that specified the following: I could only be on Facebook for thirty minutes a day after homework, I wasn't allowed to befriend anyone I didn't know, I wasn't allowed to share personal information like my address and phone number, I had to be friends with her, and last, I had to report any bullying behavior I witnessed. She'd made me sign it, then hung it up on the fridge with a Red Sox 2004 World Series Champions magnet.

When Callie got my friend request, she was ecstatic; she'd been a member for nearly a year by the time I joined. In those days, there was a tradition on Facebook known as "de-virgining" someone's wall. It meant being the first person to post on a new member's page—something crude. Within ten minutes of joining, Callie had "de-virgined" my wall: Rachel's no longer a virgin! I'm popping her wall cherry!!!

Naturally, my mom went ballistic. "Why does EVERYTHING have to be sexualized?" she pleaded. "You're thirteen. *Thirteen!* I don't think this is a good idea." She regarded my dad, who was standing in the doorway. "Ray, I think we reserve the right to change our minds about this, yes?"

He looked at me and smiled. "Apparently, your mother has recently joined a convent."

She continued to fume. Few things made her angrier than not being taken seriously.

He softened. "Honey, she's a teenager. Teenagers joke about sex."

Simultaneously, they stared at me. Was I capable of lewd humor?

Formatively speaking, I was well behind my classmates. Both parents saw to it. Their tactics were clever: If they could paint me a picture of the choices I'd have to make later in life, maybe I'd become terrified and want to remain a child forever. *Someday,* they'd say, *you'll have too much to drink at a party. You'll think about driving home. But please don't. Just call us. We'll come get you, no questions asked.* I was seven the first time they presented me with this particular scenario, and we were at McDonald's. I was eating a Happy Meal and I had no idea what the hell they were talking about. A year later, my dad presented me with his one rule for dating: *Don't get knocked up.* We were at Pizza Hut this time and I'd just taken a big bite, stuffed-crust-first. It's fair to say that when it came to dating, my mom had far more rules, the keep-doors-open, two-feet-on-the-ground sort of rules, lessons about cows and milk. But my dad always waved them all off, telling me to remember his.

At this moment, my dad was smiling. "You remember the rule?" he asked.

I looked at the Facebook contract my mom had just made me sign. I knew he wasn't talking about that. "Don't get knocked up?"

"See, Michelle!" He raised his hands in victory. "She's paying attention!"

My mom huffed and said, "Fine." She pointed at me. "But I'm watching you!"

Like that ever *wasn't* true.

She set a timer on the microwave. "You have fifteen more minutes."

I sent a friend request to almost everyone I knew. I checked to see if Ethan had a profile yet, but he didn't. Within a few days, pretty much everyone had accepted my request, even people like Misty Everett and Shorty Simpson. That was my favorite thing about Facebook: People who wouldn't be your friend in real life would on Facebook. Misty and I weren't going to walk down the halls of Waterbury Junior High together, but she was allowing me into her online world. It felt, finally, like the doors of popularity might be starting to open just a crack. Of course, I realize now that I wasn't Misty's friend so much as one of her loyal subjects. If the name of the game was adoration—and it absolutely was—then you had to accept everyone's request, even the people you didn't like. Well, almost everyone.

A couple of weeks after I joined, Ethan did, too, and I would have squealed with delight if my mom weren't at the kitchen sink doing dishes. She was sticking hard and fast to the rules she'd laid out. I had three minutes left on the microwave when Ethan's request came in.

I accepted immediately. His wall had already been "de-virgined." It was Brad who got there first. THEY SAY YOU NEVER FORGET YOUR FIRST. SUCKS TO BE YOU MONROE!!!! For Brad, I actually thought this was pretty clever.

Some of the west end girls had already posted, too. Misty wrote: Finally! and Shorty: OMG your profile pic is the CUUUUUTEST.

It was cute: his soccer team photo with him bending a knee, soccer ball in the crook of his arm, his smile unselfconscious—just a kid grinning because he loved soccer. Life was simple.

"Two minutes," my mom warned.

I couldn't log off without writing something, but two minutes wasn't enough time to think of anything that would stand out. I considered just poking him. Or throwing a sheep. But I knew that was a cop-out. Nobody liked to be poked, not virtually, not in real life. I settled on **Welcome to Facebook, Ethan!!!** and then the microwave started beeping.

· · ·

I need to go on and ask someone about a newspaper thing," I told my mom. It was a blatant lie, but the fact that I was editor made her so endlessly proud, I knew by mentioning it I could get away with all kinds of shit.

She stared at me for a long time, then at my dad, but he just looked back, unfazed. He simply didn't understand the problem. She returned to the cheese grater. "Ten minutes," she said. "Then I need you to empty the dishwasher."

When I logged on, I had a friend request waiting for me. I hesitated before clicking on it.

"I hope you know," my mom continued, from the other side of the kitchen, "professional reporters don't set up interviews on Facebook."

"I know, Mom," I said, even though I was fairly certain she was wrong about this; professional reporters set up interviews any way they could.

When I clicked on the request, my face puckered like I was sucking on a lemon. It was Alison. I clicked on her page, but it was all private. I'd need to accept her request to see her friend list. When had she sent it? How many of my classmates had gotten a request? How many would accept? What the fuck was she doing? Didn't she get enough grief offline?

She likes it.

I closed her page and logged off without accepting.

"All done," I said to my mom.

She smiled at me and I unloaded the dishwasher.

On days when I didn't have newspaper after school, Callie and I would meet at Dunkin'. She'd tell me the gossip I'd missed since lunchtime, or, as she referred to it, "the real news."

The day after Brad asked Alison about boners at lunch, Callie had been waiting for me, fizzing with details. When I arrived, she had in front of her a Boston Kreme donut and a Blue Raspberry Coolatta, both untouched, because only losers ate donuts alone. She absent-mindedly stroked her plastic cup of blue sludge, her foot tapping below the table. "I've been waiting for you!"

Truth be told, I'd lied to Callie and said I had to do some work in the library after school for a geography project. I knew I had to be home by four and the longer it took me to get to Dunkin', the less time I would have for Callie's conspiracy theories. I ordered a chocolate frosted donut with sprinkles, no Coolatta, because my mom would only give me enough money for one or the other. To have both was, in her words, *obscene*. My butt had barely hit the orange bucket seat before Callie launched into topic number one.

"You missed everything!" she exploded, then thrust herself onto the straw of her Coolatta, like she'd been roaming for days in the desert and just stumbled upon a lagoon.

Callie's green eyes bugged out of her head and her voice went up an octave. "Brad and Misty are going out!" Her tongue was blue.

"Really? Since when?" I took a bite of my donut.

"Since like five minutes ago! Apparently, Misty was on her way to field hockey practice and Brad stole her stick and he made her kiss him to get it back!" Callie took a big bite out of her donut and the cream filling rocketed out the other end and landed with a *thud* on the hot pink table.

"Made her?" I asked. It sounded like one of my mom's terrifying dating warnings: *Boys will try to make you do things.*

Callie ignored my question. "So Misty was like, 'Since I've kissed you, that means we're going out now.' And he was like, 'Okay fine.'"

"Wow. How romantic. Where did you hear this?"

"Micah."

Why did I even ask?

Callie scooped up her fallen blob of cream with her index finger and dipped it into a scattering of sprinkles that had fallen from my donut onto the table. It was a shame that most of the time I spent with Callie was around food, because she had several disgusting habits. Thankfully, our donut-eating days were nearly done. In another year, we'd abandon them in favor of anything with a low-calorie sticker on it—for me, Smartfood White Cheddar Popcorn and for Callie, Yoplait Light and Fit.

"And he told me something else, too."

I braced myself for Micah's next decree. "What?"

"Brad didn't get a friend request from Alison on FB."

"That's not a surprise."

"He's the *only* kid in our class who didn't. She's totally provoking him."

"Or maybe she just doesn't want endless taunting messages on her wall."

"Then why join at all?"

I'll admit, I'd had the same question, but I wasn't quite willing to give in to Callie's theory that Alison was starting an all-out war with Brad.

"She's provoking Brad and hoping Ethan will save her. One hundred percent." Callie took a victory sip of her Coolatta. "It's not a bad plan. I wish I'd thought of it."

Speak of the devil and he shall appear. The door to Dunkin' swung open and Brad waltzed through, howling like he'd done at lunch the day before, chest puffed, making fists at his sides. The rest of the soccer team followed behind him, laughing, egging him on.

There were only a few other tables around: some of the theatre kids, some seventh graders, a mom and her toddler. Everyone stared.

Brad surveyed them all, like Dunkin' was his kingdom, then his eyes fell on me and Callie. "Hamel. Nerdelli. What's shakin'?"

He clomped closer, still cleated from soccer, and hovered over our table in his grass-stained Purple Puma uniform while the rest of his teammates ordered Coolattas and donuts. "You guys know the deal? Right?"

"What deal?" Callie asked, excited.

"Everyone is going to friend Alison on Facebook. Tonight."

Callie smiled like she thoroughly understood his diabolical plan.

He concentrated on me. "You got a request, right, Nerdelli?"

"Yeah." I shrugged.

"I'm the only one who didn't." He looked directly at me, then lied, "That hurt my feelings."

Callie giggled.

"I think I'm going to send her one," he said. "What do you think?"

"Why? You obviously don't want to be her friend."

Brad put his hand on his heart, like I'd offended him. "You miss the point, Nerdelli. How would you like it if you were the only kid in class not to get a valentine?"

I was pretty sure I wasn't the one missing the point. Instinctively, I looked over at Ethan, still in line for a donut. His normally pristine auburn hair was getting a little long and he had to shake his head to keep it from getting in his eyes. Every shake was a little earthquake in my heart. What did he know of his teammate's plan?

When I turned back to Brad, he smiled. "Don't worry about him. *I'm* going to need your help."

"Mine?"

"I need everyone, but especially you, Nerdelli, not to write anything on Alison's page. Got it?"

"Why?"

"*I'm* de-virgining her wall."

I gulped. "What are you going to write?"

He grinned now, Cheshire-cat style. That was all I needed to know, but he wasn't done. "If your *buddy* doesn't accept my request, I'll need you to convince her."

Callie was nodding along.

"Why me?"

He lifted an eyebrow like, *Really?* "I'm counting on you, Nerdelli."

I walked home alone. Callie didn't have a curfew and she was on her way to the west end playground where Micah spent his afternoons trying to land bar spins on his BMX.

I put my earbuds in. I'd recently inherited my mom's old iPod and it still had all her music on it. I hadn't yet replaced it with my own music because, at the time, though I would never have admitted it, I liked her old sentimental mom music. I was working my way through all of it on shuffle. So far, my favorites were Boyz II Men, Whitney Houston, Sarah McLachlan, and Tracy Chapman. That afternoon, halfway home from Dunkin', Celine Dion's "The Power of Love" started playing. *This song you really* will *hate*, I told myself and prepared to rage listen, but then the song crescendoed big-time and I was entranced. This bass drum kicked in like a heartbeat and suddenly Celine was wailing about being a lady and some guy being her "man." She wanted him to reach for her. She was going to do whatever she could. She was scared, but ready to learn. And I was like, *Holy shit.*

I looked back at Dunkin', where Ethan was still inside. I imagined his hand around a Coolatta, condensation dripping, and I wished I was that Coolatta. The urgency in Celine's voice was nothing like the love songs of 2008 with their ukuleles and "do-di-dodos." I wanted what Celine was selling—kisses and groping and satin sheets.

My house was only two minutes away, but I slowed my pace so I could hear the whole song. I even leaned down and pretended to tie my shoe.

Was this what love was like? Did people actually look into each other's eyes? Was the whole experience like getting caught in a thunderstorm? Wet and warm and invigorating? Had my mom been thinking about my dad when she listened to it? I tried to imagine Dad being like the guy in the song, but his voice wasn't warm and tender. He was a Mainer, for Christ's sake. Half of the alphabet was lost on him. I supposed he would *reach* for my mom sometimes, but usually it was to slap her ass or wipe mustard off her face. Was *that* the power of love?

My mind kept returning to Ethan, in the mythical satin sheets, wearing his usual khakis and Puma T-shirt, the two of us moving closer and closer together, his hand on my face for some reason.

After tying a double knot in my laces, I felt flush, rose too fast, and there in front of me, like an apparition, was Ethan.

"Hi!" I croaked.

"What are you listening to?" He was still straddling his bike, wearing a helmet like the good son he was. Over the summer, his voice had changed. I was still getting used to its new depth.

"Nothing," I said, quickly shoving the device into my pocket. The action yanked the buds from my ears.

What was he doing two minutes from my house? He was headed the wrong way.

"I have that iPod," he said. "In black." He smiled and it was beautiful.

Conversely, my upper lip was sweating. I was pretty sure my iPod was still playing in my pocket and I hoped he couldn't hear it. "Cool," I said, and I didn't know what else to add.

He didn't move, so I didn't move either. He smelled like the inside of an Abercrombie & Fitch store, a scent so alluring to my fourteen-year-old senses, I wanted to rip off his sweatshirt and eat it.

"This stuff with Alison," he said finally, mumbling down to the browning grass between the cracks in the pavement.

"Yeah," I said, staring at the same spot, ashamed.

"Did you ask her to write it?"

"What?" I looked up, confused. I thought he'd been talking about Brad. "The soccer article?"

"It's not just soccer. Also mathletes, because I got a perfect score last time. It's like some student-of-the-month thing. Did you pick me?"

"No. I didn't know you got a perfect score in mathletes." I didn't even know what that entailed. *What is he talking about?* "She asked if she could write about soccer."

"She said it's called 'The Renaissance Corner'? I'm the first one? It's just, you're editor, right? I thought you knew."

I had no idea. Had she spoken to Mr. Beal behind my back? "Alison does things without asking sometimes."

"Can you stop it?"

"I don't know." I honestly didn't.

"But you're editor?" A sticking point he obviously felt desperate for me to understand. "It's just, she's . . . too much."

I nodded. "I'll try talking to Mr. Beal, if you like."

He smiled again. "Thanks," he said and hovered for another second. "Are you going to the dance?"

I shrugged. "Probably."

"Cool," he said, then pushed off his pedal, and he was on the move, back the way he came, without a good-bye.

That night, over mushroom Bolognese, my parents accosted me with questions about school, about the paper, about the dance. All I could think of was my chat with Ethan, Alison's friend request, her article. I couldn't tell my parents about any of that, not without opening a Pandora's box of follow-up questions, so instead, I told them about Brad and Misty, how he stole her field hockey stick and demanded a kiss for its return. I should have known this wouldn't go down well either.

"That's not right," my mom said. "He can't demand a kiss. He can ask for one."

Dad regarded her, smirking. "Michelle? Can I have a kiss?"

Her answer was quick and decisive. "Not now."

He stole the fork out of her hand, a little spaghetti wound around it. "What about now? A kiss for your fork back?"

"It's my fucking fork, Ray." She grabbed it from him. "I'm trying to teach our daughter something important." She looked at me, very seriously. "Don't let a boy steal something from you, then demand some sort of payment for its return. It's manipulative behavior. Boys will manipulate you to get what they want."

My mom had many of these lessons. She doled them out plentifully. Men were not to be trusted, full stop. In particular, she hated the myth of female power attributed to women like her. People often said she wore the pants in her marriage and that aggravated her. Once, in sixth grade, I'd made the mistake of saying to her, "You have Dad so whipped." We were in the car on the way to Walmart and she actually pulled over, right on the side of George Mitchell Drive, and stared me down, her face bright red and her eyes filled with tears. "That kind of power isn't real. You understand that, right? You know your father makes more than twice what I make? He goes to work every day and people listen to what he says. Without him and his paycheck, I'd struggle to feed and clothe you. Convincing your husband to put the toilet seat down is *not* power. Only a *man* would tell you it is."

"Maybe he was just trying to tell this girl he really likes her," Dad suggested. "Maybe he was nervous? Maybe if she had said no, he'd have handed the stick back, brokenhearted."

Mom and I both looked at him, unconvinced. We all knew Brad.

"Just maybe give the kid a break," Dad said.

I wondered if he'd still feel that way if I told him how Brad treated Alison.

"It's just a funny story, Mom."

"I don't think it's funny," she said, then turned to my dad. "I can't believe we're at the boy stage already."

They both scrutinized me. *Were we at the boy stage?*

I'd have sooner volunteered to perform brain surgery than sign up for whatever sordid act the two of them were clearly imagining me doing at that moment. Until that day, I'd still considered myself a floating head. I'd paid no attention to my body except to lament all the changes I'd found intolerable. The mere sight of it in the mirror made me uncomfortable. I'd have been relieved if the whole thing was replaced by robot parts. Until now, until

Celine and "The Power of Love," until Ethan and *Are you going to the dance?*

Again, I felt sweat forming on my lip.

Shit. We were at the boy stage.

Later that evening, I asked my dad if I could log on to Facebook. He was watching *SportsCenter.* "Done your homework?" he asked, looking away from the TV only briefly to smile at me. When I nodded, he said, "Thirty minutes," and returned his attention to the show, satisfied that he'd enforced all the rules.

Alison's friend request was sitting just where I left it. I clicked Accept and suddenly, I had access to her wall. It was still "virginal" as Brad intended, but she had more than three hundred friends. His plan was working. Callie was there, so were Micah, Misty, Shorty, and, yes, Ethan. Pretty much everyone but Brad.

I didn't know what would happen next. I stared at her profile picture—a shot of her in front of Cinderella's castle in Disney World—for so long it was like I willed her to log on. A private chat box popped up:

> ALISON: My article with Ethan is going to be different than assigned. I cleared it with Mr. Beal.

Hello to you, too, I thought.

> ME: I know. Ethan told me. The Renaissance Corner or something?
>
> ALISON: Why did you speak to him?
>
> ME: Cause he wanted to talk to me.

Could you feel someone seething from a mile away, through a computer? I could.

ME: And you should have asked me first.

ALISON: It's a good idea.

ME: We need an article about soccer.

ALISON: So write one.

ME: I assigned it to you!

ALISON: You were right. Someone should interview Brad. I don't think I'm the best person for that job. He's your neighbor. And your friend.

What was she talking about? I wasn't friends with Brad. But then I recalled Brad smiling at me at Dunkin'. *I'm counting on you, Nerdelli.*

ME: He's wondering why you didn't send him a friend request.

ALISON: Because he and I aren't friends.

Neither are you and I.

Why was I helping him? Why was I lying? There was just something about her presence on Facebook that enraged me. This is the one place where I could exist without her, where she wasn't always in my peripheral vision, in my way. Until now. Surely she knew she didn't have three hundred friends, that all this was fake.

Did *I* know that?

I had 260 friends. Except, of course, I didn't. And because fucking Alison joined, I now had to acknowledge that.

ME: Give him a break.

And I logged off.

Waterbury Eighth Grader Succeeds On and Off the Field
BY ALISON PETRUCCI

If you're a student at Waterbury Junior High, odds are you know Ethan Monroe. If your last name starts L–P, you probably know him from homeroom. If you're supersmart, you know him from the high-track classes like Honors English and Algebra II. The *really* smart kids know him as their mathletes teammate. And if you've ever kicked a soccer ball, Ethan Monroe probably blocked it from going into the goal. But to Ethan, it's all the same. He excels whether the challenge is mental or physical. I sat down with him to ask a few questions:

ALISON: First of all, hi. Thank you for taking the time to speak with me about all the amazing things you're doing. Let's start with mathletes. What do you like about competitive math?

ETHAN: I don't know . . . I like that you can get a perfect score. Math is the only subject where you can strive to be perfect and achieve it.

A: Wow. That's fascinating. What about soccer? What do you like about that?

E: I don't know . . . I like to run fast and kick the ball hard. You have to do both those things well if you want to win. I can kick the ball really hard.

A: I know, I've seen you kick it all the way down Allerton Heights. (Full disclosure, Ethan and I are neighbors.) Do you think you prefer one over the other, between soccer and mathletes? If you had to choose?

E: I guess I'd pick soccer because it's definitely more fun, but I might pick mathletes because I want to go to MIT and it would look good on my application.

A: I want to go to Harvard! That'd be cool if we both got into our top choices, we'd still be neighbors! I think I know the answer to this next question, but what's your favorite subject in school?

E: Probably math. I also like orchestra. It's like math, but with sound.

A: I forgot you were in orchestra. Wow. That's amazing. Least favorite subject?

E: Yeah, I guess, kinda, probably English? I find it hard to sit still and read.

A: Totally. I can see that. I mean, there must be a book you like reading just for fun? Like, I love the Twilight series.

E: I guess the Harry Potters are pretty cool. I like *Goblet of Fire*. If the Triwizard Tournament was real, that'd be pretty awesome.

A: Yes! Totally. Who do you want to win the presidency, Ethan? Obama or McCain?

E: Oh. Um. I don't know. I think my parents want Obama. But I know lots of cool people whose parents want McCain. I don't think it really matters.

A: Right. Last question. We know Ethan Monroe succeeds academically and athletically, but what about romantically? Does he have a girlfriend?

E: What? No.

A: If you had to pick an actress to be your girlfriend, who would you pick? I'd pick Zac Efron to be my celebrity boyfriend.

E: I have to say someone?

A: Yep.

E: Alright . . . I guess, maybe the actress that plays Hermione? I don't know her real name. I guess she's okay.

A: Emma Watson! Good choice! You heard it here first, ladies. Ethan Monroe likes smart girls!

After I read her interview, I lobbied Mr. Beal not to publish it, just like Ethan had asked me to do.

We were huddled around a computer in the lab, placing articles on Quark.

Surprised, Mr. Beal said, "What do you think we should put in this blank column if we don't run Alison's interview?" He was the kind of the teacher who never said no. He preferred to guide you with a series of leading questions designed to highlight your stupidity.

"I don't know."

"Why are you concerned about running it, Madame Editor?"

"I just mean, it's obvious she likes him."

"Nothing wrong with that."

When I turned to look at him, he quickly pushed back in his rolling chair. Being a feminist teacher was clearly a tightrope walk for Mr. Beal. On the one hand, he was always trying to uplift female students by giving them positions like editor in chief on the newspaper. On the other hand, such recognition of female existence and intelligence made girls fall instantly in love with him. The tortoiseshell glasses didn't help. Anyway, with me he didn't have to worry. I wasn't fantasizing about whipping off those glasses. When I looked at Mr. Beal all I saw was a guy who probably, like my dad, called his pants "slacks."

"It's what we call a 'human interest' piece, Rachel," he continued from a distance. "It's meant to bring joy and inspire. We don't always need to be looking under stones for worms."

I wanted to tell him that he was missing the point, that the article amounted to a social murder / suicide pact, but he'd accuse me of being dramatic.

"Are you sure you're not a little jealous?" he asked.

"No, I'm not," I said, defensive. Then I couldn't help myself. I asked, "Jealous of what?"

"Alison had a pretty good idea." A wave of relief washed over me. I thought he'd been referring to my crush on Ethan. "If you want a shot at writing 'The Renaissance Corner,' maybe you and Alison can switch off for the rest of the year?"

"No, it's fine," I said. My hand on the mouse, I dangled the text above the empty column and it pinged into place.

Ethan likes you," Callie said at lunch the next day. Her tone suggested I should watch out.

"No, he doesn't."

"He borrowed your calculator in math class." This was her proof.

And though it struck me as proof of nothing, it was technically true. The day after he asked me to stop Alison's article, he'd turned around, out of the clear blue sky, and asked if we could switch calculators. The request made no sense. He already had a fancy scientific calculator with lots of graphing buttons. Mine was the solar-powered kind with large buttons for old people who couldn't see the numbers.

"So what?" I said to Callie. "It's just a calculator."

Except I was lying. When I'd turned it on, I saw he'd left me a note using the calculator's text function. ANY LUCK WITH ALISON? it read.

Callie shook her head at my pretend indifference. "What are you going to do when he asks you out? Everyone is coupling up before the dance."

Even though I didn't think there was a snowball's chance in hell of that happening, I still started to sweat. I hadn't told Callie about my chat with Ethan a few days earlier, that he'd asked for my help with Alison or that he'd asked me about the dance. I knew she'd enjoy it too much. She'd want to coach me on how to respond. *Wear something slutty to math class.* I also hadn't said anything to Callie about Alison's article. I guess I just kept hoping I'd find a way to cut it.

"Maybe Ethan's flirting with you to send Alison a message?"

Because she said her name, I had to look over at Alison, alone in her usual spot, reading some book about fairies. Her interview was coming out later that day. "What do you mean by that?"

"Like, maybe he hopes that if Alison sees him flirting with you, she'll back off, because, like, you and her are kind of the same. But you're better."

"Thanks?"

Callie shrugged and shoved a Dorito in her mouth and the triangular corner stabbed her cheek like an alien fighting to get out.

I was worried she had a point. Maybe Ethan was using me as some sort of shield?

I looked over at Alison again. She closed the book she was reading around her bookmark and squeezed its spine. Satisfied at how far she'd gotten, she then looked at Ethan, who was putting the remnants of his lunch in a brown paper bag. I watched him, wondering if he'd notice she was staring at him. Of course, by that point, I was staring at him, too. Somehow, I'd convinced myself it wasn't the same thing.

That afternoon, sitting in the computer lab alone—I had permission to miss gym class on publication days—I watched the paper print. My job was to collate the pages and staple them together, then I'd stack them at the school's entrance before math class. The front page just kept coming: "Waterbury Eighth Grader Succeeds On and Off the Field, On and Off the Field, On and Off the Field, On and Off the Field . . ."

Normally, I loved this, delivering my hard work to the masses. That day, I dreaded it. I hated the idea of abandoning the papers there by the school's double doors, Alison's article sitting on top like a bleeding heart, Ethan in the crosshairs of her self-delusion.

Twenty minutes later, pages collated, I was walking past the eighth-grade locker bay, teetering with the tall stack of papers in my hands, when Brad sidled up to me.

"Boo!" he said, hoping I'd drop the stack. "What's all that, Nerdelli?"

"You know what it is," I said and tried to pick up the pace, thinking if I got ahead of him, maybe he'd leave me alone. God knows why I thought this would work. He was captain of the soccer team, for Christ's sake. Running people down was his thing.

He grabbed a paper off the top.

"Well, well, well . . ." he said. "Ethan, Ethan, Ethan . . . Isn't he so wonderful?" he added with a little flamboyant flick of the wrist.

"Cut it out, Brad."

"He's going to get so much shit for this."

I glanced at him sideways. "Not if you don't start it."

He looked at me like, *Fat chance, Nerdelli.*

"Did you convince your buddy Alison that this was a good idea?"

"She's not . . ." I faltered; it felt so horrible to say it even though it was true. "She's not my *buddy.*"

He clawed at the air with his hand, suggesting a catfight. "You're both fighting over Monroe. Tell me, why do losers love him so much?"

"You're just jealous."

"Ha!" He put the paper back on my lopsided stack. "You think I want attention from Princess Alison of Allerton Heights and Nerdelli? I could never be jealous of Monroe."

"I thought you were his friend?"

"Sure. We're buddies. But I'm not jealous of him."

"So, if you're his friend, maybe leave him alone."

He scoffed at my suggestion. "And how are you doing on the little assignment I gave you?"

We were by the front doors now. I desperately wanted to set down the papers, but something about having three reams between me and Brad felt safer. Thankfully, the bell rang, signaling the end of fifth period. It didn't even occur to me to question what he was doing out of class. Brad did what he wanted.

"I told her to give you a chance."

"She hasn't. No new friend requests."

I shrugged.

"Guess I'll just have to send her one. Of course, I'll need you to put in another good word."

"I don't want any part of what you're planning, Brad."

"Too late, Nerdelli. You *are* a part of it."

I looked at him pleadingly.

"You know what I'm going to do when she accepts?"

I gulped.

"I'm not just going to de-virgin her wall. I'm going to rape it."

I didn't know what he could possibly mean, but it put the fear of God in me. "Why are you doing this?"

"She's going to get what's coming to her, Nerdelli. And if you're not careful, so will you." He put his hands in the pockets of his baggy cargo pants and shuffled off.

12.

While Jen waited for me to give her the name of anyone Alison could have met at Pleasant Pond, I imagined Brad and Alison on the shore together. The image was ludicrous; I struggled not to laugh. Brad may have had it in for Alison when we were kids, but it's hard to imagine he'd want anything to do with her these days. I couldn't fathom why he'd lure her to a pond eight years later. There's only one guy I could picture her meeting there and that was Ethan. He was at Yale, surely?

I imagined them having an argument at the pond. He told her that her crush on him had to stop. *I don't love you. Get over it. You're pathetic.* He grabbed her. *You said you wanted it.*

Wait. No. That wasn't right.

I winced and rubbed the back of my legs. They were suddenly hot and stuck to the denim of my jeans.

"There's no one," I said to Jen. "She only kept in touch with this guy Ethan, but he's at Yale."

She looked deflated.

"But if she's still in touch with him, maybe he's worth talking to," Lindsay pressed. "He could know something. Are you friends on Facebook?"

"Yeah." I sighed.

"See if he's online."

I glanced at Stannard. I wanted her to say what my mom would have. *Professional reporters don't set up interviews on Facebook.* Instead, she made a face like, *Worth a shot.*

I pulled up his page. His profile pic showed him with his arm around some girl. They each had a red Solo cup in hand, smiling.

Jen looked over my shoulder at his page. "He kinda looks like Cam."

"What? No, he doesn't." *Does he?*

"There's a similar preppy vibe."

"Isn't that all college guys?" I asked.

"Unfortunately," Jen said, rolling her eyes.

"Well, he's not online."

"Message him anyway," Lindsay said.

"I don't know. That doesn't feel right."

"Why?"

"I haven't spoken to him in years, then suddenly I'm getting in touch because his neighbor is dead?"

"That's the *job*, dude," Brie said.

Lindsay and Jen were nodding like she had a point. Stannard, I think, understood my dilemma, maybe finally understood how much I was hiding from them.

I typed out a message while Brie and Jen watched.

Hey, Ethan, I'm sorry to get in touch like this. I'm sure you know the horrible news about Alison. We're writing a piece

about her for the Denman paper and I wondered if we
could talk?

I looked over at Brie, who'd gone back to placing ads. Jen was
still waiting. I felt sick.

"I think that's alright," Jen said. "I'm sure he'll appreciate it's
coming from you."

She looked away then, when a text flashed up on her phone.

"You might not get a response for this issue, but it could prove
useful for the next," Stannard suggested.

"I suppose." My fingers lingered over the Send button. I looked
behind me one more time. Satisfied that no one was watching, I
clicked out of the conversation. "There," I lied. "Sent."

"Jen, is that her suitemates responding?" Lindsay asked.

"No," Jen said, looking up. "And I don't think they will."

"Who are they?" Brie asked. "Maybe we can check their social
media? We can quote that, right? If it's public?" She directed these
questions to Stannard.

"It's not ideal," Stannard said. "This is a small community. They
could feel betrayed."

Jen rambled off their names anyway. I didn't know any of them.
I was barely paying attention. My mind was still stuck back at the
pond, the idea of Alison meeting someone there. It didn't make any
sense, but something about junior high felt important, felt lodged in
my brain.

Then it came back to me. I winced. *Be nice to her! Don't be like
Brad Hutchins!*

That's what I'd shouted at Alison on Saturday night. I hadn't
shouted it because I really wanted this guy to be nice to her. I'd
shouted it because I wanted to see Alison's reaction. I wanted her
to know there were consequences for invading my turf. Had she

reacted? A flinch, maybe? When was the last time she thought about Brad? Did she think about him every day? Did she know he was still in Waterbury, working the forklift in Walmart? I knew he had a daughter of his own. All this I learned from bumping into him over the summer, an ill-fated night at the dive bar, the Low Down.

. . .

It was Cam's idea to go, the one weekend all summer that he came to visit me in Waterbury. I knew the bar was popular with my old classmates, but I'd never actually been there or to any bar in town for that matter. I'd only recently turned twenty-one and I hadn't kept in touch with anyone from school, not even Callie, who'd moved to Augusta to attend the University of Maine, though she would frequently come home for Saturday nights at the Low Down.

Cam was visiting under protest. All summer he'd convinced me to visit him in Cape Cod, where his family had a beach house, but I hated going there. Since I had a full-time summer job at the Epicurious Farm, I could never go for more than forty-eight hours, several of which were taken up by two buses each way and a lengthy stopover in Boston's South Station. When I finally arrived, I was confronted with Cam's mom, a cold woman who made me sleep in a different room, as if that was going to stop her son's insatiable sexual appetite. He'd just sneak into my room at two a.m. for sex, then go back to his own bed. His father, who spent all his time in his study, either didn't know I was there or was purposely ignoring me. But in Cam's mind, these trips were a win-win. He got laid and I got to take in the beautiful sea views.

I was at my wit's end when I invited him; I regretted it immediately. We'd been talking on the phone and he was in one of his long-distant-relationships-don't-work moods, even though we'd both be back at Denman in less than a month. Three and a half weeks is a long wait for a college guy when sex is what he's waiting for. But I'd just been down to Chatham the previous weekend and I wasn't going again. "If you want to get laid, come to Waterbury!" I said. The line was silent for a few seconds, then he said, "Fine."

He came prepared. He already knew about the Low Down before he'd even arrived at my house. He'd been looking up Waterbury dive bars and told me within five minutes of walking through the door that we were going to go.

On his second night in town, we took an Uber that dropped us on a busy road just a couple blocks south of the Walmart. The Low Down was the type of bar you couldn't see into, but we could hear it was hopping. JLo and Ja Rule had the small, wooden-framed building thumping. The lights glowing inside were unnaturally yellow, like Velveeta.

Cam was wearing a wide grin when he slammed the Uber door. "Yes. This is perfect." He put a hand in the back pocket of my jeans and looked down my low-cut tank top. *Low cut for the Low Down.* He was wearing an oxford shirt, untucked, and khaki shorts, his best attempt to blend in. "Let's do this, Nardelli."

Inside, the place was packed. The long bar to the left was three rows deep with customers trying to get drinks. To the right were high-top tables, all shellacked pine, populated by girls I vaguely recognized from the years above me at school, drinking cocktails the color of Listerine. In the back was a dance floor, sparsely populated this early, a strobe light turning the pine room occasionally purple, pink, green.

Cam pointed to a chalkboard announcing dollar-fifty Jell-O shots.

"Bud Light is fine."

"Oh, you're getting both." He pulled me in. "I know how to treat a lady."

I made a sour face. I'd barely touched a drop of booze all summer, just the occasional beer with my parents. Spring of junior year, I'd embraced the partying life a little too much. I was frightened by how easily I'd learned it was difficult to stop once I'd started. That and blacking out at Cotillion. Over the summer, I'd decided it was just easier not to start.

Cam took my hand and we forced our way to the bar. I tried to place everyone around me. *Amy Something over there? Was that Trinity Whatsherface behind the bar? By the dance floor, was that Shorty Simpson in Daisy Dukes and a pink cowboy hat?* I found myself looking down at my feet, hoping nobody would notice me, even though I knew it was Cam's mission to be best friends with everyone by the end of the night.

Cam handed me a Bud Light bottle and a red Jell-O shot in a little plastic cup intended for ketchup or tartar sauce. "Down the hatch." We cheers-ed our Jell-O and threw them back. "Alright. Let's get down with the townies." He bobbed his head to Blackstreet, like he was trying to blend into one of those high production, pool party hip-hop music videos. "Has anyone told this town it's the twenty-first century? Do they know Y2K ended up being a whole lot of nothing?"

I scowled. When I started dating Cam last fall part of my calculation was expanding my horizons beyond Waterbury, maybe even leaving it behind. I was thinking martini bars in skyscrapers, wine bars in the Village, not Jell-O shots at the Low Down.

"Nerdelli? No fuckin' way."

It wasn't just the nickname. It was the sound of his voice, completely unchanged. When I turned around, he was in a Patriots jersey with a Dodge Ram baseball cap sitting precariously on the top of his head.

"Brad. Hey."

Cam put an arm around my shoulders and whispered in my ear, "What did he call you? You on a last name basis with this guy?" Clearly, he thought Brad had said "Nardelli," and I wasn't about to correct him. Cam reached out a hand to Brad. "Cameron Parker."

Brad ignored the invitation, took a swig of his own Bud Light. "You been around all summer, Nerdelli?"

I shrugged.

"Bunch of us got a table over there." He pointed in the back, between the bar and the dance floor, where I was pretty sure I had spotted Shorty before. "Hang with us." He gave Cam a long look. "If the professor doesn't mind?"

"Oh, we're not sticking around," I said.

Cam pulled me in tighter, but he regarded Brad. "Was she like this in high school?"

"Like what?" I asked, trying to get out of his grasp.

Cam laughed. "Antisocial."

"Nerdelli's always been too good for us," Brad said. He locked eyes with me and said, "Isn't that right?"

"No," I said. I could hear how unconvincing it sounded. I didn't think I was better, it's more that I didn't fit, square peg / round hole stuff. At least that's how I chose to see it.

Brad raised an eyebrow. "Good news for you. Ethan's home."

Brad made his way back to our classmates, expecting us to follow.

"Old boyfriend?" Cam asked.

"Who? Brad? No way."

"But there's one back there, isn't there?" Cam grinned.

"I didn't want to come here," I said.

"No. You didn't want to come to *Chatham*. Now, *I'm here* and you're getting what you asked for." He nudged me, grinning. "NERDelli."

I spotted Ethan right away, sandwiched between Misty and Shorty. When Brad rejoined the group, I saw Callie—wearing another pink felt cowboy hat to match Shorty's. She jumped on Brad and bit his ear. He seemed to nibble her back, although the exact action was unclear under the strobe lights.

When she looked up from his neck, she saw me and screamed "RACHEL!" She ran toward me in a tube top that was more bra than shirt, just a black band around her chest. She had a pink rhinestone belly-button ring in her still fleshy midriff and green highlights in her hair. "Fuckin' A! You never respond to my texts, bitch!"

"Callie." I gave her a reluctant hug. Over her shoulder, I locked eyes with Ethan for a split second.

I pulled away and my hand found Cam's. I squeezed, hoping to impart some sort of *help me* message. What's the point of having a significant other except to be able to say *save me* without saying anything at all? "This is my boyfriend, Cam," I said to Callie—well, to everyone, because the whole group was now staring at us, except Ethan, who was looking at a condensation ring on the high-top table they were gathered at.

Even Cam looked nervous now. He needed to be in control at all times, but I think it dawned on him just then that he wouldn't be among this group. He squeezed my hand back. "Hey," he said to everyone and took a swig of his Bud Light.

"I found them at the bar trying to hide," Brad said.

"Sorry, I didn't know you guys were back here," I offered.

"I need another one of these," Cam said, shaking his empty bottle at me.

"I'm good," I said, though he didn't ask.

"I'll go with you!" Callie said, linking arms with Cam. "Rachel's here. We need shots!"

Cam smiled at his new coconspirator. "So, you're *the* Callie?"

"You know it!"

And then they were lost in the crowd.

I turned to Brad. "So, you and Callie?"

Brad winked. "Only on Saturdays."

"Okay . . ."

"Don't judge, Nerdelli. You're always judging."

"I'm not."

His expression said, *Bullshit.* "She's got a guy up in Augusta, and I'm still technically with my baby mama. Callie and I, we have fun."

"That's cool," I said, even as I was thinking *car crash.* "Wait. You're a dad?"

"Yeah! Where have you been? Luna Hutchins is two next month."

I tried to picture Brad as a father, but I felt my lips start to form a sour expression, one Brad would certainly pick up on, so I stopped myself.

Thankfully, we were saved.

"Rachel, how's Denman?" Misty was on my other side now. That she and Brad had gone out in junior high was now ancient history. She had a big diamond ring on her finger. It caught the strobe light when she lifted her hard seltzer to her lips.

"Yeah, school's good. Sorry, are you engaged?" *Why is everyone so grown-up?* I still had a summer job. I still didn't sign up for classes earlier than eleven a.m. so I could sleep in.

"Ha! Yeah!" She leaned in and whispered, "We go to USM together, his dad owns a construction company down in Portland."

"Nice," I said, peering past her at Ethan, who was disengaged, playing with his phone.

"When we get married, we're going to expand to Central Maine."

"Cool, so you're going to join the family business?"

"I'm studying marketing, so yeah." She winked at me and said, "Maybe we'll put the Petruccis out of business!"

I didn't have words, but I felt my eyes widen by way of response.

Cam and Callie came back each carrying a tray of Jell-O shots. Everyone except me and Ethan cheered.

Callie grabbed my arm, pulled my ear to her lips. "You've always had a thing for rich guys."

I looked back at where Ethan was standing, but he was gone and Shorty had taken his place. Clearly drunk, she was staring at the ceiling and singing to herself.

"How amazing is the ring?" Misty said, flashing her engagement ring under my nose.

"It's . . ." *Ugly. Huge.* "Yeah. Amazing."

"Don't get any ideas, Nardelli." Cam handed me another Jell-O shot. "It's not in the budget right now."

Cam's budget. He was in love with it—a five-, ten-, and twenty-year plan for investments and career projections along with what he hoped to be able to afford: a new car at twenty-two, an apartment in the Upper East Side at twenty-five, a house in Greenwich at thirty. A two-carat Tiffany's engagement ring was scheduled for age thirty-one. Ten years.

"Who's the lucky guy?" Cam asked Misty.

"The heir to a construction company," she bragged.

"Wait, wait, wait!" Cam, excited, downed another shot. "The guy with the trucks! We see them all over Denman."

Everyone except me started laughing. Cam regarded me, confused.

"Can you imagine if Alison had a hot brother?" Misty mused. "That would have changed everything."

"Alison?" Cam lightly shoved me. "Rach? The girl at the coffee shop? That Alison?"

"Yep."

He turned to everyone else. "You guys friends with her? She goes to Denman and Rachel won't talk to her."

I shoved Cam harder than he shoved me.

Everyone else was quiet.

"She's home now," Brad said. "Hangs around that overpriced coffee shop."

"Probably owns it," Callie scoffed.

Misty laughed. "Ethan told me she still flirts with him and it's really uncomfortable."

Everyone looked at me, then Callie said, "Ugh. The worst."

"Jesus." Cam laughed. "What did she do? Murder somebody?"

After a couple shots, Callie dragged Cam onto the dance floor at the behest of Destiny's Child, who assured us the Low Down was now jumpin'. I watched the two of them flail, trying to work out how close to get to each other with me watching. Callie was grinding at his side. Cam was working out where to put his hands: her ass or her bare midriff? He looked to me for guidance and I shrugged. It was so uncomfortable to watch that I went and stood next to Shorty.

She was hammered, her pink cowgirl hat on the tilt. She was sucking hard on the straw of a drink that was long gone. She tried to focus on me through her red, bleary eyes. "Raaaachel. Crazy."

"Hey, Shorty."

She pouted and said in the baby voice I remembered so well, "No one calls me that anymore. I miss it."

I offered a perfunctory smile.

"Elizzzzabethhhhh," she said, like she was vomiting up her own name. "So gross, right? Like I'm old-timey." She was lilting, then suddenly, serious eye contact. "Right?!"

"I don't think it's so bad."

She scoffed, then looked at Cam and Callie. "She'll steal your boyfriend, you know. She's such a ho."

I laughed.

"I'm serious, Rach-uuul! I was seeing this guy at UMA and she totally stole him. And Brad! His girlfriend is soooooo nice! She draws *blood* at the hospital."

Far too much information to process, so I said, "I thought you were at Union College?"

"Yeah, for like a semester."

I didn't ask. Instead, I said, "I don't think I need to worry. I'm pretty sure Callie scares the shit out of Cam." I watched them creating awkward angles around each other. I snorted to myself, grateful that they were, for the moment, amusing each other instead of harassing me.

"Where did Ethan go?" I ventured.

Shorty smiled at her drinkless glass, only a few ice cubes remaining. "You and Ethan."

"No," I said. "Nothing like that. We haven't spoken in years."

"Right." She popped one of the ice cubes in her mouth, sucked it like a lozenge. I worried she would choke. "He said he had to go home and call his fancy Yale girlfriend."

The night ended with Cam and Brad each taking one of Shorty's arms and escorting her out of the bar and into the back of a cab.

I looked on as she flopped into the back seat, laughing and yelling, "Where's Misty?" Misty had already gone home, leaving her best friend to be everyone else's problem.

"Callie! Callie! Come home with me!" Shorty shouted, flailing like an upturned turtle.

Cam thought this was hilarious, but Callie wasn't paying any attention. She and Brad had retreated; he had her up against the side of the building.

Shorty turned her attention to me. "Rachel, come here."

"I can't go home with you, Shorty."

"Just come here. You can go home with moneybags, just come here first."

"Oh, I like that," Cam said. "Can you call me that from now on?" He practically shoved me into the car, he was so curious about what she would say.

The inside of the car reeked of cigarettes and air fresheners. The driver pretended he was somewhere else. I helped Shorty sit up.

She wavered and tried to give me her pink felt cowboy hat. "Take it!"

"No thanks, I'm sure you'll want it tomorrow."

She shook her head violently, no.

"Take it," she said, shoving it at my chest, then, "Look at me." When I did, her bleary eyes were sharp, almost possessed. "Don't come back here."

13.

Lindsay was restless, fiddling with her phone, then her watch, then back to her phone.

I'd barely typed a word since Stannard arrived. My professor had pulled out a stack of papers and was reading them with her signature green pen in hand. Why was she still here? We technically had a faculty advisor, though classics professor Samantha Altman, known as "Easy-A Altman," had yet to make an appearance in our newsroom or even respond to an email. We had our doubts about whether she even read the paper.

"Jen's student quotes?" I ventured. "Is that a separate article or am I adding them to this one?"

"I've got so many," Jen said. "We could put some in your article since it's thin. And do a whole separate article."

"It's not thin. We just don't have much info."

Jen's eyes bugged. "It wasn't a criticism. Chill."

"I like that idea," Lindsay said. "Let's put some in Rachel's article, then have another piece about what students are doing to stay safe."

"Boom," Brie said, mostly to herself, dropping a Domino's ad into place.

Jen nodded. "A lot of people told me they thought this was related to the election. Like, not specifically, obviously, but that if a woman becomes president, hostility toward women will get worse."

"That's insane!" Lindsay said. "They're suggesting we shouldn't elect a female president to *protect* women?!"

Stannard was shaking her head.

"Yeah, get working on that article," Lindsay said. "Jesus Christ."

I didn't find this particularly surprising. With the upcoming election, our outlooks had progressively been getting darker. Maybe the jobs we thought were waiting for us after college wouldn't be there, and even if we were lucky enough to get those jobs, would they be at 80 percent of the pay that our male classmates would get? And five years down the road, would the effects of this widening wage gap mean we'd have to choose between our low-paying jobs and having children? What made us think we'd be any different? Sometimes it felt like if we couldn't have it all, then we'd have to settle for nothing.

"I'm lacking a computer," Jen was quick to point out.

"Write it out; when Rachel's done, hop on her computer." Lindsay consulted her watch again. "We only have three hours to get this all done. Ben at the printer's is being really nice and giving us the one a.m. slot."

Jen stared at me not typing but didn't argue, just opened her notebook and started writing.

Instead of typing, I was thinking about Alison on Saturday night, when she was telling that guy about her plans after graduation. Applying to Harvard? Something about a fellowship? Was she not as pessimistic about the future as the rest of us? Or was she just *that* used to getting what she wanted? Was this why she was dead? Had Alison been killed for her ambition?

I understood how these women on campus were feeling. Ambition seemed so stupid now. How had we ever dared believe we were allowed such a thing? It was dawning on us how much we'd lost— not only Alison but also a sense of safety, a sense of freedom. Until Alison, if you'd asked any young woman at Denman whether she ever feared for her life, she'd have probably said no. I think we all settled for physical safety that night. Gone was our desire to thrive; there was only the imperative to survive.

But Lindsay was having none of it. "I'm furious!"

Brie reached out and rubbed her back, then pulled her in sideways, kissing her on the forehead.

Jen, Stannard, and I all looked at each other. Jen and Stannard shared a smile, then Jen looked at me, her smile growing. "Maybe these two have the right idea?" When I didn't smile back, she handed me a stack of her quotes. "Here. Use any of these."

I flipped through the quotes:

"This is crazy," said Margaux Jennings, '18. "College is supposed to be safe."

"I didn't know her. Why would anyone want to murder some random girl? It makes no sense," Dean Pritchard, '17.

"I think maybe she lived down the hall from me freshman year? She was nice. She had this really fancy portable speaker and she would lend it to people," Sarah Evans, '16.

"I really want to know what happened," Cassidy Philbrook, '19, said. "I've only been on campus for, like, a month and this happens? Are we safe? Was she a target or could it have been any of us?"

"Just got a message from my friend Maddie," Lindsay said. "She goes to Williams. They've all heard."

I regarded her but said nothing.

"She says there's this guy on social media? Daniel Boulter? Apparently, he got rejected from all the northeastern liberal arts colleges and there's a theory that it was him." Lindsay reported all this in a monotone, reading directly from her phone screen. "He is going to kill a girl at every college that rejected him. Oh, there's a picture of him!" She reached out her phone to me, but thankfully, Brie intercepted to get a look. "Maybe we should write a story about this guy?"

I couldn't bear to look at the photo. What if it was the guy at the party? Or what if I wasn't sure? Again, I imagined myself in police interrogation. *Is that him, Rachel? Is that the guy you let kill Alison?*

"Sorry." Jen looked up from her notebook. "This guy actually *said* that? That he is going to kill a girl at every school that rejected him?" She paused for effect. "Like, is there any actual evidence for this theory? Or is this another one of those internet shaming things?" She took the phone from Lindsay's hand to get a look. I suspected that, like the photo of the pond earlier, they would also project their own judgments onto the photo of this guy they didn't know. And sure enough, Jen shivered audibly, dramatically, and said, "He does look kinda evil," before handing Lindsay her phone back.

It was on the tip of my tongue to ask, *What's evil supposed to look like?* But I continued typing Cassidy Philbrook's quote. The only one that felt worth using.

A moment later, Lindsay had more. "Okay. So. He's been post-ing angry messages on Facebook about how liberal arts colleges are discriminating against white men. He thinks women and minori-ties are the reason he didn't get accepted."

"Yeah, *that's* the reason," Jen said sarcastically. "Not because everyone in admissions was going to slit their wrists if they had to read another 'fishing with my grandpa' essay."

Stannard chuckled but didn't intercede.

For a moment I allowed myself to fantasize that the guy in the photo wasn't the guy I saw Saturday night but *was* the guy who killed Alison. Maybe the guy I saw her with really *was* her boyfriend who went to some other college. Maybe she dropped her boy-friend off at the bus stop early on Sunday morning and that's where this creep found her. What's seedier than a Greyhound stop at six a.m.? My dad used to sit with me at the Waterbury stop when I was on my way to Chatham. He didn't like the characters who hung out there. This scenario was totally feasible, right?

Lindsay continued to scroll.

"He's been missing for three days!"

"Yeah, but did he say anything threatening?" Brie asked. "He could have gone fishing, for all we know."

"To be fair," Jen chimed in, "isn't the other stuff he said threat-ening in its own right? I mean, a lot can be inferred from his state-ments about women and minorities. He doesn't have to say he was going to kill someone to be the killer. His attitude, his spreading of misinformation, *that's* threatening, right?"

"Isn't that just free speech?" Brie wondered.

"No, it's hate speech. Surely?!" Jen raised her voice, simultane-ously sure and not so sure.

Stannard was doing what she would do in fiction workshops, letting students duke it out and come to their own conclusions. She wasn't going to interrupt until we got stuck. Still, I could see her eyelids fluttering while she listened to the debate.

"Okay, Jen," Brie said, "but I've heard *you* say at least half a dozen times that you hate white men."

At this, Lindsay started giggling uncontrollably, which caused Brie and Jen to start laughing.

I turned back to my article.

"Yeah," Jen shouted over the laughter. "But I only say that to you! I don't announce it on social media, like a fuckin' psycho!"

I could feel them all watching me, but I just kept typing.

When asked about footage from the school's security camera's, Chief Levesque reiterated that they were still going through tapes from Saturday night and Sunday morning. Levesque encouraged any students who might have seen

I let the cursor pulse while my heart raced.

"Also, Brie, white men are the oppressors, not the oppressed," Jen clarified.

Lindsay's giggles were relentless now. "Yeah," she squeaked. "But what about poetry guy?!"

"Hashtag not *all* white guys, right, Jen?!" Brie shouted.

Jen didn't look at Brie, just gave her the finger.

"Rachel?"

"What?" I turned to Lindsay.

"Have you heard a single thing we've said?"

"I'm listening, but I'm also trying to finish this."

"Do you want to follow up about this guy or should I?"

She held out her phone to me, but I didn't take it. "I don't need to look at him," I said. "This guy could have nothing to do with it.

We would be ruining his life if we report on social media hearsay. Not to mention the reputation of the paper."

I regarded Stannard, hoping for backup, but she only nodded her head thoughtfully, then turned to Lindsay for her rebuttal.

"I see what you're saying, Rach, but what if we took a different angle? Like, what if we don't name him, but we write about some of the fears being stoked on social media?"

"I still don't like it. I think *we'd* be the ones stoking the fears if we gave journalistic credence to these rumors."

Finally, we all looked at Stannard.

"I hate to put police work ahead of journalistic pursuit. I *really* hate it. But maybe you should consider sharing that info with the cops or the dean. Let them investigate." Maybe she was looking at me because she knew me best or maybe she thought I'd be most likely to agree with her, but it felt like she could see through me. There was no way she could have known what I saw on Saturday night, but because of my short story, she did know I was the girl who let Alison get bullied.

"Rachel, do you want to call the dean or should I?" Lindsay asked.

I didn't even have a chance to answer before Brie chimed in, "You do it, Linds."

"But no one has actually said they've seen this guy on Denman campus, right?" Jen asked for clarification. "If we're going to tell the dean about this, we should make that clear."

What if I had? What if that was him?

"Give me the phone," I said, grabbing it from Lindsay before she could call the dean's office. It took a few seconds for his features to organize and clarify in my mind; curly light brown hair, square glasses, pudgy cheeks, straight-faced. The photo was grainy, probably a close-up from a larger group photo. I'd never seen this guy before in my life. Maybe he was a murderer, by all accounts he was a bigot, but he didn't walk out of a dorm party with Alison on Saturday night. I handed Lindsay her phone back. "Yeah. Call."

The phone was ringing when Brie said, "Hold up."

"Like hang up?" Lindsay asked.

"Yeah," Brie said; she was scrolling on Lindsay's friend Madeleine's feed. "They found the piece of shit. Apparently Daniel Boulter just moved to Colorado, like, last week."

Lindsay hung up the phone. She looked crestfallen. "Fuck. Who did this?" It wasn't a journalist's question. It was the question of a terrified young woman.

None of us could answer. It was the first time it had occurred to me that we were in that basement alone. We all knew the murderer could still be on campus, though nobody would say it. I surveyed the room and noticed Jen and Lindsay were doing the same. Stannard would have comforted us if she could. She was grasping for any words that might help.

"I brought my oar," Brie said, pointing to the corner of the room. It was the one she kept in her dorm room, a commemorative one from a winning race in high school. "I'm not afraid to beat the shit out of anyone who comes in here."

We all laughed, relieved, because we believed her.

"You guys? Do you think the murderer is a student here? A guy Alison was dating?"

I spun back around to my computer screen, where the cursor was still pulsing, and finished my sentence: anything suspicious this weekend to report it to campus police or contact the dean's office.

No one responded to Lindsay, so she tried to answer the question herself. "I mean, it could be one of the guys on campus, right?"

"Of course it could," Jen said. "That's why everyone's walking around in huddled masses."

"But he's probably not a serial killer, right? I mean, there's not, like, a guy on campus who's suddenly wanting to kill female students. It doesn't make sense."

"No matter how you explain it, it'll never make sense," Brie said.

"It was probably some trust fund creep who thinks he can have whatever he wants whenever he wants it," Jen said.

I spun around and glared at her.

"What?"

"You mean Cam?" I asked. *I was with him all night,* I thought. Which was not exactly true. Not long after Alison left, I'd blacked out. I couldn't say for certain what he did after that. But what possible reason could Cam have for killing a girl he didn't even know?

"I didn't *say* that, Rachel."

"You implied it."

Lindsay couldn't handle the tension. "I don't think Jen meant Cam, Rach. Just someone *like* Cam."

I turned back to my article, and we all fell silent again. I thought about what Cam had said earlier in the car: *Last thing I want is my semen at the crime scene.*

. . .

When Cam came to visit me in Waterbury, my parents really did try their best. On the first night, Dad suggested we all crack a beer and sit on our back deck. We lacked the sea view that Cam was used to at his family's own summer home; we only had a view of the rotting apple tree, where, when I was nine, a police officer shot a racoon in the face, from point-blank range, because it was foaming at the mouth. Beers in hand, we told Cam this story. Everyone laughed, then we fell silent.

My dad tried to cut the silence with a little teasing, a little light-hearted sports banter with Cam, a Yankees fan. "Yeah, but you wish you had Mookie. Yeah, but you wish you had Pedroia."

Cam wouldn't take the bait. He just took a swig of his Boston Lager, smiled at the label on the bottle, and said, "Yeah, but we're the Yankees."

Dad skulked off, back into the house, muttering to himself, "Fourth in the division, Yankees."

My mom stayed for a few more minutes and we all listened to a song sparrow's high-pitched call, then she went to check on my dad.

"What was that?" I asked Cam.

He wouldn't look at me. "I was defending my team!"

"You have no interest in making a good impression on my dad."

He turned to me. "I have no *chance* of making a good impression on your dad."

Mom made a pasta-bake for dinner, one of my favorites from childhood.

Cam, trying a little harder now, had a second helping. If he noticed our cracked table, the one we got from Marden's when I was ten—$79.99!!! the neon yellow price tag had said—he pretended not to. "So, you guys listen to a lot of NPR?"

Neither parent responded.

Once we were all full, the table was silent again. It was awkward, the thought of Cam and me going into one room, my parents into another. They'd said it was my choice how we wanted to sleep, I was an adult, so Cam and I would be sleeping in the guest room, my mom's sewing room, because my childhood room still had my old twin bed.

After all that pasta and a bottle of wine, it was clear none of the

Nardellis at the table wanted to contemplate what was going to happen if we all went behind closed doors.

Mom suggested playing cards. Gin rummy.

Cam had to be taught how to play, but he picked it up quickly. He was a natural at card games. He played a lot of poker with his roommates, and he had a saying, one he happily shared with my parents: "No such thing as a bad hand, only bad players."

"Huh," my dad said.

My mom smiled, tightly, and shuffled the deck. When she made a bridge with the cards, Cam nodded, impressed. She didn't react, just dealt.

He won the first hand he played.

"Beginner's luck," my mom said. She shuffled again, dealt another hand.

He won again. And again. And again.

"You sure you haven't played this before?" my dad asked.

"No. I just know my way around a deck of cards."

My mom snorted.

Cam smiled and shrugged.

"One more?" I asked. "Or are we done?" I'd come last or second to last in every game. Normally, I was pretty good, but there was an energy at that table telling me to hold back. I think my dad was getting that vibe, too. We both watched my mom and Cam.

"Sure," my mom said. "One more."

My dad dealt this time. Cam picked up his cards and smiled. Mom clocked it.

I went first and discarded a jack.

Cam cracked his neck, then picked up the card.

He doesn't need it, I thought. *He's faking out my mom, trying to make her think he's collecting jacks.*

Cam discarded an eight. My mom smiled to herself and picked

up the card. She discarded a jack and waited for Cam to react. He cracked his neck, again.

Dad and I looked at each other, then he shrugged and took a card from the pile, immediately discarding it.

I did the same.

Cam drew a card, chucked the jack from earlier onto the pile, and turned to my mom. "Your turn, Michelle."

Mom's eyes grew wide. She drew a useless card and discarded it, sighing heavily.

On Cam's turn, he drew a card and smiled. He slid it into his hand and removed a different card, placing it face down on the discard pile. "Gin." He laid his cards on the table. Four threes and a run of clubs four to nine.

Mom slammed her cards on the table.

Cam watched her, pityingly, and I wondered if actually I hated the guy whom four hours previously I thought I loved. "Want me to tell you what you're doing wrong, Michelle?"

She didn't respond, just looked at me. She got up from the table and pushed in her chair, letting us know she was done for the night. "I'm going to bed."

So, are you a Republican now?" my mom asked once Cam was on his way back to the Cape.

I was preoccupied when she said this, watching Cam turn left out of my parents' driveway when he should have gone right. *The highway is the other way.* I had on his stupid nautical flag sweatshirt. I'd thrown it on that morning to make coffee and Cam had made some joke about me keeping it to remember him by. I was about to have a shower and shove it in a drawer until I could return it to him at Denman.

Mom plonked down at the kitchen table and I watched her finger trace the cracked tiles.

Sitting down across from her, I said, "Is this because of the sweatshirt?" She didn't smile. "I was just cold. I promise, I don't know what any of these stupid little flags mean."

Mom nodded, slowly, but didn't look up. "Well, if you're going to join that world . . ." She trailed off.

"What world?"

"Cam's."

"I'm not joining anything."

She studied me for a long beat. "For now."

"Jeez, Mom—"

"It's not easy to maintain your own identity when you enter a world like Cam's."

"It's not a cult."

"Men?" she continued. "They're not so good at being flexible. I know you wish that wasn't true. I know you wish you could date Cam and keep your liberal friends and get a job writing funny essays for *The New Yorker*, but those things don't go together. You have to choose." She stood up then, as though suddenly she couldn't bear to be around me. "If you really like Cam, if you want to spend your life with him, you need to get used to a life of editing the yacht club newsletter."

"It's just a stupid sweatshirt, Mom."

"It's not stupid," my mom said, walking away. "It's ugly."

A week later, I'd still been thinking about what Shorty had said to me. *Don't come back here.* I'd considered it a gift, a pearl of essential wisdom: *Don't get stuck here, Rachel.* Sometimes drunk people can see things the clearest. The Low Down wasn't the place for me or anyone who didn't want a life frozen in amber. I had no desire to go back. I was only two weeks away from being back on campus and hopefully only a year away from being someplace completely different. I pictured myself writing in an NYC apartment at night, bagging groceries at a Whole Foods by day, a fantasy I hadn't shared with anyone because I couldn't bear the likely response. Who graduates from a college like Denman and goes on to bag groceries?

I was contemplating all of this behind the register at the Epicurious Farm, when the bell above the entrance jingled and Alison came through, tanned under a flowing sundress. She lifted her big sunglasses onto her head.

"I've been in Rome," she said, unprompted. "Just got back last week. Henry James spent a lot of time there. Did you know?"

"Cool."

"I'm writing my senior thesis on why so many Victorians loved the Eternal City."

"Sounds more exciting than a summer in Waterbury." My thesis was "The Ethics of Anonymous Sources in Journalistic Practice." I was bored just thinking about it, that's why I was fantasizing about fiction and Whole Foods. But I knew I had to have a practical thesis if I wanted to get a *real* job someday, the kind with a salary and benefits. Only rich people got to study things as fancy and useless as Victorian literature.

Alison smiled. "It's nice to be home, too." Standing in place, she spun around. "My mom sent me here for tomatoes. The really ugly ones that cost so much."

I pointed behind her to the wicker basket overflowing with eight-dollars-a-pound tomatoes.

"Great, thanks. How's your summer been?"

"This, mostly."

"Not long now, though," she said. "Soon, we'll be back at

school." She loaded tomatoes into the crook of her arm and wad-
dled over to the register, trying not to drop any. "Think this'll be
enough for a caprese salad?"

She plopped eight tomatoes on the counter.

"I'd say so. Depends on how many people you're feeding."

"Just Mom, Dad, me, and Ethan."

"Yeah," I said, swallowing my rage. "This will definitely
be enough." I shook out a paper bag and loaded it with the tomatoes.

"Mom and I are making ravioli, too. I bought this amazing cookbook in Rome. Nothing but filled pastas. Seriously, you
would not believe the things Romans pair with ricotta. Chest-
nuts! Oranges!" Then, emphatic and serious, she added, "So deli-
cious."

I didn't give a fuck about her fucking cookbook. "How's
Ethan?"

She took a moment to size me up before answering. "He's really
good. I mean, I've hardly seen him. I haven't been back long, and
I've had visitors . . ." She lingered on this point, keen for me to know
there were people in this world who desired to spend time with her.
"Next week he goes back to Yale for soccer. You've probably seen
way more of him." She knew this wasn't true, and I swear to God
she slightly smiled to herself.

I pictured Ethan at the Low Down, staring at the stupid condensation ring on the table. "No, haven't seen him."

Grabbing the brown bag of tomatoes, Alison said, "I'll see you
back at school." It was an odd thing to say. It seemed to imply that
it wouldn't be a mutually agreed-upon event.

She swung open the door again and lowered her sunglasses
over her eyes, then sauntered down the street, her dress catching
the breeze. Had she come into the shop purely for the opportunity
to enrage me? *She does it on purpose. You know that, right?*

14.

"Rachel, it's eleven. Ben needs the paper by one. Jen still needs to write her story."

"I know."

Brie pushed away from her computer. "Take this one, Jen. I'm nearly finished." She got up from her chair and moved past Lindsay and Stannard to grab her oar. "I dare anyone to come in here," she said, swinging the oar like a baseball bat. "I was born to take some prick out with this."

Jen took over Brie's seat. She stole a momentary glance at what I was writing before focusing on her own screen.

Stannard held out my notebook. "My quote," she said. "For your article."

I reached back for it and held her gaze as urgently as I could but I had to drop my hand when Lindsay said, "Read it. I want to hear it."

Stannard returned an odd expression. She wasn't getting my telepathic message. *They don't know about your class.*

When I shrugged, defeated, she started to read, "'I was very fortunate to have Alison in my fall fiction workshop.'" The other three were all watching Stannard thoughtfully, but none reacted. I breathed a sigh of relief. "'She was a talented and generous story-teller with bright prospects ahead of her. My heart is broken that this promising future was stolen from her. And her stories stolen from all of us.'"

I felt my eyes welling up at the quote's poignancy as well as my own immediate envy. Did Stannard think Alison was a better writer than I was? What would she have said if I was the dead one? I reached for the quote again and said, "Beautiful. Thank you."

The other three agreed.

I set the notebook next to my keyboard and stared back at the sentence where I was currently stuck. I was in the middle of describing the crime scene. Pleasant Pond is predominantly a local fishing spot, located off Route 3. The walk from the parking lot to the pond is half a mile through dense wood. As a student at Waterbury Junior High, Alison would have been familiar with the pond, which was visited annually by students on their final day at the school.

I started to delete the last sentence, then retyped it several times. Stannard must have noticed because she asked, "What's the problem?"

"I'm trying to decide if I should add something about how Alison would have been familiar with the crime scene. Maybe I should take it out?"

Stannard got up from her seat and dragged it over next to mine. "Do you have a disclaimer at the beginning of the article about how you knew Alison?"

"Should I?"

"I think so," Stannard said. "Just a little disclaimer—"

"Wait," Jen said, staring at us. *"You're* in Stannard's fiction workshop this fall, aren't you?"

Fuck. I nodded.

Now Brie and Lindsay were staring at me as well.

"This morning you claimed you didn't know her at all. But you've known her since childhood *and* you were in a class together this semester?" Lindsay tittered in total disbelief. "The fuck, Rachel?"

Jen rolled her chair closer to Lindsay, as if I was dangerous. "Why do you keep lying?"

NERDROE

arrived in math class with Brad's words ringing in my ears—*rape her wall*. My eyes fell on Alison right away, already in her seat, two behind mine, sitting at attention, notebook open and none the wiser about what was in store for her. *She's going to get what's coming to her, Nerdelli. And if you're not careful, so will you.*

Ethan was in his seat, too, drawing soccer logos in his notebook, when I took my place behind him. Normally, I'd imagine running my fingers through his hair and maybe down his neck—Celine style—but not then.

Rape her wall.

I crossed my legs tight.

Callie waved from her seat two rows over and plugged her nose to indicate that Carter Girard, who was sitting in front of her, stank.

Mr. Jensen stood awkwardly in front of us, hands in his pockets, swaying, waiting for everyone to settle in. He and Mr. Beal were best friends, even though nobody thought Mr. Jensen was as cool as Mr. Beal. He *was* tall, but not in a handsome way, more treelike. His neck always had shaving rash and his buzz cut was far too severe to be hip. We all thought it was nice of Mr. Beal to be friends with him.

For the past several weeks we'd been working on simplifying algebraic expressions, which I was terrible at even when I was trying. The entire point of the exercise seemed designed to torture me. Worse, Ethan was amazing at it, getting one hundreds on all his quizzes. Only Carter Girard was worse than I was. He kept referring to coefficients as codependents.

"Take one and pass it down," Mr. Jensen said to the room, and I prepared myself for Ethan to turn around by readying my smile.

"Thanks," I said when he handed me the worksheets.

"Sure," he replied, and once again, I was staring at the back of his head, disappointed.

"Rachel!" said Max, directly behind me. I spun around and handed him the worksheets with an apologetic smile. When I turned to face forward again, there was Ethan's calculator, in its hard case, sitting on my desk. He'd taken my shitty one.

I picked it up gingerly, like it was hot. Then, God knows why, I brought it to my nose and inhaled its scent. I couldn't have described it other than to say it smelled like Ethan. I wanted to rub it all over my face.

"Let's solve these together," Mr. Jensen said. "Who wants to go first?"

Not me. Max had his hand in the air right away. I was safe.

I returned my attention to Ethan's calculator, sliding off the case. The screen of his TI-84 Plus Silver Edition lit up when I pressed ON. It was in text mode and there was another message.

Will you go out with me, pls?

I looked around the room like an idiot, wondering if everyone else already knew what it said. They were all staring down at their worksheets.

I read it again. My ultimate dream was right there, typed out on a calculator. He'd used a comma and everything. And then I thought about what Callie said earlier that day: *Ethan's flirting with you to send Alison a message.*

I carefully set the calculator on my desk, not wanting to disturb the message. Max continued to recite a series of numbers and letters. Callie shot me some side-eye, then started blowing me kisses. Did she know or just suspect?

"Eleven X minus twenty-three," said Max resolutely.

"Well done, Mr. Nugent." Mr. Jensen always referred to the boys in class formally. "How about the second one?"

Misty Everett raised her hand. "I'll give it a try."

"Go ahead, Misty." Mr. Jensen had no such formality for the girls.

I deleted Ethan's message and prepared myself to respond. Say yes, and all my dreams could come true. I imagined us gazing into each other's eyes, waves crashing around us for some reason, as we leaned in to kiss. As I imagined our lips getting closer, I felt saliva gathering in the corners of mine. I remembered Callie's disastrous first kiss, all the spit. What if I was a terrible kisser? And what if I touched him? He'd find out about my sweaty palms. What if, attempting to kiss, I accidentally bit him? The satin sheets of my mind were now covered in my spit and sweat, and Ethan's blood. *No,* I assured myself, our teeth might knock a little, but I wouldn't bite him. I could control that. Maybe, even, I was a good kisser? Shit, what if I was *too* good a kisser? Would I get a reputation?

Say no, and I could avoid all of this, but I also wouldn't be Ethan Monroe's girlfriend.

Just to see what it looked like, I typed YES. I'd sit with it for a bit and see how it felt. Then maybe I'd type NO and see how that felt.

"How about you, Rachel?" Mr. Jensen asked. "Number three?"

I looked up at my teacher. "Sorry," I said, flustered. "I need more time."

"Alright. Raise your hand when you're done."

Mr. Jensen was still looking at me, so I attempted to simplify the stupid algebraic expression, $5y^2-y-(3y^2-6y) + 8y$. I knew I needed to start by "eliminating the parenthesis," so I crossed them out. Next, was to "combine like terms," so $5y^2-3y^2$ is $2y^2$. Easy. Then, $-y-6y + 8y$, so that's . . .

When I looked up everyone was staring at me. I tentatively raised my hand.

Mr. Jensen nodded. "Rachel."

"Two y squared plus y?"

Mr. Jensen surveyed the room. "What did Rachel do wrong?"

"Two negatives make a positive." It was Alison, of course. Math was just another one of her fairy tales where two wrongs make a fucking unicorn. "If you put negative one in front of the parenthesis," she continued, "it becomes negative three y squared *plus* six y, because negative one times negative six y is *plus* six y."

"Excellent. So, the correct answer is?" He looked at me first, but then away again when he saw how lost I looked. "Alison?"

"Two y squared plus thirteen y."

"Well done." He smiled. "Rachel, let's pay attention, okay? Stop playing snake on Mr. Monroe's calculator."

"I wasn't," I croaked.

"And, Mr. Monroe, maybe stop lending it out."

"Sorry," Ethan said. He whipped around to snatch it back and returned my lame one.

SHIT.

When the bell rang, Ethan walked out of math class without even turning around.

Callie and I walked behind him to the locker bay.

"He borrowed it again," she said.

"He won't anymore, not after what Mr. Jensen said." I couldn't tell her about his message; I was convinced he'd already changed his mind. To know it was real, I needed him to look at me first.

"Want to get ready for the dance at mine tomorrow night?"

Shit. The dance. The dance with a boyfriend?

We reached my locker. Ethan was at his, three lockers over, still not looking at me.

"Sure," I said, turning the dial on mine right, then left, then right again. "Help me pick an outfit?"

"Seriously?!" She spun me around, grinned.

But I wasn't paying attention anymore. Brad was coming toward us, his index finger pressed against his lips. He came up behind Ethan and pulled the back of his teammate's T-shirt up over his eyes, blinding him.

Instinctively, I looked down to where Ethan's T-shirt had lifted, revealing his midriff and the seam of his plaid boxer shorts, a thin rim around the top of his khaki pants. Callie noticed and made another kissy face.

Fighting off Brad with an elbow to the ribs, Ethan adjusted his shirt, then spun around to pound Brad on the chest.

Suddenly all the soccer guys were crowding around, along with several kids whose last names started with K–R. We had two minutes before final period. The eighth-grade locker bay was fizzing with the compressed energy of fourteen-year-old bodies that would be forced to sit for another forty-five minutes before they could go outside and POP!

"Monroe," I heard Brad say. He slung an arm around Ethan's shoulder, pulling him into a headlock. He whispered something I couldn't hear into Ethan's ear and I tried not to notice.

"Sure," I said to Callie. "Plan my outfit."

She jumped up and down, excited.

"Hey, Nerdelli?"

Fuck. "What?" I said, but didn't look at Brad, just pretended I forgot something in my locker, turning the dial again.

"What should your couple name be?" Brad leaned his back on the locker next to mine. He was talking to me, but it was imperative that everyone in earshot be able to hear him.

Callie grabbed my arm, "WHAT?"

"She didn't tell you, Hamel?" He laughed. "Nerdelli? You're not embarrassed to be going out with Monroe are you?"

"No," I said to the inside of my locker.

"I'm thinking Nerdroe. That's better than Ethal or Rachan. Mondelli could be good." It took him a few seconds to conclude he'd tested all the variations. "Nerdroe, I think." He seemed satisfied, maybe even planned to let the topic go, but then the mischievous smile returned. I spun around to find Alison, clutching the newspaper. "What do you think, princess?"

She ignored him and looked over at Ethan, who'd returned to burying his face behind his locker.

"Tell Alison the good news, Nerdelli. If you're not embarrassed."

I waited for Ethan to intervene. *You tell her,* I thought. *Tell her you prefer me.* I stared at the door of his locker, but he didn't come out. I didn't know who I was angrier at in that moment, him or Brad.

Brad nudged me. When I turned back to Alison, she was waiting for me to tell her the news, but with the tears welling up in her eyes, I knew she already knew.

Brad shook his head at me. "What's with her?" he said to Callie.

Callie nudged me, hard.

Everyone watched, silently, as Brad approached Alison. He took the paper from her hand and a pencil from his cargo pants. "Your article is out of date, princess." He pressed the paper up against the locker next to Alison's. "We all know Ethan Monroe succeeds academically and athletically," Brad put on his girliest voice. "But what about romantically? Does he have a girlfriend?"

A couple kids chuckled at his dramatic reading; Callie included.

When Ethan eventually shut his locker, we finally made eye contact, only a darting sideways glance, but neither of us knew what to do. Our mutual conclusion seemed to be *nothing*.

Brad was scratching at the paper, crossing out where Ethan's answer read, "No," and replacing it with "Rachel."

"There," he said as the bell rang, handing the paper back to Alison. "Fixed it."

It was my dad who asked about the paper first. "What's the scoop?" he said at the dinner table, reaching behind him to turn down NPR.

"Slow news week," I said. I was carving, listlessly, at my eggplant parm. I should have been happy, I was Ethan Monroe's girlfriend, but the events of the day hadn't left me with much of an appetite. My mind was still in the locker bay with Alison's red, swollen eyes. We'd all just left her there, moved on to the next thing. She'd arrived late to the next class, but I specifically hadn't looked behind me. At dinner, I kept worrying the phone was going to ring.

I kept imagining my mom reacting to Ethan's voice on the other end of the line.

When my parents kept staring at me, I put down my fork and said, "Alison's got this interview thing she's doing. It was the lead article. It bumped my pizza dough article."

At this, my dad frowned on my behalf, but Mom heard something different. "Good for Alison!" she said. "I'm glad she's coming out of that awkward phase." When I snorted, she asked, "No?"

"She's still Alison."

"You two used to be such good friends."

I shot her my *don't go there* look.

"Who did she interview?" my dad asked. Bless him, he always knew when to change the subject. "The principal?"

"Ethan Monroe."

My parents looked at each other and shrugged.

"He's in my class."

"Oh, his mom's the pediatrician?" my mom recalled. "Dr. Monroe?"

When I said yes, Dad rolled his eyes and asked, "What's so special about him?"

"He's the goalie of the soccer team. They're undefeated. And he's really good at math. It's called 'The Renaissance Corner.' Once a month, Alison interviews someone who's really good at more than one thing."

I could tell Dad was growing defensive, gripping his fork. "Lots of kids are good at more than one thing. Not just the children of doctors."

"I don't think anyone is disputing that, Ray," Mom said, then looked at me. "Is he nice?"

I shrugged to a blob of cheese I was about to put in my mouth. "Yeah. He's one of the only people that's nice to Alison. They're neighbors." I was thinking I needed to big up Ethan, but I immediately wished I hadn't said what I did. I knew what was coming next.

"You're nice to Alison?" Mom's question was more of a demand.

I shrugged again. "I guess."

She glared at me, but Dad, I could tell, was confused, grappling with his class frustration being in direct conflict with his sympathy for this friendless girl.

"Why is she so unpopular?" he asked.

If I wasn't feeling so cornered, I might have given the matter more honest thought. *Because she always has been. Because reversing that storyline will take courage nobody has, especially me.* But right then, I was only interested in one thing: getting these two off my back. "A lot of kids at school are like you, Dad."

"Meaning?"

"They don't like rich people."

Mom and Dad regarded each other, clearly unsure how to proceed.

"Then don't be like me," he said and got up from the table, putting his half-eaten plate in the sink.

"I want to see the paper," Mom said.

"It's in my bag," I replied, watching my dad walk out of the room. He'd never done that before.

I got up and pulled the paper from my bag by the door. Handing it to her, I said, "I didn't think Alison should do the interview, but I was nice and I let her." This didn't bring Dad back, and Mom looked unconvinced. "Actually, stopping her might have been nicer," I was explaining now in teenage warp speed. "Everyone knows she has a crush on Ethan. The article is embarrassing."

Mom looked at Ethan's picture, the same one as his Facebook photo. "He is cute. So what if she has a crush?"

I ignored her question, pushed food around my plate.

"I bet lots of girls have a crush on him." By the time she finished reading the article, what I'd hoped wouldn't occur to her had. She regarded me with a delighted, smug smirk. "I bet *you* have a crush on him."

I glared at her, all the evidence she needed, so I looked back at the doorway, the one my dad had passed through, and wished he'd come back to save me, to change the conversation to baseball, but he must have gone upstairs.

"Is this why you and Alison aren't friends anymore? Because you're fighting over a boy?"

I didn't know how it was possible that she could have it so wrong. Her imagination lacked that adolescent setting, or maybe she'd just long forgotten it. That Alison and I were no longer friends because it was a matter of survival would have been unfathomable to her. That Alison was so toxic that Ethan had asked me out purely as a way of distancing himself from her. Of course, Mom could never know about what happened in the locker bay that day, how in a split second Ethan and I had banded together and crossed over the line of kindness to something like the edge of cruelty.

"No," I said and pushed my plate away.

When the phone rang, I nearly jumped out of my seat. Dad answered it upstairs. I heard him say, "If it's not about schoolwork, she'll have to call you back tomorrow."

I held my breath. Mom and I were both silent when Dad's feet padded down the stairs. I wondered if she also thought it was Ethan on the phone.

Dad leaned on the doorway. "That was Callie."

I felt myself exhale.

"No phone calls tonight, okay?"

I nodded.

"And no Facebook," Mom said.

I was being punished for not being friends with Alison. I shot up from my chair. "Seriously? Why? I'm done with my homework."

Neither answered.

"You can't make me be friends with her!" I tried to storm past my dad toward the stairs, but he grabbed me and held me against his chest. I didn't realize I was crying until I felt my chest heaving.

He held me tight and whispered in my ear, "I know it's hard."

I couldn't see what my mom was doing, but I imagined her still sitting at the kitchen table, picking at the crack in the tile.

Dad pulled away and put his hands on my shoulders. He looked as serious as I'd ever seen him. That adolescent imagination that my mom couldn't conjure, my dad could. That's what he'd been doing upstairs. I knew he was disappointed in me, that he wanted me to be nicer to Alison, but I think he also understood that the situation was more complicated than that. "Alison is going to find her place in the world." He kissed the top of my head and added, like a terminal diagnosis, "And so will you."

15.

Back in the newsroom, Jen wasn't going to stop staring at me until I explained myself. Years of explanation, she wanted, condensed into a few succinct sentences that would adequately justify how I'd become such a disappointment to her.

"I don't mean to lie," I said. And I wasn't really lying so much as omitting, though the look on Jen's face suggested she didn't care about the semantics. "It's a long story, but I wasn't Alison's favorite person. It was kid stuff."

It *was* kid stuff, but I said that like it minimized what had happened. When, in fact, the errors of my childhood were the seeds of my adult trauma.

Stannard put her hand on my shoulder. She understood how difficult that must have been for me to say.

Lindsay, Brie, and Jen, who had never read the story I'd written for Stannard's class, all stared at me, confused. They had no idea of all the truth hiding in its fiction.

. . .

A couple days after we workshopped Alison's story in intermediate fiction, I heard a knock on my door. It was odd. I so rarely had visitors. Most people just texted me. My room was quiet and I considered pretending I wasn't in. It was probably a student petition I didn't want to sign. But the journalist in me prevailed. If there was a petition going around, I should know what it was.

When I opened the door, it was Alison. She peered into my room, no doubt wondering why it took me so long to answer. "You don't want to be a journalist?" she said.

It felt like she'd been reading my mind. I stumbled around a few sounds, but no words came out. How did she know where I lived?

"I mean, that's what you always wanted." She put her hand on my doorframe.

"I, yeah, I mean, I guess. Sorry, what's this about?"

"Did you know I was in Professor Stannard's workshop when you wrote that story?"

"No. Honest."

"Is that how you see me? Tragic?"

Maybe. A little. Yes.

She shook her head. "I would have thought you'd have figured it out by now."

"What?"

"Which one of us is tragic," she said, and walked away.

UR DISGUSTING

The next day—dance day—the eighth grade had turned into a pheromone-fueled free-for-all. *Who are you going out with? Who do you want to go out with? How far have you gotten? How far would you like to get at the dance?* All these questions, both whispered and shouted. It was everyone's goal to get into a couple before setting foot in the gymnasium that night. Everyone was talking about me. I was the answer to the question, *Wait, who?*

Regardless of my newfound fame, it was safe to say that going out with Ethan was exactly the same as not going out with Ethan. After twenty-four hours of being his "girlfriend," we still hadn't spoken, hadn't gotten within six feet of each other.

But now I had an invite to Misty Everett's pre-party. It had come in the form of a note slipped into my locker in Brad's hand-writing: *Nerd— b at Mistys at 6.*

At lunch, Callie stared at me, furious, when I said I wouldn't be attending.

"You and I said we'd get ready together," I told her, pretending a show of unity was my reason for skipping the party and not the fact that I was shit scared of all the alcohol and having to make out with a boy for the first time with an audience. I also knew my mom would never let me go once she found out Misty's parents didn't chaperone.

"Seriously, you're just going to let someone else make out with your boyfriend?"

"My *boyfriend* doesn't seem to know I exist."

The orchestra girls were all scowling at me. I'd stolen their hunky cello player.

"That's because you're acting all closed off," Callie said. "You need to be more *inviting* to him."

I pretended to ignore her comment, even though I'd spent all day agonizing about how to change my behavior and my look to better match my new situation. Changing my clothes, my hairstyle, and working on getting within a football field of Ethan without breaking out into a full-body sweat were all goals. It gave me some solace that he seemed to be struggling with similar apprehensions. Over my shoulder, I checked he was in his usual seat. It was Brad who caught me looking and blew me a kiss, before smacking Ethan on the shoulder, trying to get him to turn around. When Ethan finally did turn around, we looked at each other, just as we'd done the day before in the locker bay, briefly and vaguely terrified.

I hadn't looked at Alison all day. I couldn't. I'd heard rumors that she'd been crying in bathroom stalls. Micah told Callie she'd hung a calendar in her locker that was counting down the days until the end of junior high. Thankfully, since she sat behind me in classes, it was easy to ignore her, but it was unusual not to hear her voice. She'd stopped raising her hand.

Callie seemed to know what I was thinking about. "Think she'll dare come to the dance?"

———

Callie and I got ready at her house. She dressed me in a sleeveless, short black dress with a bubble hem. After I pulled it over my head, she tied the two black strings connected to the bust around my neck, then spun me around to face her. Callie tilted her head, inspecting me like an abstract piece of art she needed to form an opinion on. "This'll work."

I reached behind me to touch where the dress hit my thighs, about two inches below my butt cheeks. "I need tights."

At this, she rolled her eyes and chucked me a blue pair, the footless kind. "Hurry up," she said. "We need time for hair and makeup."

We walked to the dance, me in a pair of kitten heels, Callie in ones much higher. We teetered down George Mitchell Drive to the school and I prayed neither of my parents would drive by and see me dressed like Katy Perry. Callie had fluffed up my hair and pinned one side back with a bejeweled butterfly clip, then painted my lips bright red. If she was going to go for a celebrity, I'd have hoped she'd lean toward Taylor Swift, but Callie only had one speed and that speed was Katy Perry. She was wearing a tight pink dress with a gigantic, gold waist-cinching belt. She was coatless, but it was October in Maine; the evening was cold, so I also had on my sherpa-lined, maroon corduroy coat. We looked ridiculous.

Coming from the other direction, we could see the west end kids approaching, probably from Misty Everett's pre-party. The girls were all wearing short denim cutoffs with black tights underneath, tight boots zipped up their calves. Misty and Shorty were wearing matching sequin tube tops. They stumbled into each other, laughing. Misty pulled a little bottle from her pocket and tipped the contents into her mouth, before handing it to Shorty, who finished it off, then chucked the empty bottle into the road.

"We're overdressed," I said to Callie, scowling.

I scanned the group for Ethan. He was bringing up the rear with the boys from the soccer team. His hands were in the pockets of his khaki pants, his shoulders were hunched up because he was only wearing a T-shirt, the one with 3 Doors Down on it—five intimidating guys staring straight ahead. Under the band was some aggressive message of defiance.

Brad was just in front of Ethan, handing out little bottles like the one Misty and Shorty just downed. When he spotted us, he came running in our direction.

"Nerdelli!" He held out a little bottle to me. "A gift from your boyfriend."

My boyfriend was twenty feet away, staring at the pavement.

I took it because Callie nudged me, but just stuck it in the pocket of my coat.

"You can't bring that into the school, Nerdelli. You gotta drink it."

I regarded Callie, nervous.

Callie stuck her hand in my coat pocket and fished the bottle out. She twisted off the cap and drank half, like she'd seen Misty do, then handed me the other half. I looked at the label—Allen's Coffee Brandy—then at Ethan, his eyes still averted.

"Just drink it, Nerd."

I puckered, swallowing the rest of the bitter liquid, thinking maybe Ethan would acknowledge me if I did. No luck. I felt the acid in my stomach rising up immediately. Swallowing it back down, I must have made a sour face because Brad started laughing. "Damn, Nerdelli." He smiled, proud. "I didn't think you actually would."

He looked back at Ethan. "He never drinks." He took the bottle from my hand and chucked it onto the hard shoulder.

"What?" I said. "But . . ."

"Don't worry about it," he said, slipping me a piece of gum more covertly than he did the bottle. "You'll need this to get in." He handed another piece to Callie.

"Have you seen Micah?" Callie asked.

"He was at Misty's. Said school dances are a form of mind control."

"So what?" Callie didn't think there was anything wrong with mind control so long as she got to dress slutty while it was happening.

"He's coming. He was just going to smoke a lot first." This was classic Micah. He believed being high was like building a charm barrier against fascist ideology. *They can't penetrate a free mind.*

I popped the gum in my mouth and stared at Ethan. *Look at me.*

He was talking to a kid called Todd, who had a curly mop of hair that exploded out from the sides of his backward baseball cap. Todd had terrible acne around his lips and chin. The rumor was you could always tell who'd kissed him at Misty's last party based on which girl was forming a giant chin zit. Shorty was looking a little spotty recently, even though she claimed to have a boyfriend who was a high school freshman in Augusta.

We started moving en masse toward the doors on the side of the junior high, the ones closest to the gym. We could hear CeeLo Green crooning that he thinks we're all crazy.

Mr. Beal was at the door, bobbing his head to the beat, greeting students. "It's the gum brigade," he said, looking at all of us suspiciously. His eyes landed on me, uncomfortably, my stupid hair and red lips. "Check in with Mr. Jensen, then coats in the band room, okay?"

We all nodded, except for Misty and Shorty, who were giggling uncontrollably. Mr. Beal squinted at them, then at me, like he expected we shared some special tattling signals.

That's when Ethan came up beside me. "Give me your coat."

I was so surprised by his proximity that it took me a moment to remove my coat. Now both Mr. Beal and Ethan were looking at my dress, or lack thereof. I felt a head rush, the alcohol. Could Mr. Beal see it in my eyes?

Freaked out, I spun around to Mr. Jensen, seated at a fold-out table that blocked off the hallway to the rest of the school, taking everyone's three dollars. I held out a wad of dollars bills, sweaty in my hand.

"You're all set, Rachel." He nodded in Ethan's direction.

Having ditched our coats, Ethan was now staring into the dark gym at a big disco ball spinning in the center of the room, roughly a hundred kids surrounding it, leaning against the walls and sitting on the few rows of bleachers that had been pulled out.

"But I'm asking everyone," Mr. Jensen said, trying to regain my attention. "What song are you most looking forward to dancing to tonight?"

"Oh, um . . ."

"She's looking forward to the slow ones," Brad said, nudging me.

Mr. Jensen nodded, knowingly. "Leona Lewis?"

"Yeah, sure," I said, looking around for Callie. There was no point in explaining I was more into Celine Dion, not in this crowd.

"Keep bleeding . . ." Mr. Jensen sang to Mr. Beal, who pretended to rip his heart open to Mr. Jensen.

Brad started laughing, I heard him whisper in Ethan's ear, "So gay."

I don't know whether Mr. Beal heard Brad, but he caught my

eye again. "Have a good time," he said in a cautionary tone, then Callie took my hand and pulled me into the gym, because Katy Perry was playing.

Within seconds, Callie was flailing on the dance floor, lip-synching into her fist. Shorty and Misty were drunk enough to join her. Now all three of them were leaning into each other, singing into their "microphones," and I watched until I felt an arm around my shoulders. Not my boyfriend's. Brad's.

"Why weren't you at Misty's?"

"My parents wouldn't let me."

He removed his arm and looked at my outfit, as though it was evidence of the opposite. "You have a role," he said. When I just stared at him blankly, he added, "*She* showed up at Misty's looking for Ethan."

"Alison?" I couldn't picture her at Misty's.

"He needed his girlfriend to be there."

For the record, Ethan was nowhere to be seen when Brad and I were having this conversation.

"What happened?" I asked.

"She was all dressed up." He snickered to himself. "She made a beeline for your boy."

The beat slowed to something hip-hop adjacent. Shorty was now grinding up against Misty. Callie, feeling left out, tried to grind up against Shorty.

"Ethan had to walk her home and come back."

"He walked her home? Alone?"

"Yes, Nerdelli."

I finally spotted Ethan, under the disco ball, his hands deep in his pockets, talking to Todd.

Brad pulled me back to his attention. "We need to deal with her. I sent the friend request."

"She won't accept. Not after what you did to her article."

Brad smiled. "That's where you come in."

"Please, I really—"

"Nerdelli, Ethan and I both need you to do this."

I said nothing and watched Ethan out of the corner of my eye. His hands were now out of his pockets. He and Todd were playing that think-fast game, the one where you try to slap each other's hands.

Brad leaned in to me, confidentially. Even though the music was so loud, everything said was a secret right then. "Tell her I like her."

"What?"

"Tell Princess Alison that you heard I have a crush on her."

"What about Misty?"

"She knows I obviously don't."

"Alison won't buy it."

"Yes, she will." He looked over at Ethan, then said, "Trust me."

Suddenly, the mood of the whole room changed. There was just the sound of an organ, then a woman's voice, then drums. Brad smiled, then dragged me by my arm into the center of the room, where Todd and Ethan were still slapping each other. He shoved Todd out of the way and presented me to Ethan. Brad took my hands and placed them on Ethan's shoulders, like I was a puppet in his control. Ethan put his hands on my waist and we both stared at our feet. I felt a third hand on my back. Brad's again. He must have had his other hand on Ethan's back, because suddenly he'd pushed us together. My head was over Ethan's shoulder, his over mine. At least this way we didn't have to make eye contact. I don't think I'd ever been that physically close to another human being who wasn't one of my parents hugging me.

I kept my hands on his shoulders; I didn't know what else to do with them. At the very least, I figured his T-shirt could absorb their clamminess. He was drenched in that mall cologne scent that made me simultaneously itchy and ravenous. I looked out into the room as we spun around slowly. Leona Lewis sounded desperate, like she was warning me that love was violent: *Fall in love and you'll end up splayed out on an operating table in need of a blood transfusion.* I kept thinking, *Please don't cut me open. That sounds awful.* I hated that song.

Everyone was staring at me and Ethan. Callie and Shorty were in the distance, watching us, leaning into each other, whispering like they'd been best friends forever. Brad had found Misty and they were dancing next to us. As our rotating took them out of my view, I felt Ethan's hands creeping down to my butt. I did my best not to react at all, just let them rest there. It didn't feel invigorating, like Celine suggested it would. It was more like Ethan and I were the flaps of a cardboard box that had been folded together.

Mr. Beal was now walking through the couples on the dance floor. "Brad, cut it out," I heard him say. "Misty's not an ice cream cone."

I felt Ethan's hands go back up to the small of my back. I put my cheek on his shoulder and closed my eyes to avoid looking at Mr. Beal. I stayed like that for a few rotations, because that part actually did feel nice, even if my cheek on his shoulder was basically bone on bone. After a while, I started to feel like we were floating, and the alcohol had gone from feeling like a fireball in my gut to a warming flame. As the song was ending, I opened my eyes to the pores on Ethan's neck, thinking maybe we weren't such a mismatched couple. Maybe now he'd say something to me?

But when I lifted my head, I was facing the door to the gym, and she was standing in it.

Everyone's eyes suddenly followed mine and we were all staring at her. Ethan let go of me.

Alison had on a pink, sparkly top and white jeans. She'd had her brown curls blown out. She looked pretty, really pretty, not that it mattered one tiny bit to anyone in the room.

When my hands dropped to my sides, Ethan grabbed one of them and squeezed. She saw the gesture and bolted.

Brad and Callie were right. The only thing that kept Alison away from Ethan was me.

When the music went back to a thumping beat, everyone returned to gyrating. A male rapper and a female singer were accusing each other of being promiscuous. Callie and Shorty immediately shot their arms up in the air, aggressively shaking their asses. Brad and Misty knew all the words, singing in each other's ear. Misty would get up close to Brad, then pull away at the last minute, laughing. Brad would grab her back and bite his lower lip as he humped her side.

Ethan and I just stood there in the center of the room, holding hands, watching the empty door. Would she return?

Mr. Beal and Mr. Jensen were now leaning into each other, having a serious conversation. After nodding in agreement, Mr. Beal approached the DJ, gesturing with his finger at this throat and the song stopped to loud groans, replaced by Coldplay and even louder groans. I turned to Ethan, but he'd let go of my hand; he was no longer beside me.

Back at the entrance, Alison reappeared, this time with Micah at her side. She exchanged money with Mr. Jensen: a five-dollar bill and a one. Was she paying for him?

Enthralled by her new friendship with Shorty, Callie hadn't noticed Micah yet. When she spotted I was alone, she pulled me in with her, Shorty, and Misty, who had now rejoined them. "He had his hands on your ass!" she shouted, and they all giggled. "Did he have a boner?"

At the time, I had no way of knowing, no frame of reference. I know now that if he'd had an erection, I would have felt it. Thankfully, I could ignore Callie's question. I knew something she'd want to know more. "Micah just walked in with Alison."

Callie's head swung toward the door. Micah was now leaning on the wall. I couldn't find Alison.

"He's not with Alison. Why would you say that?"

"I swear! They walked in together."

"Whatever. It was just a coincidence." She didn't go over to him.

We all looked around for Alison, but we couldn't find her. Instead, I spotted Brad, beckoning me again.

"She's here," he said ominously.

I shrugged. "She's allowed to be."

"Ethan's over there." Brad pointed to the back wall by the equipment closet.

"Is he hiding from her?"

"He's waiting for you," Brad said, and shoved me in Ethan's direction.

"Hi," I said, when I found myself suddenly in front of him again.

"Hi," Ethan said to the toe of his sneaker.

The dance floor flooded when "Crazy in Love" started playing. Even Mr. Beal and Mr. Jensen were dancing, a crowd of kids surrounding them—two grown men, purposely embarrassing themselves in the name of keeping the peace. But Ethan and I stayed where we were.

"Have you told her?" I asked. "That you don't like her in that way?"

Ethan didn't answer.

"Maybe she'd leave you alone if you told her."

He still didn't say anything; instead he looked at the kids gathered around our teachers. Mr. Jensen was confused, doing

Beyoncé's "Single Ladies (Put a Ring on It)" dance. I wondered if, like me, Ethan couldn't wait to be an adult. They looked so unburdened, our two teachers. I contemplated what it would be like to feel that confident in my own skin. Would I ever? I smiled at the thought and reached out my hand to grab Ethan's. I'd start now. I'd pull him onto the dance floor, my boyfriend.

He responded, taking my hand firmly enough that it caused me to glance at him before I could pull him to the dance floor. He was looking straight ahead, not at me, but at Alison, who'd stopped Mr. Beal's dancing with a tap on the shoulder. I started to say "What the—" when Ethan lunged at me. His kiss was so forceful that I felt the back of my head pressing into the cinderblock wall. Then his hands were on my hips and his mouth was open, enveloping mine. I tried to open my lips, to get some purchase before he swallowed my whole face. When that didn't work, I found myself grabbing his T-shirt, which must have looked like I was trying to pull him closer to me.

Ladies and gentleman, my first kiss ended there, when the music stopped and the lights in the gym went on. I used all my strength to push Ethan off me.

Under the disco ball, still spinning in vain, Alison was standing beside Mr. Beal. Both were staring at me. I turned to Ethan, but somehow, he had disappeared again.

"Dance is over!" Mr. Jensen shouted.

Callie found me, pulled me away from the wall. "We gotta go."

"What's happening?"

"Alison told Mr. Beal about Misty's party, about all the little booze bottles in the street."

"Why would she do that? She just making things worse for herself."

Callie glared at me. "Because she saw you and Ethan kissing."

I caught a glimpse of Micah in the corner of the gym, snickering while kids huffed and growled at the abrupt end to their evening. That's when I realized that there's no way Alison would have noticed the little bottles in the road. Micah had told her. She'd paid his way in, but they both wanted to shut down the dance. I thought about something my dad said when I asked for my three-dollar entrance fee. "What about kids who don't have three dollars? They don't get to dance?" Maybe dances weren't mind control, maybe he was just embarrassed that school events cost money he didn't have.

Callie kept pulling me toward the door. Shorty, Misty, Brad, Ethan, and the soccer team were all gone.

"Micah helped her," I said to Callie, but she scoffed at that.

"Rachel," Mr. Beal said. Alison was behind him, scowling at me. "You came in with Misty and Brad and that crew. You want to tell me about the party?"

"I wasn't there," I said.

"Why was everyone chewing gum?"

I shrugged. "Brad gave it to me."

I looked right at Alison and asked, "Where did Ethan go?"

"Home," she said, all smug with the knowledge.

"Ethan's mother has collected him," Mr. Beal said and gave me a long look. "Were you and Callie about to sneak out?"

"No," I said, even though the answer was obviously yes.

"Sit on the bleachers," he said. "Parents are being called."

How was it possible that Ethan's mom came that quickly? Had Alison warned her about Misty's party?

While we waited for our parents, Callie continued to glare at me.

"I'm telling you," I said. "Micah conspired with Alison. He told her about the bottles in the road."

"Why would he do that?"

"Because of what Brad said. He thinks dances are mind control. He doesn't like school stuff."

"So what if he did?"

"Did you even talk to him tonight?"

"Oh, so you're a fucking relationship expert now?"

I was meant to spend the night at Callie's house. That no longer sounded fun, but I had to go. Otherwise, my parents would see my outfit and I would get in trouble.

But it was my dad who showed up. I watched while he and Mr. Jensen shook hands and chatted at the door, very chummy. All the teachers in Waterbury knew each other. When Mr. Jensen gestured to Callie and me, the smile dropped from my dad's face. He'd seen us when he came in but hadn't recognized that one of those girls was his own daughter. A second later, he spotted Alison, now sitting at the far end of the bleachers. I knew he was thinking about our chat the night before, because he waved to her and smiled like he would have to someone chronically ill.

She waved back and smiled, warmly, before turning to narrow her eyes at me.

Callie scoffed, then said, "Don't tell your dad about the *bottle*."

"I won't," I said, even though I was remembering my parents' *someday you'll have too much to drink* speech from when I was seven.

"Rachel, Callie, Mr. Nardelli is here for both of you."

Originally we'd planned to walk home. My guess was Callie's mom, anticipating an evening on her own, had gotten into her wine and asked my parents to collect her kid, too.

When I stood up, I tugged on my dress, hoping to cover more of my legs from my dad.

"I need to get my coat," I said, plowing past him and Mr. Jensen into the band room.

After I found it in a pile on the conductor's podium, I wrapped my coat tightly around myself, hoping the tighter I wrapped it the more my dad could unsee my body.

Callie, coatless, had no such issues.

Dad smiled, relieved, when I emerged. "Sounds like that was an eventful evening," he said. It hadn't occurred to me until then that he wouldn't anticipate I was involved in any of the mess that got the dance shut down. He put his arm around me. "Some kids just love to cause trouble, don't they?"

When we dropped Callie off at her house, I asked if I could go in and change back into my other clothes.

Dad gave me a look. "It's late," he said, even though it was only eight. "You can get them tomorrow."

Callie smiled when she shut the car door. I was in trouble for once, bigger trouble than she was.

He observed me in the rearview mirror. "Anything you want to tell me before your mother starts asking questions?"

Nothing, and also so much, I thought. I looked down at myself, wearing the little black dress of a grown woman. But buckled up in the back seat like a child, I felt so uncomfortably on the cusp of something, yet so far away. "I hate this dress," I said.

"Glad to hear it," he said, and put the car in drive.

When Dad and I returned home, my mom was at the kitchen table ready and waiting. "Have you been drinking?"

I forgot to lie. "There was this little bottle going around. I just took a sip," I said. "I shouldn't have, but I didn't want to be singled out and I knew it wouldn't be much. I'd never have drunk the whole thing." I was reasonably certain that last part was true.

She shook her head, then stared at my dad before turning back to me. After taking a second to look me over, she seemed to determine the outfit under my coat was a secondary problem, at least for the moment. "They said there were several little bottles in the road outside the school."

"That wasn't me."

"Who handed it to you?"

"Brad Hutchins."

"Since when does my daughter do what Brad Hutchins tells her to?"

Suddenly, my dad had a brain wave. It happened so swiftly that he couldn't think better of asking his question in front of my mom. "Wait, was it Brad you were kissing?"

"WHAT?" My mom was glaring at me like I'd started a house fire.

I narrowed my eyes at my dad and said, "No." He shrank back and let my mom take the lead.

"Rachel! Who were you kissing? And for that matter, take off your coat. What are you WEARING?"

When I removed my coat, she flinched.

"What is going on?!" she asked my dad.

"Rachel was seen kissing a boy when the dance was cut short. Mr. Jensen didn't tell me who. Said we should ask Rachel about it."

They both looked at me.

As a grown woman, I would now have all manner of responses to my parents in this situation, the most persistent being, *It's my body, I don't have to tell you what I do with it.* But my right to bodily autonomy wasn't something I knew anything about at age fourteen, and besides, I know my bodily autonomy had nothing to do with that kiss. Ethan had lunged at me, stolen it. None of this was clear to me then, so I answered Mom's first question truthfully, "Ethan Monroe."

"The boy from the newspaper article?" my dad asked.

Mom turned to me. "The boy Alison has a crush on?" I didn't

know what disappointed her more, the fact that I was kissing a boy or the fact that I was hurting Alison in the process.

"She doesn't own him," I said.

"Yes, but you knew she liked him."

I should have said that I was just as infatuated with him as she was, that I'd loved him from afar for years, but none of this seemed to square with the new reality, the disappointment of actually going out with him.

"He asked me out," I said. "We're in the same classes," I added as though it provided justification.

"Whose dress is that?"

"Callie's."

"Never again. I approve all your outfits before you see Ethan." She pronounced his name like it was in a foreign language. "And I want to meet him. No more dark corners for the two of you until he sits down with me and your dad."

Dad looked as uncomfortable with this demand as I was.

I could barely get Ethan to look at or talk to *me*. How on earth would I convince him to sit down with my parents? I pictured my dad telling him his one rule.

"Whatever," I said, and stormed off.

I should have been at Callie's house. We should have been on the end of her bed, giggling about Ethan's hands on my butt and Mr. Jensen's dorky dancing.

There was only one person to blame for this.

I got up early, before my parents, so they wouldn't see me on Facebook. I was just going to leave Alison a message telling her it was wrong to shut down the dance, that she was only making her situation worse. I wasn't expecting her to already be online.

ME: Why are you trying to punish everyone?

ME: You ruined the dance.

ALISON: Misty and Shorty were obviously intoxicated.

ALISON: They ruined the dance, not me.

I looked at her empty page, her growing friend list, all Brad's design. *Tell her I like her.* When I'd first logged on, I thought for sure I was going to do it, but now I wasn't so sure. How could she not know something was up? Why was she walking straight into the lion's mouth?

ALISON: Also, you should give Ethan space.

How dare . . . What on earth was she talking about, *give him space*? He's either fifty feet away or forcing himself on me.

ME: Stay out of it.

ALISON: Ethan and I talk.

ALISON: He doesn't want a girlfriend until high school. That's what he told me last night. He's going out with you because he feels he has to be going out with somebody.

He's going out with me because he doesn't want to go out with you.
I imagined her and Ethan walking home from Misty's the night before, side by side as he told her what she wanted to hear, not lying but also not telling the truth. Sure, I was a place filler, a means to an end, I knew that. But fuck her for saying it. She went to Misty's be-

cause she knew he'd have to walk her home. Her boy across the street. He'd always be more hers than mine. *He's* why she was walking straight into the lion's mouth. *She likes it.*

> ME: Brad said he sent you a friend request, but you didn't accept.
>
> ME: Maybe if you stop this war with him you two could get along. Maybe he feels bad and is trying to reach out?
>
> ALISON: He should feel bad, but he doesn't.
>
> ME: Brad and I talk, too.
>
> ME: I think he really likes you.
>
> ME: I think he's bored with Misty.

I waited several minutes for a response. In that time, I rode a roller coaster of emotions. First, vindication, then I started plummeting to regret. All the way down at the bottom was the truth of it: Brad's mission. *I'm going to rape her wall.* So much had happened since Brad had used those words. Despite them, somehow, he'd become my friend. I'd led myself to believe that all he would do is knock her off her perch, tell her to stop being so smug and righteous.

She never responded to me. I didn't know what to make of it until five minutes later when I got this message:

> BRAD: Good job. :)

I logged off without even responding.

The rest of the weekend I hid in my bedroom in a state of panic. I didn't dare log on to Facebook. I told my parents I was studying hard for a math test, so they left me alone and tried to go back to being proud of their kid, an act of love that gutted me because I knew I wasn't someone to be proud of.

I finally logged on Sunday night, once I'd managed to convince myself that if he'd posted something, Callie would have called. Maybe he'd decided not to. Maybe he really did have a crush on Alison. Maybe they'd start going out and everything would change. I imagined that maybe she could be happy with Brad, and I could be happy with Ethan, and all could be right with the world.

Or maybe he was waiting for maximum impact.

The post had only been up for ten minutes when I saw it.

BRAD: Hey Virgin Princess. Cant get anyone to fuck your wall? That's cuz no1 wants 2 touch u. U actually think I like u? Ur disgusting.

16.

let her get bullied in junior high." I looked at Jen as I said it. She responded as I knew she would, with the same astonished face she'd given me the day I'd admitted to not knowing about June-teenth. I still had further to plummet in her estimation. I didn't think I had much chance of pulling myself out of her deep well of disappointment, so I dug down farther. After a deep breath, I added, "*I* bullied her."

Jen scrunched her face tight, but kept her narrowed eyes on me.

"Why would you do that?" Brie asked.

I opened my mouth but nothing came out.

"Who cares why?" Jen said. "There's no excuse."

"Kids didn't like her because she was rich, but mostly it was this one kid, Brad. He wanted to torture her, and I helped him."

Everyone stayed silent, disbelieving.

"She and I used to be friends. Until I ditched her."

"Rachel, that doesn't seem like you," Lindsay said.

I was grateful that she felt that way, but Jen glanced at her like,

Really? For Jen, it was all starting to fall into place. She'd seen me laughing at Alison's Facebook page freshman year. Seen me scoffing at all the photos of Alison and her chem-free tribe. She'd listened while I embellished stories of Guinevere the Unicorn and Alison's extensive Hannah Montana T-shirt collection. *You laughed at those stories*, I wanted to say to Jen, but I didn't because maybe I was mis-remembering that. Maybe she never laughed at my Alison jokes. Jen rarely drank; she grew up in a wealthy family, too. Why would she?

Stannard was rubbing my shoulder like my mom used to do when I needed courage.

"It was wrong," I said. "I'm very ashamed of it. Back then, it felt like I only had two choices. Let her be tortured or be tortured my-self. It's stupid to think that way. I know that now. It's not a good excuse, but it is the reason. I wrote a story about it for Stannard's workshop before I knew Alison was in the class."

Brie and Lindsay regarded each other.

"I should have said something. I'm sorry."

Jen stared at me like I'd killed Alison myself. "Did you at least apologize?"

THE COOL TABLE

Some days I tell myself that all the stuff that happened with Alison in junior high wasn't such a big deal. We were just kids. It doesn't define me. Sure, I'd given Brad a little help, but *I* hadn't called her disgusting for everyone to read. *I* hadn't picked on her in the cafeteria. *I* hadn't asked out Ethan or humiliated her in the locker bay. With hindsight, I understand perfectly what a coward I was, how inaction can be just as damaging as action. *Silence is violence.* Sometimes I wonder how much of my life has been determined by all the moments I've tried to avoid.

After what Brad wrote on her wall, I couldn't sleep. I couldn't even listen to Celine and lie to myself that I did it for love. I tried to justify my actions by wondering if Alison already suspected what he was going to do when she accepted his request. Was all of this a way to drive Ethan into her *poor me* arms? I was desperate to believe this. I wanted Alison to be the ultimate puppet master, but deep down I knew that Brad's message must have crushed her. He hadn't called her smug or a know-it-all. He'd gone straight for the teenage-girl jugular. He'd called her disgusting. All I'd wanted him to do was knock her off her high horse. I wanted her to admit that she couldn't have everything she wanted.

But how did I know what she wanted? Maybe all she wanted was to be liked, like everyone else. Like me.

I considered faking illness the next morning, but I knew my mom wouldn't buy it, so I steeled myself for what was coming and vowed to keep my head down. I would feign interest in *Because of Winn-Dixie*, *por* versus *para*, the culture of Uruguay, and badminton. But when I got to school, someone had decorated my locker, covered it in hearts that read, "Rachel and Ethan 4-eva!"

I looked over at Ethan's closed locker, blissfully devoid of paper hearts. I could sense a few of my classmates smirking at me as they shut their own lockers and left. Relief washed over me once I got the door open and the hearts were hidden, but not for long. When I put my coat inside and closed it again, there was Alison.

"I didn't do it," I said, rushing past her. I was referring to my locker, but it rang so false, because we both knew what I did do. When she said nothing, I glanced back at her. She was staring at my locker. I darted to homeroom.

Alison never went to homeroom or any of our morning classes. By break time, it was all over school that she'd told on Brad. He'd been pulled into Principal Corrigan's office. The rumors were rampant—he'd been suspended, he'd been expelled, he'd been arrested—so when he was in his usual spot at lunch, I was surprised. The other soccer boys hadn't yet arrived, and Brad sat there alone with a face like thunder.

I carried my brown bag to my table, pretending to be interested in something out the window, cringing, waiting for him to call out for me. The orchestra girls were already seated at our table, but there was no Callie; she always showed up before me. I looked around and spotted her by the back wall of the cafeteria, waving me over. Next to her was Shorty. They both took seats at one of the tables reserved normally for only field hockey girls.

When I approached, Shorty was smiling. She pulled out an additional chair they'd stuck on the corner. "I had no idea you could be so bitchy, Rachel."

Sandwiched between her and Callie, I looked back and forth between them, confused.

"You told Alison that Brad had a crush on her," Callie explained. "Everyone knows it was you."

I shuddered. Would I be called to the principal's office, be expelled or arrested like Brad?

The other field hockey girls appeared suspicious at my and Callie's sudden presence at their table. All their sticks had been lined up against the wall to make room for us.

I pulled my sandwich and apple from my lunch bag, suddenly nervous about chewing in front of a new group of girls. I left my sandwich in its plastic bag and polished my apple. "How did everyone hear about my conversation with Alison?"

"Brad," Misty said, and all the other girls nodded in agreement.

"He's in *deep* doo-doo," Shorty said.

I regarded Misty, who seemed unfazed to be going out with the class criminal.

"He doesn't look like he's in that much trouble," I said, peering over my shoulder at Brad. From my new seat, his back was to me. Ethan was just taking his seat, and we locked eyes. I smiled self-consciously.

"Omigod, you guys are so cuuuute," Shorty said.

Utter bullshit, but I still blushed.

Farther behind him, Alison took a seat at her usual table. Everyone in the cafeteria went a little quiet when she pulled a notebook from her bag and started writing. We all thought she'd gone home. *Had the principal wanted a written statement from her? Was she providing information to the cops?* There was a rumor she'd hired a lawyer and was suing Brad for defamation, a word that Micah, who'd clearly started the rumor, had to explain. There was another rumor that Alison's parents were actually Brad's mom's landlords and he and his mom were being evicted. (Another new word Micah was happy to explain. He knew all the legal jargon. You had to when you were a one-man fascism-fighting machine.)

I couldn't see Alison as well from my new seat, one of the bonuses of sitting at the cool table, I guess: less access to all the depressing shit. Over here, I could pretend there was no sadness in the world, no bullying. All these rumors were just stupid gossip. Really, everyone was friends with everyone.

Facing the girls again, I tried to embrace my new status. "So did one of you decorate my locker?"

Callie and Shorty started giggling.

"Ethan saw us," Callie said. "He turned beet red."

"It was so cute," Shorty added.

"Don't take it down, Rachel. It'll be funny when Alison sees it."

"She already has," I said to my apple.

Callie and Shorty reached over my head and shared a high five. Now that these two were thick as thieves, I briefly fantasized about pulling Misty aside and asking her if she wanted to strike up a mellower, less cruelty-loving friendship, but my fantasy was cut short when the cafeteria suddenly went quiet.

When I turned around again, Brad had pushed out his chair

and stood. It was like he was suddenly ten feet tall. When he started walking away from his table with a tray containing the remnants of his lunch, people started whispering. *Is his mother here to collect him? The cops? What is about to happen?*

He moved, slowly, aware he had the attention of the whole room. When he stopped at Alison's table, I swallowed my bite of apple before I was ready. The chunk stopped for a moment in my throat. I swallowed again, harder this time, and the apple shifted, but it felt like it was still there, my little, guilty lump.

"I know you think you're better than everyone," Brad said to Alison loud enough for all of us to hear. "Well, you're not," he added.

I craned my neck to see her reaction. She stayed focused on her notebook.

Ethan and I locked eyes again, and his seemed to be begging me to make it stop. Couldn't he? I just shrugged.

Brad started to fume. "Say something."

At this, Alison looked up at him with a slight smile, one that said, *I'm better than you, at least.*

And with that, he tipped the contents of his tray onto her notebook and added, "Bitch," before chucking the tray on the floor. It bounced around before settling, motionless, like the rest of us.

As Brad walked away, I kept my eyes on Alison. She just sat there, staring at the mess Brad had made.

No one said a word. No one moved a muscle, until Callie and Shorty, looking across me, smiled at each other and pushed back their chairs. Quickly, they collected all their trash. When Callie stood up, she looked at me and pointed her head toward Alison. I shook my head and kept my butt firmly on my seat. Disappointed, she stole my half-eaten apple. She and Shorty carried their lunches calmly to Alison's table. Other kids began to understand and rose with their own trays and waste.

Callie was the first to reach Alison, who looked up right away this time, but Callie stared her down. Callie dumped the contents of her brown paper bag, her fluff-covered crusts and Dorito dust and my apple core next to Brad's trash, then let the grease-stained bag fall from her hand. Shorty did the same.

Brad stood in the doorway of the cafeteria, observing, to see which of his classmates would testify on his behalf. Soon, two lines formed: one to Alison's table, another to the trash cans. The line to Alison's table was much longer. The other girls at the field hockey table got up and joined it. Most of them, including Misty, set their brown bags, passively, on the edge of Alison's table, fully intact. Most of the skater kids and half the theatre kids, led by David Bullock, followed with their trash. David had only a banana peel to offer. He kept his unopened pudding cup. The orchestra girls went to the trash cans and so did the mathletes and some of the other theatre kids.

Micah leaned against the back wall in the corner, observing, same as Brad. *He* was the one Brad should have been mad at. *He* was the one who started the rumors. When he saw me staring at him, Micah pushed himself off the wall, shaking his head as he walked past me, then he leapt over the railing and sped down the ramp. His hot lunch was still steaming where he'd left it. Micah wasn't going to harass his coconspirator, the girl who'd paid his way into the dance, but he wasn't going to testify on her behalf either. Didn't he understand that he wasn't absolved? He had a role in this, just like me.

The lines dwindled down and I stayed seated.

The soccer team got up and supported Brad. All except one.

When the bell rang, everyone else rushed to abandon their

waste on Alison's table or in the trash cans. Only three kids were still sitting: Alison, next to a mountain of trash, Ethan at the soccer table, and me. Some kids fled the scene, others hung around to see what Ethan and I would do.

When Ethan stood, I honestly had no idea what to expect. He grabbed his brown paper bag and walked briskly over to me. He held out his hand and said, "Come on."

I focused on my own brown bag, paralyzed, until he grabbed it, lumping it with his own bag. He took my hand, pulling me up and dragging me along with him. I was instantly grateful that he would make the choice. When we got close to Alison's table, he slowed down. He kept hold of the two brown bags. He kept hold of my hand.

Alison's eyes were full of tears, mixed with the pride of not letting them spill over.

"Sorry," he mumbled to Alison.

I opened my mouth, but nothing came out.

Ethan pulled me along and dumped our bags into the trash can. Once we were out of Alison's view, he let go of my hand and ran down the ramp.

Alison's parents called mine. Things had "gone too far" was the way they'd described it. They felt the two families should meet to discuss it.

When I got home from school, I found my parents in the kitchen. Mom was at the dining table, worrying away the tiles, while Dad stood in front of the sink, head down, arms crossed.

They both looked up when I came through the door.

"Get in the car," my mom said.

"Where are we going?"

"The Petruccis'," Dad said. "Come on."

"I don't know what's gotten into you," my mom added, "but it stops now."

"I didn't put trash on her table," I said. "Lots of kids did, but I didn't."

The expression on my mom's face suggested she didn't know about the trash incident.

"Kids were throwing trash on her table? Who does she sit with?"

"She sits by herself."

Red with fury, she stormed out to the driveway. She flung open the passenger door, climbed in, and slammed it shut.

Resigned, my dad said, "Car, Rachel."

I sobbed the whole way there, a full-on tantrum, like I was three years old again. Completely inconsolable. My parents remained stony in the front seats.

We parked in the middle of Alison's crescent driveway. Getting out of the car, I looked across the road at Ethan's house and wondered which bedroom window was his and if he could see my beet-red face. In his front yard, there was a soccer goal set up with a ball tucked into the corner. As I walked up the steps, I looked back and forth between the goal and Alison's deep, wraparound porch. I could imagine her sitting on the porch swing, shadowed by the eves, watching Ethan, kick after kick. He'd probably never even known she was there.

"Rachel, let's go," my dad coaxed.

The front door was already open and Alison's dad was standing in the entry, a tall, tanned man with a sizable, protruding gut, wearing khaki pants and a salmon pink polo shirt. He extended his hand to my dad.

"How are ya, Ray?" he asked jovially, considering the situation.

"Doing alright, Bill. Thanks." I heard the phoniness in my dad's voice, the way he was leaning into his Maine accent, as they shook hands. Both men were born and raised in Waterbury, one in the west end, the other in the south. Worlds apart. My mom and I were a step or two behind. She kept her hand on my arm, like she expected me to bolt.

"Will we have you back on the team next summer?" Bill asked, his hairy hand squeezing my dad's shoulder.

"That depends. Are there any houses in this town left to paint?"

"Always," Bill said. "Thank goodness for the harsh Maine winters, or we'd be out of work. Right?!" He slapped my dad on the back.

What's this we? I wondered. When was the last time Alison's dad had been up a ladder? And my dad had another perfectly good job without Bill's scraps. Only then did it occur to me how hard it must have been for my parents to show up at this man's house, admit wrongdoing, and ask for forgiveness. And it was all my fault.

"Come on in, Nardellis."

Alison's father led us through the foyer to the living room, which looked out on the backyard and pool. My mom explained to me once that any room with a sofa but no TV was a "living room." Growing up, I came to understand that such rooms only existed in west end houses. Often, they had a living room *without* a TV, a family room *with* a TV, and usually a finished basement or "rec" room with another TV. At our house, we had just a family room. No surprise, Alison's house had even more rooms than normal west end houses. Back when I used to come over, she would call the room we were now entering "the conservatory." I once repeated that word to my dad and he muttered to himself, "It's a goddamn screened-in porch."

It had probably been two years since I'd been inside, but it felt like a lifetime. Everything was just the same, like I was walking into a museum of my own childhood. There was the wicker furniture in the conservatory, where we used to leave our naked Barbies after they'd been for a swim in the pool. And the glass table that we used to fog up with our breath and write each other secret messages.

Alison and her mom were sitting close together on a wicker love-seat. Alison was in a hoodie and sweatpants, something I'd never seen her wear before, like she'd spent the day home sick. *If only.* Patricia, her mother, was running her fingers through Alison's hair. It made me uncomfortable to watch it. My mom wouldn't have dared do that to me in front of other people. She knew if she tried, I'd slap her hand away. The truth of it made me feel awful.

"Hi, Rachel, dear," Patricia said. Her voice was kind. Either she was being polite, or she wasn't nearly as disappointed in me as my own mother was.

"Patricia," my mom said. I thought for a moment she might curtsy.

Rising, Patricia greeted her warmly. She was a tiny woman with dyed blond hair, each shoulder-length strand perfectly blow-dried into place. Her denim wrap dress stopped just at the point where her brown leather riding boots began. Taking in Patricia, my mom ran her hand over the top of her messy ponytail and adjusted her baggy red fleece. Alison stayed seated. She hadn't looked at me yet.

Patricia motioned for us to sit down across from her and Alison. The four us sat in uncomfortable silence for a minute, my dad and Bill having disappeared. I surveyed the familiar room: the Persian rug under the glass coffee table, half a dozen porcelain vases filled with flowers, strategically placed. When we were little, Alison and I had strict instructions not to run around those vases and we were the type of girls who followed instructions. The two men returned with a pitcher of iced tea and several glasses, which screeched as they made contact with the table.

When the men took their seats, I was flanked by my parents, Alison by hers.

"So," the dads said in unison, causing both Alison and me to stare down at our feet.

"I suppose," Bill began, raising his voice over my dad's, "Rachel has told you everything that's been going on."

Both my parents looked at me.

"Actually," my dad said, "we're feeling a little left out on the details."

"Rachel," Patricia said, her own heavily mascaraed eyes starting to go glassy. "Do you want to fill your parents in?"

I shook my head, no. There was nothing I wanted to say.

"Rachel." Dad nudged me.

The Petruccis now looked hurt and confused by my silence. They only wanted for the world to love their daughter like they did. They didn't understand how their own good fortune made that impossible.

My hands began to shake and my eyes again filled with tears. Alison and her parents went blurry in front of me. "I'm sorry, Alison," I blurted into my lap.

"Sorry for what?" my mom asked, rubbing my back, cajoling me.

"Brad wanted to write something mean on Alison's Facebook," I said to my knees. "But he couldn't unless she accepted his friend request. I convinced her to accept."

"And you knew he was going to write something mean?" Mom's tone was getting harsher.

Rape her wall.

I nodded, too cowardly to affirm with my voice.

"Why would you do that, Rachel?" my dad asked.

I gave him a pleading look. These weren't answers I wanted to share in front of Alison or her parents, but Dad didn't care. He stared me down until I spoke.

"For Ethan," I said. "Brad said Ethan needed me to do it."

My face felt puffy, my tears were getting sticky on my cheeks. When I finally broke from my father's gaze, my eyes met Alison's. She shot up from the loveseat and skittered into the foyer, then up the stairs to her bedroom. I pictured her throwing herself on her bed, covered in stuffed unicorns and plush bears.

Patricia and Bill regarded each other gravely, then looked at my parents.

"Alison hasn't got many friends at school, but I think she's always considered the Monroe boy to be one," Bill explained.

My parents nodded, ashamed. All three of us Nardellis fixated on the same red dot on the Persian rug.

"Sorry, is this connected to what happened in the cafeteria today? Something about trash? Was Brad behind that, too?" my mom wanted to know. She was crying now, using the sleeve of her fleece to wipe her eyes until Bill offered a box of tissues.

"Alison said neither Rachel nor Ethan threw trash on her table." Patricia smiled at me. "Thank you."

I nodded, but Patricia and I both knew that I didn't deserve to be praised for not making worse a problem I'd helped cause.

"Why is no one standing up to Brad?!" Mom raised her voice, looking at the ceiling.

I knew the question was why *I* wasn't standing up to Brad. I also knew it wouldn't do much good telling her that there were moments when I did try, but I was weak. She already knew I was weak.

"Alison's going to take some time off school. We're exploring the possibility of getting a restraining order against the Hutchins kid," Bill said.

My parents looked across me at each other. This was the kind of legal action the Petruccis could afford to take. It would never have occurred to my parents to do something like that.

Still, my dad said, "I'd probably want the same."

"I've had it with this school system," Bill continued. "Next year, private high school."

Another solution my parents would never have at their disposal. It went silent again. I suspected we were all thinking, *It's only October.* How would we survive until next fall?

Alison never came back downstairs, and ten minutes later my parents and I were back on the porch, dazed. "I don't want to cook," my mom said, regarding the last of the sunlight, moments from setting. "Let's go to Applebee's."

I was the last one out, closing the large front door, twice my height, behind me. My parents were halfway to the car, but I stalled when I saw Ethan in his own front yard. Just as I'd imagined earlier, he was kicking the soccer ball into the goal. If he noticed my parents getting into our Nissan Pathfinder, he gave no indication. Suddenly, I wanted to stay, to take a seat on the porch swing, hide away and get lost in his kick, retrieve, kick, retrieve. I wondered if his parents knew what had happened. If they were as disappointed in him as mine were in me. I wondered if we'd ever talk about it, if we'd ever talk at all.

"Rachel!" my dad yelled from the car.

That was all it took. Ethan retrieved the ball from the net and looked up. Hugging it close to him, he watched me walk to the car and get in.

"Is that?" my mom asked as I was putting on my seat belt.

"Yep."

"Why are you both pretending the other doesn't exist? Did you break up?"

"No."

My dad had his hand on the car door handle, like he planned to go out there and have a word with Ethan, but he couldn't figure out what to say. It didn't matter. Before Dad could work it out, Ethan had gone back into his house.

"Coward," I heard my dad whisper under his breath.

I wondered if he was referring to Ethan or himself. Or me.

17.

No, I hadn't apologized to Alison. At least, not with the sincerity I should have. I suspected that Jen could tell, that all the girls and Stannard could, too. Sitting silent, staring at my feet, I could have been back on that wicker sofa in the Petruccis' conservatory. I was being punished all over again for the same crime. Although, really, in the past eight years, had I ever stopped punishing myself?

"When I was made to," I said finally to Jen. I looked at my lap to avoid more disapproval. Then, out of nowhere, a flood of tears. I'd just realized I'd never have the chance to apologize for real, to show her how much I really meant it. "I never did it properly."

Everyone sat silently while I cried. Stannard continued to rub my back. I suspected the other three were having conversations with their eyes again.

Finally, Lindsay asked, "Rachel, is there anything else we need to know?"

I nodded but said nothing. The words were stuck in my throat. I felt sick, suddenly hot and dizzy. I needed to talk to the cops.

But whenever I imagined it, it was never just a conversation with the police. It was also with Jen, Lindsay, and Brie. Cam and Professor Stannard and the dean. My mom and dad were there, too. And Ethan. Brad and Callie. The Petruccis. And looming larger than all of them was Alison. Everyone would stand behind her, waiting silently while she asked me the one question we all wanted the answer to: Why are you such a coward, Rachel?

Jen threw her hands up in the air.

"What else, Rach?" Brie asked, wheeling her chair closer to me. She put her hands on my knees. Stannard's hand was still on my back. Were they comforting me or preparing to restrain me? Did they think I killed her? Did they think I wanted her to die? *Did I?*

"She was at Cam's party on Saturday night. She left with some guy. I didn't recognize him." I took a deep breath, then choked on it. Coughing up my sobs, I said, "I chased after her. Told the guy to be nice to her. Told him not to be like Brad, her bully. I was really drunk. I blacked out after that." I glanced at Stannard; her reaction was the one I was most afraid of. She held my gaze, expressionless. I watched her swallow the lump in her throat.

"Jesus. Fuck, Rachel!" Jen said. "You need help."

Lindsay was silent for a moment, her nervous giggling finally overtaken by rage. "I can't believe you kept all this from us. You're off the article, Rachel."

I nodded. She was right.

"And you need to talk to the cops," she added.

Stannard's hand on my back turned into a grip on my shoulder. "Agreed."

"That means Cam should know something, right? It was his party." Brie looked at Lindsay. "We should call him."

Lindsay shuffled papers on the desk, looking for her phone.

"He definitely knows something." I said it without thinking. Or maybe I thought I could get them back on my side. But mostly, I just couldn't carry it anymore.

They stared back at me, mouths open.

"What?" Jen asked. "What does he know?"

"I asked him if he saw the guy, but he said no. I think he was lying."

"Why do you think that?" Lindsay was holding out her phone to me now. She'd pressed Record.

"Seriously? You're recording me?"

We all looked at Stannard, who just nodded at Lindsay.

They'd all returned their focus to me, but I regarded Stannard a little longer. Betrayed.

"Rachel?" Lindsay prodded. "Why do you think he was lying?"

"Because he's competitive. If there was another guy in the room. If there was a guy in the room he didn't know, he would have sussed him out."

"So, he's protecting a friend," Jen scoffs. "Typical."

"Maybe." But that didn't feel right. I hadn't even considered that he'd protect a friend. It wasn't in his character to do that, probably why he didn't have many. Cam only looked out for Cam.

The beer on the guy's shirt. Its source was suddenly clear to me: Cam had walked straight into him, purposely. A bunch of freshman girls had just arrived and Cam had to walk past Alison's friend to greet them. He elbowed him, left the guy bracing himself with his hands in the air, looking down at his wet shirt.

"And he knew his way to the pond."

Nobody said anything. It took them a while to process. I was processing right along with them.

"Why would he lie?" Brie asked.

Then I remembered Cam pulling out of my driveway this past summer. He went left. Toward Allerton Heights.

I opened my mouth to speak, but Stannard got there first. "Because he was jealous."

Lindsay called Cam, but I knew he wouldn't answer. "Right, I'm going over to his dorm," she said.

"You're not going alone!" Brie shot up from her chair. "He could be dangerous."

I shook my head. At what, I wasn't sure. I didn't think he was capable of killing Lindsay or Brie, and I didn't think he was capable of killing Alison either.

"Hold on," Stannard said. "Let me call the dean."

Stannard left the room to place her call. Lindsay's and Brie's eyes followed her out of the room. Jen returned to her computer, jaw clenched. She had nothing left to say.

"He *knew* her" was all I could manage, shaking my head.

Stannard returned quickly. "The dean is in a meeting with the detective now," she said, hanging up. "Apparently, they're following up on something. She'll call me back."

"Following up on what?" Lindsay asked hopefully.

"She wouldn't say."

"Rachel, can you go sit on the couch?" Lindsay got up and hovered over me. "I need to work on your article. Shit, I also need to call the printer and change our run. We're definitely going to need more time now."

I didn't object. I was ready to ditch the article, ditch the newsroom entirely. It was in the back of my mind to run, but only for a split second. Where would I run to? I had no car. I imagined myself running all the way to South Waterbury, finding Brad's apartment, and asking him if I could stay there. He was the only person who I could imagine would have me right now. But just as I didn't have the courage to speak up, I also didn't have the courage to run. I plopped down on the sofa.

Another text from my Mom. **Please call me. I just ran into Dr. Monroe. Ethan is so distraught.** I buried my phone between the sofa cushions.

Stannard came over and sat down next to me. "We'll speak to the dean together," she said. "You're doing the right thing. I know it doesn't feel like it, but you are."

Brie rocked pensively in her chair, jangling her lanyard in the pouch of her hoodie. "Hey, Rach?" She leaned forward. "Remember last year at Cotillion? When you got so drunk? You kept saying 'I wish it never happened.' Was that about Alison?"

· · ·

Cam and I had been together about five months when we went to Cotillion our junior year. I didn't understand the point of it. But growing up in Greenwich, Connecticut, Cam was all too familiar with that kind of nonsense, so he was eager for us to go. He joked it was my one chance to be a debutante. "Anyone at a debutante ball with a last name ending in a vowel is usually wearing an apron," he said, then kissed me to make up for the insult.

When I went home for spring break, I told my mom about Cotillion and she rolled her eyes but offered to take me to the Macy's in Portland to look for a dress. We found a nice, simple black slip dress with spaghetti straps on the sale rack. Twenty-five dollars and that was that.

Before the event, Cam had several tuxedoed and gowned people over to his room. We all played flip cup and arrived on the dance floor tipsy and underfed. Denman had no ballroom, so we were in an auditorium-like space often used for bands and improv performances. It had a large, open floor space as well as a balcony that surrounded half of it. Later in the evening, Cam would drag me up to that balcony and force me against a wall. He would kiss me and tell me he loved me for the first time. As drunk as I was, I wondered if he was confusing love with lust. I said I loved him, too, because I didn't know for sure that I didn't. And because, at the very least, I so desperately *wanted* to be in love.

Of course, there were no debutante balls in Waterbury, Maine, not even for the likes of Alison Petrucci, so it shouldn't have surprised me that she'd show up to the Denman Cotillion in a full-on ball gown. It also shouldn't have surprised me that she'd show up with the one date she'd been dreaming of since she was tall enough to look out her bedroom window, but I still stopped, frozen, when I saw Ethan standing there among Alison and a group of her friends.

He spotted me, too, and pretended to be really interested in what one of Alison's male friends was telling him. Just then, Cam handed me a flask of rum and asked me to keep it in my bag. We were meant to share it, but I immediately took a giant swig. When he asked for it back twenty minutes later, it was already drained.

Everything after that remains blurry, like a series of floating scenes in a dream, the order unimportant. I can recall dancing with Cam, his erection when he pulled me closer, I remember him asking me about Alison, *Who is that girl who keeps looking at you?* I remember Brie and Lindsay arriving. I was already so drunk by then that I had flung my arms around both of them.

I remember being on the balcony a couple times, order unknown. There was the moment when Cam pressed me up against the wall: He loved me; he remarked also that he'd be able to remove my dress in less than two seconds. There was also me and Ethan on the balcony. I think Cam had gone back to his room to refill the flask I'd downed. I don't remember how it went exactly, but I remember confronting Ethan on the dance floor. *What you did was wrong*, I said, or something like that. He said, *Can we go somewhere else?* We ended up on the balcony, where he told me he didn't want to be there, but Alison had begged him to come. He had no interest in dredging all that up again. I think he got in his car and drove back to Yale after that. Later, Brie and Lindsay found me in the bathroom stall, passed out.

The next morning, I woke up in the health center, sentenced to mandatory alcohol counseling. When they released me, I went to Cam's, still in my slip dress. Somehow, the night before, I'd managed to vomit on everything but the dress.

"What the fuck was that about?" He wasn't angry, he was laughing.

"Too much rum," I said. "I have to do alcohol counseling."

"This campus is run by prudes," he said, then he whipped the dress over my shoulders in less than two seconds, just like he had boasted he could, even though, for me, the room was spinning.

• • •

I'm still pissed at Cam for that night," Lindsay said. "He just ditched you."

I didn't want Stannard to hear any of this. She was the only woman in this room who dared sit next to me, the pariah. I didn't want them to give her a reason to get up. And it was humiliating, the thought of her knowing how drunk I could and would get, all to avoid my own feelings. And I didn't want her to think Cam had ditched me that night. He hadn't. I regarded her instead of Lindsay. "No. I was hiding, embarrassed. I didn't want anyone to find me."

"You could have choked on your own vomit." Brie was less concerned about humiliating me.

Stannard smiled and said, "I had a few nights like that in college.

I thought I could drink away wanting to be a woman." She chuckled because everyone was staring at her. "Turns out alcohol just makes you want what you desire even more."

"True that," Brie said. "That's why I don't drink when I'm sad."

I regarded Stannard and shook my head. *Congratulations, Brie, for being so well adjusted.*

My professor understood. "We all process differently." Then her phone rang.

"It's the dean," she announced, then answered. "Dr. Fishman, are you on your way to the newsroom?" I couldn't hear the dean's response, but then Stannard held out the phone to me. "She wants to speak to you."

I took it with my shaking hand. The three girls and Stannard watched me stutter before saying, "Dr. Fishman, I saw Alison on Saturday night. She was at a party in Cameron Parker's room. She left with a guy I didn't recognize."

"We've heard this from some other sources. No one seems to know who he was. There's an officer who's taking descriptions. I'll add you to the list of people to contact. Keep your phone on."

"I will," I said, slightly relieved. "You might want to speak to Cam."

I'd ask if they're putting their focus where they should be. On the townies.

The dean was silent a moment before saying, "Yes, alright."

"Can I talk to her?" Lindsay was holding out her hand for the phone.

"Lindsay would like to talk you, Dr. Fishman." I handed over the phone without getting the dean's permission.

"Can we print Rachel's account of the party? Talk to other students who were there?"

"Well done," Stannard said.

"Other people saw what I saw," I said. Why did it still feel like I knew more than everyone else at that party?

"That's good."

I shrugged. "It won't bring her back."

"No, it won't."

Now that I'd spoken to the dean and Lindsay had told me I was off the article, I couldn't fathom a single reason to stay in the newsroom, especially not with Jen scowling at me every couple of minutes. I needed to speak to Cam before Lindsay did. He'd never tell her the truth; I needed to get it for myself. "Professor Stannard, will you drive me back to my dorm?"

Lindsay was bobbing her head to the muddled words from Dean Fishman on the other end of Stannard's phone. She put her hand up for me to wait. "Thanks, Dr. Fishman, will do," she said. "I'd like to contact Cameron Parker, too."

I shook my head at Lindsay. "He won't speak to you."

She hung up the phone. "That's what Dr. Fishman said."

Why had Fishman said that? Had she already spoken to him?

I didn't have a chance to say anything before my phone was ringing. A number I didn't recognize.

"Is this Rachel Nardelli?" asked a man on the other end of the line.

"Yes."

"I'm Detective Massey. I understand you saw Alison Petrucci leaving a campus party on Saturday night."

"That's correct."

"I'm going to ask you to answer a few questions for me. Then we'd like to see you at the police station tomorrow morning for a full written statement, okay?"

"Okay," I said, swallowing hard, imagining the interrogation room.

"When you saw Alison leaving the party, was she with someone?"

"Yes."

"Did you know him?"

"No."

"Can you describe him for me, please?"

"He was taller than her, maybe like six feet." I looked at Lindsay, who'd once again hit Record on her phone. "He was white. Brown hair. It was short with lots of product in it. His shirt was plaid or something, like a button-down. Blue, I think. It was like he was kinda dressed up. Khakis, I think."

"Were you drinking that evening, Miss Nardelli?"

"Yes."

"Would you say you were intoxicated?"

"Yes."

"Did you engage with them?"

"When they were leaving, I told him to be nice to her."

"Can I ask why?"

I put my head in my free hand. "Alcohol, probably. I knew her as a kid. I was teasing her a bit. She wasn't the type to go home with guys."

"Did he react to your comment?"

"He smiled."

Brie and Jen were exchanging looks. I felt Stannard's hand kneading my tensed shoulder.

"Just one more question."

I braced myself for a question about Cam. What could I tell him that he wouldn't already know? *Of course*. Cam knew Alison. She was at his party. Only an idiot like me would take so long to tumble to that conclusion. I needed to get off the fucking phone and confront him.

"Do you know someone named Ethan Monroe?"

The fuck?

I went quiet, but Massey didn't fill the silence.

Jesus, had I been suspicious of the wrong boyfriend all along? Just how bad was my taste in men?

"Yes," I said finally. "He went to school with me and Alison. Why?"

I couldn't imagine why he'd come up here and kill Alison. Could he not take her relentless crush anymore? Was she making things difficult with his Yale girlfriend? None of this was reason to kill her, certainly not with his road to success being so well-paved. But he could be a real shit. I knew that. What had Lindsay speculated about the killer? *Maybe he raped her but didn't mean to kill her?*

"His was the last number she called. Any idea where he might be?"

"Yale, probably. That's where he goes."

"Okay. Thank you, Miss Nardelli. We'll see you in the morning?"

It was just past midnight. "What time?"

"Anytime between nine and noon."

"Alright."

I hung up the phone and yelled into my own hands, before composing myself. "I have to do it all again tomorrow in an official statement." I'd finally done the one thing I should have done twelve hours ago and I didn't feel any better. I felt worse. She was fucking gone. Whether I'd spoken to the cops or not, she was just fucking gone and I'd let her go. "I could have stopped him," I said, and no one had a response for that.

Stannard wrapped her arms around me. "You've done all you can do," she whispered in my ear.

"Rach?" Lindsay asked. "I'm going to print all this, but keep you

223

anonymous. Since you went to the pond, your name will be on the article, but I'll need to put a note at the beginning to say you recused yourself."

"Yeah. Okay."

Stannard nodded at Lindsay. "I'll take Rachel back to her dorm room for some sleep. But I'll be back. Get that print time pushed back."

"Shit!" Lindsay reached for her phone, scrolling for the printer's number. "Brie, can you call while I write?"

Brie took the phone as Lindsay spun back around to her computer. They were busy. They needed nothing else from me. Maybe they never did. Jen took a second to watch me, expressionless, while I put on my coat. I nodded to Stannard and we left.

I knew if I asked her to take me to Cam's she'd protest, so I allowed her to take me back to my dorm. I'd head to Cam's once she left.

"You know, there's one in every year?" Stannard said as we walked to her car.

I looked at her, confused.

"Cam? There's one just like him in every year, a young man that confuses his privilege with authority. I shouldn't say there's just one. There's plenty, but there's always one who is, shall we say, the best at it." She tried a goofy grin. "You know he once wrote me an email to tell me he liked my Op-Ed in the *Times,* along with a long list of all the things he actually *didn't* like about it?"

"Shit. I'm sorry."

She chuckled. "I wouldn't get in the habit of apologizing for him, or you'll find yourself doing little else."

"He's always going on about how being a bystander isn't a crime.

But I feel guilty as hell. Why doesn't he? What does he know? Why won't he tell me?"

"It's disconcerting, isn't it? Writers are never used to the questions in our heads being real. We're used to everything being solved on the page, choosing our own adventure. I know you have questions; I know you're scared, but try to trust that when the real answers come, you'll be able to handle them." She pointed her car beeper into the parking lot and the headlights of a Subaru Outback flashed. "I hope you weren't expecting a Porsche." She was doing her best to cheer me up, and I loved her for it. "Hop in."

Sliding into the passenger seat, I glanced over my shoulder into the back, where an empty car seat was covered in mysterious stains and crushed Goldfish crackers. This glimpse into my professor's domestic life caught me off guard. I'd never imagined Stannard, the *New York Times* bestselling author, standing in line at Hannaford, her shopping cart full of Goldfish, Fruit by the Foot, and juice boxes.

"How about a little turbo boost, K.I.T.T.?" Stannard said to the car radio.

I regarded her blankly.

"*Knight Rider?* No?" She shrugged. "It's better that you don't know. Believe me. I wish *I* didn't know." When she turned on the ignition, the stereo blared, someone playing the piano. It sounded like a toddler banging on the keys. I stared at the volume nob, willing it lower. Before taking her foot off the brake, Stannard hesitated, then said, "You like Monk?"

"Sorry?"

"Thelonious Monk." She pointed to the stereo, then turned it down a little. "He once famously said, 'The piano ain't got no wrong notes.' I've always loved that. Imagine knowing your craft so well that it's impossible to play it wrong."

I listened a little more intently to the recording, confused. "Honestly, if you told me this was your son playing, I'd have believed you."

Stannard shook her head and sighed. "Melody is overrated," she said. "Disharmony is progress."

I wasn't sure what I was supposed to do with this plum of wisdom. After the day I'd had, a little order sounded good. But like most of what Professor Stannard said, it would probably take a while for the message to become clear, so I filed it away.

You going to be alright, tonight?" she asked, dropping me outside my door.

"I think so."

I told myself I'd go up to my room and wait for her to drive away, then I'd go to Cam's.

"Would you like me to come back tomorrow morning? I can take you to the police station. Nine?"

I nodded and reached for the door handle. "Professor, how come you were in the newsroom tonight?"

"Did you know that Lindsay asked me to be the faculty advisor to the paper this year?"

"No."

"I turned it down." She sounded ashamed. "I told her I thought you girls could handle it on your own, but honestly, I didn't want the extra work. Didn't want to be involved in the campus politics. I wanted to be at home with my wife and my kid." She regarded me, her eyes watery this time. "I'm sorry I let you down."

"You didn't," I said. "I didn't even know."

"No, but I think *I* did. I was tired of all the bullshit and told myself nothing important ever happens at Denman that's worth my valuable time, and, well, campus politics can be draining for someone like me, when everyone thinks your very existence is up for debate. But after I saw you at the press conference, I knew I was wrong. I called Lindsay and said that at the very least I wanted to be with you ladies to offer moral support. We all make mistakes, Rachel. Every once in a while, when you see the chance to rectify one, it's a gift."

18.

When I flicked the switch, my narrow dorm room lit up, uninviting, like a hospital room or a prison cell or that bedroom van Gogh painted before he went nuts. The twin bed that I'd slept in only a handful of times was pushed up against the wall. On the other side was my desk, where my laptop sat, closed. My copy of *Sidereus Nuncius* was still on the floor where I'd dropped it that morning. Next to the door, a chest of drawers was tucked into a wardrobe. All the furniture was made from the same yellowy wood composite, the lacquer peeling away like Scotch tape.

I walked over to the window and looked out. Stannard's car was still parked out front. She was sitting in the front seat, looking at her phone. Did she not trust me?

My phone started ringing. My mom.

I was running out of excuses.

"Sorry," I answered.

"I thought you were dead."

"I'm okay, Mom," was all I could muster.

I could hear her take a deep breath.

"Have you spoken to Alison's parents?" I asked.

Her breath was getting shorter now. She started to cry, which in turn choked me up. "I've tried so many times to pick up the phone. I can't do it. I feel like such a coward."

I nodded even though she couldn't see me. I understood her dilemma better than she could comprehend.

"How could someone *do* this?"

"I don't know," I said. Then, after a moment, I added, "I might have seen him, Mom. At a party. Alison was leaving with some guy I didn't know."

My mom's silence was long enough for me to imagine her hand covering her mouth. "How awful," she said finally. "I didn't think you and Alison were traveling in the same social circles these days."

"Neither did I. The girls at the paper are handling the story without me. I guess I'm too close to it."

"That might be best."

I couldn't tell her my suspicions about Cam. She already had plenty of her own before all this. "I told the police everything I knew. I have to give an official statement tomorrow."

"Oh, Rachel, you're carrying all of this. Want me to come tomorrow to be with you?"

"My creative writing professor is taking me in the morning. She's been helping Lindsay and the others finish the paper."

"Okay." She sounded hurt.

"The police asked me about Ethan."

"Really?" Her voice seemed to go up an octave.

"Apparently, he was the last person she called."

"But no, they don't think? You don't think?"

"I assume he's at Yale."

"He was a good kid, right?" My mom contemplated what little she knew about Ethan. "He wouldn't want to hurt her?"

"I think she called him when she knew she was in trouble."

My mom sighed. "Sounds about right."

I couldn't believe I was crying again. It came on like a giant wave. Because I tried to suppress it, it went through the phone, into my mother's ear, as one bloodcurdling shriek.

"Rachel!" she said. "What's going on?"

I took in the sharpest intake of air I could, then exhaled as slowly as I could, just like the therapist last year had taught me. "Sorry," I said.

"Rachel, honey, please. What is it?"

Another long inhale, and even longer exhale. "Something happened when we were kids that I never told you about."

THE POND

The eighth-grade trip to Pleasant Pond was a much-anticipated event on the Waterbury adolescent calendar. The final day of junior high. We were high school bound. People were going to stop calling us kids. They were going to start taking us seriously. Only summer stood between us and growing up.

Or at least I thought I'd have the summer.

It was a hot day, one of those freakish ones that come only weeks after the wintry chill. I had my tankini on under denim cut-offs and a tank top. I remember the way the dark green vinyl of the bus seat stuck to my bare thighs on the ten-minute drive to the pond. This would only be my second summer of shaving my legs and armpits. I wasn't a fan. I couldn't get used to the idea of a blade that close to my skin. Callie warned me that I'd better shave my bikini line, so the night before, I did that for the first time. Now I had red itchy bumps and I didn't understand why this was better.

On the big yellow bus, Ethan was sitting next to me. Miraculously, we were still together. We'd celebrated our six-month anniversary in April. He'd given me a necklace with a little silver dolphin pendant, which I wore all the time. Everyone considered us inseparable, which I guess we'd become even though we still treated each other with awkward trepidation.

After the incident in the cafeteria in the fall, it was a few weeks before Alison and Brad returned to school. It was in their absence that Ethan and I finally gelled. During those weeks, he started to turn around in class. We sometimes called each other at night, though neither one of us was good on the phone. When we were still too nervous to touch each other, he taught me how to simplify algebraic expressions and I started doing better in math. Eventually, my parents insisted on going to one of his soccer games. They took us both out for Subway after. Ethan clammed up again, of course, but this time my dad seemed to find it gratifying rather than cowardly. I made Dad promise not to say anything to Ethan about his one rule. With the parental meeting over, that seemed to open the door to more physical contact. Mostly, I'd go over to his house, because he had the basement rec room and we'd make out and play video games. Every fifteen minutes, his mom would poke her head down from the top of the stairs and ask if we needed anything. I was always thankful for that. I think I spoke to his mom more than I did him.

Callie and I continued to sit with the field hockey girls at lunch. As Callie and Shorty got closer, Misty and I could sit back and breathe a sigh of relief. We never became great friends, mostly we were each just thankful that the other wasn't hell-bent on destruction. Ethan continued to sit at the soccer table and sometimes he'd come over and give me one of the Hershey's Kisses that his mom put in his lunch. This simple act was enough to make my relation-ship the envy of every girl in eighth grade.

Brad came back first, a week before Alison. It was like he'd never been suspended. He just slotted right into place. Without Alison to pick on, he went back to his equal opportunity form of torture, one that everyone, including Principal Corrigan, agreed was preferable. Alison came back in the middle of November but never returned fully. I don't know how it really went down, but the rumor was that her parents and the superintendent went head-to-head on the conditions of her return, the main stipulation being that Alison was allowed to have her lunch in the library. For the rest of eighth grade, we never saw her in the cafeteria, only in class. Her empty table was odd at first, but by Christmas, it was like she'd never sat there. By January, Callie, Shorty, Misty, and I started sit-ting there. Sometimes, Ethan, Brad, Micah, and Todd would join us. Shorty had finally admitted she had no high school boyfriend and it was Todd who was causing her frequent breakouts.

Once, I went into the library at the end of lunch, to check out a book for a science project, and saw Alison sitting there, munching on a Milano cookie and reading *Jane Eyre*. I smiled, but she had no interest in my pity and didn't smile back.

She did stay on the paper, but she stopped coming to meetings. Her only assignment was "The Renaissance Corner," now a bi-weekly column, where she mostly interviewed seventh graders and a few of the eighth graders from orchestra and theatre who hadn't put trash on her table. I continued in my position as editor in chief, although I felt like Mr. Beal was always disappointed in me. I don't think he ever knew how I'd helped Brad, but he could see who I was hanging out with and I know he was trying to send me telepathic messages: *Be better, Rachel.*

Alison and Ethan remained family friends outside of school. It was something Ethan and I both quietly agreed would be for the best. Their parents had dinner parties, went on Saturday day trips together to Portland or Acadia National Park. Sometimes he'd call me after and tell me all about just how *Alison* Alison still was.

It took five buses to transport all of the eighth grade to the pond. Ethan and I were seated two rows from the back on what we childishly considered the "cool bus." Misty and Brad were behind us, Callie and Shorty were across the aisle. Micah was angry at Callie for something and chose to go on a different bus. They were in the midst of one of their many twenty-four-hour breakups that Callie was confident she could repair with the iridescent mermaid-style bikini she was wearing.

I'd planned to spend the day lying on my towel and listening to my iPod while watching the boys splash around in the water. After growing sick of the saccharine songs my mom had loaded on there, I'd recently become obsessed with another band she had on there. R.E.M.'s "Nightswimming" was now the song I had on repeat. I loved listening to it and imagining the summer Ethan and I were going to have: swimming, barbecues, and pickup football games at the west end playground.

At the pond, Callie, Misty, Shorty, and I laid our towels close to the shore and the boys ran at the water like dogs to puddles. Callie brought us fashion magazines, the kind my mom wouldn't buy because she was convinced they would body-shame me. We were going to take all the quizzes. We were laughing as Misty answered questions for the "Is My Boyfriend Too Good to Be True?" quiz, when I saw Alison camping out several yards away on the grass, by herself. She'd come on a different bus, of course. I was surprised she'd come at all, figuring that like with lunch, she'd have permission to skip. She was shaded by a huge black straw hat and a matching coverall. Occasionally she'd stand up and we four girls would watch as she removed the coverall to reveal the black one-piece coating her hourglass figure. She tiptoed to the water. She'd get in to about her waist, glide her fingers across the surface of the water for a couple minutes, then get out and go back to her towel to once again pick up *The Hunger Games*. A couple of times, I spotted Brad watching her, too, with an expression that I could never quite interpret.

Otherwise, the soccer team was constantly in and out of the water. They'd kick a ball around for a while, then go over to the picnic tables and eat potato chips and drink Sprite. Sometimes they'd try to force us girls to eat the chips, then oink at us if we did. At one point I walked past them, munching away, on the way to the bathroom to rub aloe on my bikini rash. I'd been keeping my shorts on because I was so embarrassed by it. When I came back, Brad, Ethan, Callie, and Shorty were gathered around my towel. I knew they'd been talking about me, because they were quiet when I sat down, but Ethan quickly kissed my cheek and Callie and Shorty cooed. When the boys went back into the water, Callie advised me to take off my shorts.

"Why?" I said.

"'Cause if you do, Ethan will get an erection when he gets out of the water."

I rolled my eyes. So far I'd been evasive with Callie about "how far" Ethan and I had gotten. At that point, I felt I was becoming a pretty competent kisser. I could go for hours, if necessary, but that was it. Seven months in and we still kept our clothes on, which was perfectly fine with me. Any other scenario would have been virtually impossible given that both of our mothers never left us alone for much more than fifteen minutes.

When they got out of the water, Callie's words were ringing in my ears and I blanched. Looking the other way, my eyes caught Alison's, who was never afraid to stare at Ethan, especially in board shorts. When I turned around, Ethan was standing over me, his pond water dripping on my tankini top. "Come on," he said and offered me a hand.

"The water? No thanks."

"Let's go for a walk," he said.

When I got up, Callie, Shorty, and Misty all started making kissing noises.

Ethan and I had been on plenty of walks, usually to one of the playgrounds where we could make out on the swings uninterrupted by parents. That afternoon, though, we walked quietly, holding hands, back up the path to the parking lot. I was pretty sure the teachers wouldn't allow this if they saw, but they were all having a relaxed day, too. Their last day of us. Mr. Beal and Mr. Jensen were drenching the theatre kids with Super Soakers. Mrs. Morgan had brought her Labrador.

Up ahead, I noticed Micah under a tree, skulking with a lighter in his hand, flicking the flame on and off, like he was contemplating setting the whole place on fire. Though we didn't realize it yet, Micah was becoming more and more detached from the rest of the class, withdrawing from his usual gossip trade. By sophomore year of high school, he'd stopped talking to Callie and was on heavy medication for an attempted suicide. But that afternoon, it still felt like classic Micah. We walked past him without a thought.

I smiled at Ethan and said, "Alison's been watching you all day."

"I know." He shrugged. There was nothing to be done about it. Today was the last day. We kept walking and he seemed nervous. I wondered if he was about to break up with me and I got nervous, too. Was that what they'd been talking about when I went to the bathroom?

I was surprised when he led me to the bus we'd arrived on. He didn't hesitate outside it, just pushed on the folding door that I'd assumed was locked. He boarded and I followed without questioning him, absolutely convinced I was about to get dumped. At least it would be in private. When we were both on board, he pulled the lever of the door hard, latching it. I stared at it, wondering how we'd open it again. Were we stuck?

I looked at him, puzzled. "What are we doing?"

He lunged at me then, just like he did at the fall dance, unexpectedly, nervously.

I pulled away. "If they catch us, we'll be in serious trouble."

"Is that the only problem?"

I was confused by his question.

He gripped my hand tighter and led me to the back of the bus, where he pulled me into the seat we'd been sitting in earlier. It was on the shady side; the other half of the bus was bathed in sunlight. He started to kiss me again and pulled me down, so we were both lying face-to-face on the seat.

"Seriously," I said. "They're going to wonder where we are."

"They're not paying any attention," he said. "And they're keeping their eyes out for Brad and Misty, not you and me." He continued kissing me and I figured we could do this for a little while longer, then head back to the pond, and I'd have a story to tell Callie that would make me seem a bit cooler.

But then he undid the button on my shorts. It happened so quickly. His hand was down the front of my bikini bottoms. His fingers were searching.

"Ethan?" I said, but he didn't answer.

With his free hand, he took one of mine and put it down his wet swim shorts. My fingers wrapped easily around his erect penis. I'd heard of penises being described as hard, but this one wasn't really that. Walnut shells were hard. The low hanging pipe in the laundry room where my dad frequently smacked his head was hard. This was something else: rigid, but squishy.

I let go of him. "Not here," I said, as though there were another location where I would be more comfortable with this.

His expression seemed to call my bluff. "Where? Both our parents are always watching." Just then, his index and middle fingers found the hole they were searching for and I flinched in agony, but I managed to suppress any sound of it. However, the surprise caused me to grab hold of him again. His penis twitched in my hand and he said, "Don't grab so tight."

I tried to loosen my grip, but every time he twisted his fingers around inside me, like he was trying to get the last of the peanut butter from a jar, I found my fist tightening.

Was there a lever for the door? Or would I have to run into it with my whole body to get off this bus?

Using his free hand to guide me, he moved my hand up and down on his penis. By then, he'd stopped kissing me. Our wrists were tangled and his focus was entirely between our legs. "You'll have to swallow at the end," he said.

"What?"

"When I . . . You know. You have to swallow that or it'll get all over the bus."

Why couldn't I just say no? The word wasn't even on the tip of my tongue. It was like I'd forgotten it existed. He drove his two fingers even deeper inside me. If I'd worn a one-piece like my mom wanted me to, would that have stopped him?

I thought about the *Hang On to Your Hat!* video from sex ed. Was this my virtue? The video never really explained. Was I handing it over to Ethan now, just as I'd felt at the time I would? I didn't feel like I was giving a gift.

Then out of nowhere came his bizarre justification: "Brad said you'd want it." He finally looked at me and must have seen that I didn't. It was hard for him to hide his disappointment. He'd been promised something, even if not by me. He took his hand out of my suit, but when I tried to remove my hand, he held it there more tightly, then said, "Your mouth, use your mouth."

That was when a bang finally came on the back door of the bus. I heard Mr. Beal's voice say, "Rachel? Ethan? You in there?"

I yanked my hand from his shorts and quickly did up my zipper and button. My eyes filled with tears, part fear, part relief.

Ethan and I looked at each other when we heard the bus driver coming with the keys.

"We should break up," he said.

"What?"

"I don't think we should go out anymore."

The key was in the lock of the back door of the bus, twisting. When the driver swung the door open, Ethan bolted out. Mr. Jensen stopped him just as Mr. Beal boarded the bus.

When Mr. Beal saw the tears streaming down my face, the color drained from his own.

"Rachel? What's happened?"

I couldn't look at him. "We just broke up," I said, wiping away my tears with the hand that had just moments ago touched a penis for the first time. "Sorry," I said. "This is embarrassing. He broke up with me."

"Is that it? Should I get Mrs. Morgan?"

"That's it," I said, staring at my shorts. Beneath them, it burned. I wondered what Ethan was saying to Mr. Jensen. "Can I just sit here a few more minutes?"

"Rachel?" he said, lightly touching my shoulder.

I looked up at him, that's what he wanted from me, eye contact. "Please?"

"Okay," Mr. Beal said. "Just a few. I'll be right outside."

Ten minutes later, I stepped off the bus in time to see Alison and Ethan getting into Mrs. Petrucci's white BMW SUV. I wouldn't see Ethan in the flesh again for seven years. Cotillion.

19.

My mom listened, patiently, to the whole story. Finally, she said, "I'm so sorry, Rachel. Jesus. I knew there was a reason why I don't own a gun. If I ever see him . . ." She couldn't finish the sentence; the ending wasn't in her. Just that quickly, she remembered that Alison was dead, dead for real by some other guy's hand. "That's terrible, I shouldn't have said that, sweetheart. Sorry."

"You're just being protective."

She sighed long and hard. "Still."

"I'm pretty sure Alison told Mr. Beal to look for us." As soon as I said that, something occurred to me that never had before. I should be grateful to Alison for that, even if it hadn't been her intention to save me. She'd probably meant for me to get caught, to get in trouble.

Then my mom confirmed it. "Well, thank God she did. I just wish he'd found you sooner."

We both fell silent for a moment. I didn't know what else to say, but I could tell she didn't want to hang up, not ever.

"Your old classmates have created an RIP Alison page on Facebook. Have you seen it?"

"You're joking," I scoffed. "That makes me want to scream."

She sighed. "I think it's human nature, honey. People always struggle to do the right thing until it's too late. Sometimes it's just easier to look back and convince yourself it was different. So much of what we do in adult life is to make up for the things we can't fix."

Once I got off the phone with my mom, I returned to the window. Stannard's car was still there. She was talking to someone on the phone. I wondered if she was waiting on me to turn out my light. I did just that but saw no movement. I opened my laptop and logged on to Facebook. The group, "RIP ALISON," was the first thing to come up.

DAVID BULLOCK: Who remembers Gwenoveer the Unicorn? Legend.

LIZZIE SIMPSON: Oh my god! The centaur that looked like Zac Efron!

MISTY EVERETT: Hey, Hannah Montana turned out to be a total badass bitch. Alison schooled us all.

CALLIE HAMEL: She did have the best pool parties.

DAVID BULLOCK: Hamel—she had the ONLY pool parties.

I kept scrolling, message after message, I took in every single one. *What was this?* I felt myself growing angry. Weren't they haunted? I searched for a post from Ethan but I found nothing. I clicked on the private chat box again. Should I send him a message? Not for the paper this time, but for me? *Why did she call you? Did you do to her what you did to me?* I couldn't do it. I couldn't type any of it. Instead, I looked for a comment from Brad. I wondered if he was feeling like I was: devastated, guilty, confused. I didn't have to wonder long; within moments, he messaged me.

BRAD: Nerdelli. What the fuck happened?

ME: I don't know.

BRAD: They don't know who?

ME: Not yet. She was at a party with some guy. They found her at Pleasant Pond.

BRAD: The fuck?

ME: I know.

· · ·

I don't want to talk about it was my line whenever anyone asked me what happened with Ethan on the bus. There were rumors, of course. "Brad said you and Ethan went to do it!" Callie said that afternoon when I returned to my towel.

I didn't even look at her. "He dumped me," I said, then went mute.

By the time we boarded the bus back to school, everyone knew Ethan had dumped me. The delicate skin between my legs burned. Every time the bus hit a bump, I'd feel a sharp pain, like his fingers were still up there.

"Alison followed you guys," Callie said, sitting next to me now. "At least you never have to see her again."

When I stepped off the bus, junior high was officially over, and I walked home alone.

I only told my parents that Ethan and I had broken up, that it had been his decision. They didn't understand and desperately wanted to. Why had Ethan suddenly lost interest in their daughter? "I don't know," I said. "Maybe he loves Alison after all." It came out sarcastically, but when he didn't show up the first day of freshman year and word got around that he'd also gone to Exeter Academy, I wondered if it was actually true.

My dad often referred to that summer as the summer I lost my smile. He meant it like, *Chin up, kid*, but I found myself having to leave the room every time he said it, for years.

That June, my parents let me languish for about a week before they told me I had to get out of the house and see my friends. "Go to Dunkin'. Meet Callie!"

One afternoon, I lied to them and said I was on my way to meet her at Dunkin'. I figured I'd just get a Coolatta, go for a quick walk, then come back. I knew if I actually met Callie, she'd want more details. She'd been calling every night, and every night, two minutes into the conversation, I'd pretend my parents needed me.

I left the house without my iPod and felt naked doing so, but I hadn't seen it since the pond and thought it had probably dropped out of my bag. I was worried about telling my mom that, too. I'd been searching for the same make and model on eBay and didn't know how I was ever going to get $113.

At Dunkin', I ordered an Oreo Coolatta and surveyed the room for anyone I knew. I thought I was safe until Brad came through the door. His house was just a couple doors down from the Dunkin'.

"Nerdelli," he said. "Why've you been hiding?"

"I haven't," I said, taking the Coolatta from the brown-visored girl behind the register.

"Sit," he said.

"No thanks, I'm going home," I said, heading for the door.

"Who cares about Ethan? He's not so great."

I turned around.

"Come on. Sit." He'd already found his way to one of the tables, despite not ordering anything. "People do crazy shit for him. I've never understood that."

I rolled my eyes and sat down. At least I could tell my parents I'd been social. I wanted to ask him why he told Ethan that I'd *want it*, but that would have involved admitting there was an *it*. Instead I just said, "What are you talking about?"

Brad tapped his fingers on the table. "Like, why did you help me? Why did you tell Alison to accept my friend request when you knew what I was going to do? Didn't she used to be your best friend?"

I shrugged.

"You did it cause I told you Ethan wanted you to."

"He didn't?"

"The point is, he never did anything for you."

"Maybe I was afraid of what you'd do to me if I didn't help you. Unlike Alison, I didn't have Ethan to protect me."

He smiled. "See, that right there, that's the thing. Is he the reason you guys aren't friends?"

I shrugged, again. Obviously it was so much more than that. When things happen slowly, there's never *a reason*, but I surprised myself when I said, "Her friendship with him was always more important to her than her friendship with me."

Brad raised an eyebrow at my pettiness. "For the record, I wouldn't have done anything to you, Nerdelli. I like you."

"You threatened me!" I raised my voice. "You said if I didn't help you, you'd do the same to me."

"That wasn't what I said."

"You said she'd get what was coming to her and if I wasn't careful so would I!"

"I just meant you needed to loosen up, to stop wasting so much attention on Monroe."

"No, you didn't. That stuff you wrote on her wall was terrible. You'd have done the same to me."

He shook his head, no.

"Brad, you once kicked a soccer ball into my face!"

It took him a moment to recall it. "That was different."

"How?"

"It just was. And sorry. I shouldn't have done that. You and I, we're cut from the same cloth."

I scowled, desperately wanting that last part not to be true.

"Ethan and Alison, a whole different one. Like, what's the nice one?"

"Silk?"

"Yeah, they're silk, we're . . ." He reached around and pulled the tag from his T-shirt forward. "A cotton-polyester blend."

I smiled a little, despite myself. He had an odd intelligence, not the kind that would ever do well on a test. It was then that I wondered when I'd stopped being afraid of him. "So, why mess with Alison? Why didn't you just let her be?"

Now it was his turn to shrug. "I don't think I was the only one. None of you girls ever sat with her at lunch. That was mean. Every day, you did that."

"Please, Brad. You tortured her."

"So did you. Same cloth, Nerdelli." I was about ready to get up and leave him, when he started in again. "Did you know my dad lives next to Alison?"

"I knew he lives on that street."

"See, like, why would you know that? I never told you." When I shrugged, he continued, "Anyway, sometimes she babysits my twin sisters. Did you know about them?"

I nodded and took a slurp from my Coolatta. I wondered if I should offer him some, if he didn't have any money to buy his own, but he didn't seem to care about that. He only wanted to talk.

"There's lots of rumors about me. I bet you've heard about the time my stepmom called the cops when one of my sisters saw me hanging out in the woods behind their house. I bet you heard all about how the cops drove me home that day."

"Yeah, but is it a rumor or is it true?"

"It's none of your business, but it's a good story, right? I bet you loved it. That's the point."

I couldn't admit that was true, so I said, "What does any of this have to do with Alison? It was probably Micah who told everyone."

"A couple weeks before she joined Facebook, I knocked on my dad's door because I saw she was there." He tapped nervously on the table as he spoke. He watched his fingers rise and fall. "She was babysitting and I'd never been on the inside of my dad's house, so I asked her if I could come in. Do you know what she said? 'Your dad says you can't come in.'" He tapped the table harder, then looked at me suddenly. "You know what that feels like?"

I swallowed hard. "No." When he continued to stare at me, I added, "I'm sorry." And I really was.

Still. It was his dad who was the asshole. Alison was just doing as she was told.

"Go ahead," he scoffed. "Tell me it wasn't her fault. Ethan said the same thing."

"Maybe she didn't let you in because you've never been very nice to her. She was scared of you." When he glared at me, I said, "But she should have let you in. That really sucks."

"Yeah." He laughed to himself. "It sucks."

Brad's relationship with Alison must have been as convoluted as my own. The high road was a foreign concept to him. He'd never been shown it, certainly not by anyone in his own family. The fact that Alison had such easy access to it, that for her, it was paved in gold, must have enraged him. To pinpoint the exact moment the war between them was declared, and by whom, was impossible, but some part of him had to know that his aggression was excessive and misdirected.

I offered him some of my Oreo Coolatta and he took a big, long slurp, looking around the empty Dunkin'. "That Allerton Heights crowd always deserts us in the summertime."

"What about Misty?"

He rolled his eyes. "Especially Misty. Face it, Nerdelli. It's just you and me."

I sat uncomfortably with that idea for a moment, then said, "I should get home," pulling myself up.

He scoffed. I was deserting him, too, then he seemed to remember something. "Here," he said, pulling my iPod from his pocket.

"Where did you get this?"

"The pond. Ethan showed it to me. He wanted me to see all that weird old-people sex music you like." I must have turned beet red, because he smiled a little. "I told him how my mom likes all that stuff and she's a total horndog."

"Oh." I looked down at the iPod and understood what Ethan meant on the bus. *Brad said you'd want it.*

"He said there was no way you were like that. He said you're a total prude." When I took it back, he said, "See? He's not so great."

I looked away. I didn't want Brad to see the tears forming in my eyes.

He continued, "You know, Ethan was pretty pissed at me for saying in front of the whole cafeteria that Alison thinks she's better than everyone one else. You know what he told me?"

"What?"

"He said if I was going to say that about anybody, I should have said it about you." At this point, Brad finally got up and adjusted his T-shirt, still twisted from checking the label. "At least with me, you know what you're going to get. Am I right?" He shuffled to the door. "Later, Nerdelli."

• • •

What kind of resentment must he have felt that day, having to teach me—little miss straight A's—that life was never fair, not for one solitary second? How much did all of that still weigh on his mind? I didn't see much of him in high school. He wasn't in my classes, our paths never crossed much. He played soccer and I did the paper. Nobody hung out at Dunkin' after school. He wasn't the boss of us anymore, not in this newer, bigger school. Not when girls like Misty Everett started dating older guys who could kick his ass. I'd see him at parties sometimes. He'd swing his arm around my shoulder and say, "What's happening, Nerdelli?" If you could peak as early as junior high, Brad had.

BRAD: Shorty was joking that people are going to think I killed her.

ME: That's not funny.

BRAD: THANK U.

BRAD: Me and A were just starting to get along.

ME: What? Really?

BRAD: We hung out a bit this summer. She saw me with
Luna downtown and she invited us over to her pool. No way
I could say no to the kid, so we went. Went couple times.

ME: Wow.

BRAD: Luna frickin loved her.

BRAD: We got round to the past at some point and I said
sorry for being such a giant dick back in JH.

ME: I wished I could have some time with her to say sorry
again.

What a stupid thing to say. I'd had a million opportunities to
apologize. Brad was kind and didn't call me on it.

BRAD: I think she needed to say sorry to u also.

BRAD: When she saw me and Luna in town she was at that
coffee place with ur boy.

ME: Ethan's not my boy, Brad.

BRAD: Not him, the other guy.

Of course.

It had been there, in the back of my mind, inaccessible, all day.
I just needed someone else to say it. I saw it clearly now, like a slide
reel. Cam was different after Cotillion, a little cagey. He didn't keep
the door to his room open anymore. Sometimes, I'd get there and
it was locked, even if he was inside. I figured I'd crossed a line with
my drunkness at the dance. I didn't want to be *too much*, so if the
door was locked, I went back to my own room and waited for him

to text. When he came to Waterbury, he was there to visit us both. Had she gone to visit him in Chatham? He'd been lying to me all fucking day. For months. Cam, the collector of stray girls. Did he love her?

I've had visitors, she said that day at the Epicurious Farm. Didn't she and I always want the same thing? Didn't she always find a way to get it?

BRAD: Hope ur not still with him. Why U and A have the same douchy taste in guys?

ME: Good question.

BRAD: U need a d-bag detox Nerd. Hang in there. Don't be a stranger.

How had I let it happen again? Was it possible that Alison and I had our sights on the same guy for a second time? Or was this another one of Cam's orchestrations, another stunt to make everyone in the world believe they can't live without him? I had fallen for him, for *it*, so easily. I was still entrenched in it. Maybe Alison was, too? *Come to my party, Alison. You won't get this chance again, Alison.*

Had Cam gone to see her Saturday night after I'd blacked out? I thought again of Alison at the pond, only this time I imagined it was Cam with his arm around her waist. Together they watched the glistening water. Cam looked peaceful there by the pond with his arm around her, then he looked over his shoulder at me and smiled.

20.

Stannard's car was finally gone. I shot up from my desk chair and put my coat back on.

I did what every woman on campus had been told not to do: I walked its length, from my dorm to Cam's, alone, in the dark. I wrapped my coat around my waist and held myself tightly, as though that would protect me from whatever might be lurking behind Denman's carefully manicured hedges. It wasn't totally dark. The paths were lit by lamps, the pretty kind meant to look like Victorian gaslights. They cast shadows of the bare tree branches, like arthritic witches' fingers, on the paved walkway. I kept my head down, probably the last thing I should have done. My body was begging to be attacked. But I didn't care. I already knew I was walking straight toward danger.

At two a.m., there were still lots of dorm room lights on as I walked past. I wondered how anyone could sleep. I pictured couples coming together, intertwined in twin beds, guys saying stupid shit like *I won't let anything happen to you* just to get laid.

Denman's campus, like any campus, was awash with dating horror stories. There were the guys who demanded their girlfriends be completely waxed, like little girls. And guys who liked to piss on girls. And apparently, one particular guy who liked to masturbate to his girlfriend over FaceTime, claiming that the stillness of her silently reading a book turned him on more than her actual presence. I thought about Ethan Monroe and his Yale girlfriend. Was he the same? Did he put his own pleasure above hers? Did he demand blow jobs? Did he prefer fucking her tits and filling her jugular notch with semen, his own little Lake Ethan?

My body felt electric with rage because now, all these guys got to sit back, proud of themselves, thinking they were heroes simply because they didn't kill a girl.

The dining hall that had been all lit up when Cam and I had driven past hours ago was now pitch-black.

I wondered if Cam had waited for Alison outside that dining hall, same as he'd waited for me last fall. What book had he offered to read for her? How long had this been going on? Had she brought that guy to his party to make him jealous? Had it worked? And where was that guy? Dead in those woods somewhere, his body not yet found?

When I pounded on the door of Cam's suite, Mitchell answered in his pajamas, groggy. He didn't say a word, just stepped out of the way to let me in, then stumbled back into his own room and closed the door.

I had to bang even harder on Cam's bedroom door to get him to open up. When he finally did, it just came out: "Did you kill Alison?"

"The fuck?" He was still dressed, but his room was dark. There was an open beer bottle, sweating, by his lit-up computer screen. "Are you seriously asking me that?!"

"Yes" felt like a stupid thing to say, so I just stared back, tried to appear unmoving. His face didn't feel familiar. I wondered if I'd even seen this man before in my life. Who the fuck was he? He clenched his jaw. His eyes were bloodshot. "Just fuck off, Rachel," he said and started to close his door, but I stuck my hand out to stop it.

Both Brandon and Asa opened their doors. When they saw me, they closed them again.

"You've been to the pond with her. At least admit that."

He leaned on the doorway to his room, not inviting me in, but inviting a fight, nonetheless. He was drunk. "Once. Over the summer. We went skinny-dipping."

I shook my head.

"You find it so unbelievable that I'd gravitate toward someone who didn't have to be off her face to be with me? Someone I didn't have to beg?"

I felt an ache in my abdomen like a gut punch. He could do this: land a winning blow in my tender center and walk out of the ring. But I wasn't going to let him. Not anymore. I pushed past him into his room. "Tell me everything."

At this opportunity to hurt me further, he finally smiled. I wondered if he was this way with her as well.

When he shut the door, it sounded like a dead bolt. I could have been back on that bus with Ethan, behind a door it would take all my force to open.

"We met at Cotillion last year. And for the record"—he pointed at me—"you lied to me, too. I asked you who she was and you said you didn't know. You were obviously lying. You kept staring at her date. Then you got epically drunk."

"What's that got to do with anything?"

"Maybe if you weren't so drunk all the time, you'd remember

shit. You'd know, for example, that I didn't fucking kill her. I wouldn't."

I felt so stupid, so dizzy. The way he said that, *I wouldn't*. He did love her.

"She approached me at Cotillion. Apparently you lashed out at her date and he left. She was pissed at you. And that same fuckin' guy, he hightailed it out of the dive bar this summer the second he saw us. You think I didn't notice?" He flopped back onto his desk chair and took a swig of his beer. "After Cotillion, I told her to come over for a drink sometime."

"Of course you did," I said, trying not to show how much it stung.

I took a seat at the end of his bed and caught a glimpse of the picture on his desk of me and him outside the Low Down. In it, he's looking down my top, wearing Shorty's stupid felt hat. I hated that fucking picture.

I must have been scowling, because he said, "She hated that picture, too. Always turned it face down every time she was here."

I heard it: *every time*. I didn't take the bait, just shook my head.

"I'd offer you a drink," he added, "but it's my policy not to offer drinks to alcoholics who accuse me of murder."

"What happened on Saturday night, Cam?"

He turned his chair away from me. "I told her she shouldn't come. I said that you'd be here, but she showed up anyway."

"So, the guy? She was trying to make you jealous?"

"Probably."

"Did it work?"

He didn't answer, stayed facing the other way.

"Who was he?"

Finally, he turned around slowly. He looked at me with complete disdain. I felt a chill go down my spine. "No fucking clue, Rachel." He was grinding his teeth. "Your newspaper buddies probably have you wearing a wire."

"Jesus, you're paranoid."

He got out of the chair and stepped toward me. "My own fucking girlfriend thinks I'm a murderer."

"I need to know, Cam. Did you recognize that guy?"

"Oh, you need to know, do you?" He got in my face. He grabbed my waist and patted the pockets of my coat until he found my phone. He knew my code and punched it in. After he'd determined I wasn't recording him, he stuffed it back where he'd found it. "Let me guess. You think I hired him to kill her? She was going to tell you about us, so I had to off her? Is that your running theory?"

"No." I'd settled on something different: Cam went after Alison and the guy once they'd left the party. Maybe she knew the guy, brought him here to make Cam jealous and it worked. After tossing me into bed, Cam went after them. Maybe he got angry, tried to hurt the other guy but somehow ended up killing Alison by accident. It wasn't a full picture and I sure as fuck wasn't going to share it with Cam. Instead I said, "You don't feel the least bit responsible?"

He didn't answer, just stepped even closer to me. He used to do this when he wanted sex. He'd tower over me until I fell backward onto the bed. He found it hilarious, that his size meant he could get whatever he wanted with minimal effort. The window was behind me now, and I felt my back pressing into the glass.

"You shouldn't have let her leave with him," I said, determined not to back down either.

"Oh yeah, you'd have loved that, right? If I'd intervened, saved your childhood frenemy?" He grabbed my forearm tightly.

"If it saved her life!" I shouted. I pulled my arm away and pushed past him, making my way back to the door.

"Oh, please." He followed me. "You hated her. She told me about how shitty you were to her when you were kids. She told me about your story."

"I didn't want her to die!" I turned my back to him, sick of his face in mine, his horrible, clenched expression. I resolved that if he touched me again, I'd scream. Mitchell would help me.

"I'm the one who told the cops about him," he said. "I'm the one who actually loved Alison."

He did it. Finally, he said her name. It sounded like a thunderclap.

I turned back. "If you loved her so much, why didn't you just break up with me?"

He threw his hands in the air. "I knew if you and I split up, it would give the newspaper girls full license to write bullshit about me in the paper all senior year."

"You're dating me to keep your name out of the fucking *Denman Weekly Review*?"

"God, you're naïve. Newspapers are digitized. Any job I apply for next year will look me up online and see the Denman paper. If Jen had the opportunity, she'd write me out of my career before it even has the chance to begin. I'd hoped after graduation Alison and I could . . ." He let his voice fall. He was in pain.

I always knew there was something off about my relationship with Cam, but it never once occurred to me that he was using me like this.

All dexterity lost, I couldn't wrap my fingers around the handle. I couldn't unlatch the door.

He was still towering over me, still angry, but now his eyes were filled with tears. "You know who the cops told me she called when she realized she was in danger? Not me, that other prick. The one from Cotillion. The one from the bar. She didn't want me." Reaching out, he wrapped his hand around mine. "You know she only ever wanted to be your friend. All this shit you're carrying. It's your own damn fault." I prepared for him to grip harder, to crush my hand, but he just pulled open the door. "Get the fuck out."

21.

I speed walked back to my dorm, fighting off the cold and the terror of what I'd just experienced. I regarded all the dark dorm rooms once more; everyone had finally succumbed to sleep or was lying in the dark, staring at their ceilings. I didn't know who lived in any of these rooms. I'd never visited any of them. I had no idea what they looked like inside. I was only months from graduating, but I knew so few people. It struck me then that I didn't even know myself, not really. The person on this campus who probably knew me the best was now dead and she couldn't stand me. What a mess I'd made for so long. Why couldn't I have just cleaned it up?

When I got back to my own dorm, the hallway was dark until I swung open the front door, illuminating the sensor lights in the stairwell. Climbing the two flights, I listened to the eerie quiet—no hip-hop, no country, no late-night television.

My room was bright. Before I'd bolted out earlier, I'd left the lights on. I flopped back on my bed and stared at my nearly empty wardrobe. I didn't need the hanging space because I didn't have any clothes to hang. Everything I wore, I shoved in a drawer, much to the chagrin of my mother, who, for reasons I would never understand, still spent several hours every weekend ironing. Though right then, it was comforting to imagine her ironing in the family room, watching *Property Brothers*. I'd always enjoyed stretching out on the couch at times like that, the two of us laughing at the buyers with their first-world problems and million-dollar budgets. There was really no reason why I couldn't go home that weekend and do exactly that. *Property Brothers* with my mom, postseason baseball with my dad. Except such innocence only worked if Alison was alive, and she wasn't.

I recalled what my mom had said on the phone: *So much of what we do in adult life is to make up for the things we can't fix.* It reminded me of Alison's story for Stannard's class, the one I'd been convinced was some sort of revenge. Maybe it was the opposite. Maybe it had been Alison's way of saying, *It doesn't have to be this way.* I remembered what she said in class. *There's far more pain out there than there is sympathy.* Would things be different if I had listened?

I wish it had never happened. All of it, was what I'd meant when I'd wept in Brie's and Lindsay's arms at Cotillion. From puberty onward, I wished none of it had ever happened. I'd have given anything to take it all back. To have a redo. But this was how I lived now. Making decisions I knew I'd regret, because regret was the only emotion I knew how to feel. Regret and guilt. Were there others?

The next morning, I woke up to my phone ringing in my hand. I was still in my clothes from the day before.

"I'm outside your dorm in my car," Stannard said. "I got you a coffee and yet another donut. After how many times does something become a habit?"

"I've just woken up," I said, confused.

"Get dressed. I've got news you'll want to hear."

I stumbled out to her car in yesterday's jeans and a sweatshirt.

When I opened the car door, her hand was already stretched out with the coffee. "They got him."

"What? Really?" I landed hard on the seat and took an excited swig of the coffee. It burned the back of my throat.

"He's in custody."

"Who is he?"

"His name is Brett Something. They found footage of him and Alison on a security camera. They were getting in a car and the police ran the plates."

I had no idea how good it would feel to hear this news, but then I imagined myself running out into the parking lot yelling, *Stop!* and the good feeling faded. "Brett? Is he the guy from the party?"

Stannard shrugged. "I have a feeling they might want *you* to confirm that. We do know he's not a Denman student."

I nodded at the coffee in my hands. It was too scalding to take another sip. "That means I could have stopped them."

"Rachel, there's no way you could have known."

"She's dead because of me."

"She's dead because of him."

"I could have saved her."

"Maybe."

I clenched my hands around the coffee cup and the lid popped off. Stannard took it from my hands and put it in the cupholder. "Say you stopped it. Say it was the guy you saw at the party. Don't you think he would have just moved on to another party? Another girl?"

I shook my head, not in disagreement, just sheer bewilderment.

"I think he would have." When she spotted my fists starting to clench, she grabbed them. Held both my hands in hers. "For you, this is all about Alison. For him it wasn't about her at all. It was all about him."

I suspected my professor was saying this to make me feel better, less culpable, but instead, her wisdom filled me with a deep chasm of sorrow. Head to toe, hollow at the thought that in her own death, Alison was an afterthought.

"You can't save everyone," Stannard said.

I remembered Alison following Ethan and me to the bus that day. She might not have meant to save me, but she had. "I understand that, but I *should* have saved her."

"Okay. I get it. I'm not going to try to talk you out of that. Now's your chance to help put him away. Shall we go?"

I nodded.

"Eat your donut." She directed her attention to a Dunkin' bag on the dash and smiled. "Chocolate frosted with sprinkles. All other donuts can go to hell."

I'd never been in a police station before; this one smelled like Egg McMuffins and stale coffee. I felt my stomach churn, my recently consumed donut on a spin cycle.

Stannard stood by my side. She looked nervous, too.

"I'm Rachel Nardelli," I said to the woman behind the desk. "I told Detective Massey I'd come in this morning and give a statement."

The woman looked me over. She was probably about my mom's age, with a tight perm, short in the front, long in the back, not a mullet, exactly, more like highly practical. She said nothing, only picked up the phone and pressed a few numbers. "Doug. A Rachel Nardelli here for you." When she hung up, she added, "Have a seat." She gave Stannard an extra-long look, taking in her height. "You'll have to wait out here."

"Don't like these places," Stannard said, when we sat down.

"You don't have to stay," I said.

She pulled a stack of papers out of her bag. "I'll be plenty busy."

Detective Massey came out from behind a heavy metal door. "You're Rachel?"

I nodded.

"Go get him," Stannard said, and I followed Massey down a long linoleum corridor to his office.

Massey let the door to his office close behind us. When I heard it latch, I flinched.

"You found him?" I said.

"I'm going to take your statement first, Rachel." He motioned to a chair that was facing away from the door. "Have a seat."

I swallowed hard but agreed.

He tapped the pocket of his sport coat and pulled out a pair of reading glasses, rectangular ones that looked like they came from Walgreens. He took a seat on the corner of his desk and reached back to fiddle with his computer, finally grabbing a pen and note-pad. "I'm going to record you. The computer will generate a written statement, which you will read and sign. Okay?"

"Okay."

He adjusted his posture, ready to receive my information. "Tell me about Saturday night."

Even though I've never thought much about heaven or whether I'd one day end up there, the whole time I recounted my version, I imagined Alison was critiquing me from above: *Actually, Rachel, those were blue flowers on my dress, not red. Actually, Rachel, it wasn't a drunken smile I gave you, it was a polite one, the kind you give to someone you don't really like. Why is it ALWAYS you, Rachel? Why are you AL-WAYS around at my darkest moments?*

"When Alison and this young man left the party, what time was this?"

"I don't know," I said. "Probably after ten."

"Did they look like close friends or new acquaintances?"

I thought about how quickly Alison made friends freshman year. Within days, it seemed she'd formed an army and they'd already gone into battle together. I shrugged at Massey. "I don't know."

"Do you think any of the party's hosts knew him?"

"I asked Cam Parker. He said he didn't."

"Okay. Thank you, Rachel." He shuffled through some papers on his desk. "I'm going to show you a selection of photos. I want you to tell me if you recognize any of them as the young man from the party."

When he held out the printouts, several pages stapled together, I started sweating. I thought I might puke. I looked over my shoulder at the closed door.

"Rachel?" he said, putting the images under my nose.

I took them. The first page had two images. Neither one was him, so I flipped the page. Same with the second page. There were only four pages, four images left. My fingers were so shaky, I struggle to separate pages two and three.

"Take your time," Massey said.

When I finally managed to flip the page, there he was, the bottom image. "Yep," I said. "Right there." I couldn't take my eyes off the photo. He'd changed clothes. He was wearing a gray sweater. His short brown hair was messy, like they'd pulled him out of bed. He had bags under his eyes. I felt my fist tighten around the paper, crinkling it. Who the fuck was he? Why did he do this? And why didn't he do it to me, the drunk girl in the corner talking to no one? Why Alison? I could have sworn the photo was smiling at me, then it winked. I thrust the pages back in Massey's hand. "Number six."

"Thank you, Rachel." He hit a key on his computer and a printer lit up and shot out a page. "Read this and sign. Then you're free to go."

How was that?" Stannard asked once we were outside the station.

"Awful. It was him. The guy at the party."

"That's good news. They've got him." She pulled my shoulders to face her. She knew I was resisting her words. "You can't go back in time. This is the best outcome we can hope for."

I nodded and we got back into her Subaru.

"I spoke to Lindsay while you were in there. The paper is out, just in the nick of time with the news that a suspect is in custody. They were all concerned about you."

"Even Jen?"

"Remember what I told you last night? We all make mistakes? I think Jen's mistake is that she sometimes forgets that. I said I'd bring you back to the newsroom before they all crash for the day. You up for that?"

"Yeah. Okay."

"I've got ideas I want to share with all of you, too."

When we got to the newsroom, Lindsay, Brie, and Jen were all there waiting. Immediately, Jen shot up from her chair and pulled me in for a hug.

Brie and Lindsay came over to join.

"It was the guy I saw," I said, my head buried in the huddle. All three of them just gripped me harder.

We let go when Stannard said, "Well done getting the paper out this morning."

I wiped my eyes and grabbed a copy off the table. I let the headline sink in. "Alison Petrucci Murdered at Pleasant Pond" by Rachel Nardelli, Lindsay Castle, Jen Pollard, and Brie Lundqvist.

"It took all four of us to write it, Rach," Jen said.

"And the work on the next issue starts now," Stannard said. When we looked at her confused, she added, "I spoke to Professor Altman this morning. I am now your faculty advisor. I've started writing down some thoughts. We have the opportunity to put together a really important issue. There's another press conference this afternoon?"

"At one," Lindsay said.

"Alright. You all need to get some sleep, then we'll meet there. We know this guy wasn't from Denman. We might learn more about what brought him here."

"There's more than one bastard out there," Lindsay said. "I'm just not sure I want to tell this dickhead's story."

"Well, exactly," Stannard said, pointing to Lindsay. "Bretty Whatshisface isn't the point. Let's not make this next issue all about him." She looked at me then. "Let's make it about Alison, about all the women on campus."

I nodded and smiled as best I could. Jen wrapped an arm tight around my shoulder again.

"It's over between me and Cam," I whispered to her.

"I'm sorry," she said.

"No, you're not."

She smiled. "I'm sorry if you're upset."

"Thanks," I said. "It's been coming for a while."

"And let's think about the long game." Stannard was animated, just as she always was in class. She had all of our attention. "Jen, your article about women's first reactions was the best piece in this last issue. Let's keep on that. Let's ask women how they're feeling a week later, a month later, six months later . . . The point is, let's stay on this. Let's stop always talking to the administration, talk to your classmates. You could let the news turn over and go back to writing about nothing but dining hall waste and student council meetings, but who the fuck cares, right?"

"I do not," Brie concurred.

"Rachel, if you're up to it, I think an honest piece to the readers about seeing Alison the night she died could be really powerful. Would you be up for that?"

"I'll try," I said, because in that moment I thought I'd do anything for these women who were standing by me.

"Be bold, write about things you care about, not just the things you think you should. We're not just reporting the facts, here. We're telling stories," Stannard said, then she looked at me once more. "That's what you want to do, right?"

I nodded, yes, and so did Jen, Lindsay, and Brie.

"Good. Okay. Let's tell stories. Let's start with Alison's."

22.

Chances aren't handed out based on who deserves them most. I understand that now. I also understand that you'd be a fool not to take the ones you're given.

That Professor Stannard had my back was possibly the understatement of my young life. For the rest of senior year, she frequently joined our editorial meetings and continued to bring us coffee and donuts on layout nights, but that's not the half of it. After graduation, she helped me put together an application for graduate school and wrote my recommendation, which is how I ended up in the University of Wisconsin–Madison MFA program two years later on a full ride. And why I am able, now, to write these words from my own little home study in small-town Massachusetts, where a local liberal arts college lets me teach others to write, on an adjunct basis, of course. I have a literary agent, a fact that makes my dad so proud he tells everyone who'll listen and some who won't. My first collection of short stories was published by a big house, on a tiny budget, but I got a couple of reviews and no one panned it.

My boyfriend, Alex, has the much less tenuous position of assistant professor of painting at the same school where I teach. *Sexism*, Jen wrote in her last email. I responded, *He actually knows how to paint fresco, which basically nobody else knows how to do. And yes, sexism, too.*

I met Alex, a Pittsburgh native, in Madison. He was a second-year MFA painting candidate when I was a first-year. We both worked at Whole Foods. Even with my full ride, I still needed a job to cover all the other costs of life. Alex, also the son of a teacher, and social worker, was in the same boat. At Whole Foods, Alex mostly worked the register and I largely stocked produce.

"You're the only person working here without a tattoo," was the first thing he said to me.

Stacking red peppers, I inspected him, his arms covered in sleeves of color and black lines so dense I couldn't make out an image. "How do you know?" I said.

"Visible tattoo," he corrected himself. "Let me guess, you actually have Ruth Bader Ginsburg's face on your ankle?"

I lifted up my jeans and flashed him my bare ankles. "My back, actually, life-size."

He smiled. "No way. Me, too."

I smiled back and that was that.

Alex stayed in Madison while I finished my MFA. After, we tried a stint in New York City, but we both hated it. I kept thinking I saw Cam everywhere. I knew he was there, somewhere, among the millions. Despite being long, I just didn't like the odds of bumping into him.

Cam and I had said very little to each other for the rest of our senior year. I'd offered him the chance to write a piece about Alison for the paper if he wanted to, but he'd turned it down. Lindsay, Brie, and Jen were visibly relieved when I passed along his rejection.

What I know of him after college is that he's working at some big bank doing things with other people's money. *Something Something Financial Partners.* I heard he's married.

Lots of things changed after Alison died, particularly at the paper. We didn't have to cover Bretty Whatshisface for very long. He quickly confessed, so there was no need for a trial. We'd learned that before he'd made his way to Denman, he'd been chucked out of UMass Amherst that fall after female students had come forward. His embarrassed parents had told him not to bother coming home, so he'd headed north and found himself at Denman, where he had a friend. The friend had partied with him that night but lost track of him. According to Brett's confession, Alison found him sitting alone outside Cam's dorm and invited him in with her. When they left the party, they'd planned to go get a McDonald's milkshake, but that's when he changed his mind and took a detour to the pond. He'd spotted it on the map when he was headed north. Pleasant Pond. *How pleasant.* He hadn't planned to kill her until she'd said no.

With Brett behind bars, our objectives pivoted to long-form articles on topics that interested us. Jen and I took the lead together, holding focus groups with students about what they wanted to know. And what they wanted to know about was each other. *Who else was scared shitless all the time?* The answer we found: everyone. But, as the year went on, the women became less terrified about losing their lives and started to worry more about finding entry-level jobs with good benefits. "Let them worry about that, it's a good thing," Stannard told me one night when I lost my temper, shouting, "Have they just forgotten all about her?!"

Jen's back in Chicago now. When I was in Madison, we saw a lot of each other. Less so these days because now she has a husband and baby and a law practice defending those who have been wrongly terminated from their jobs. Every email she writes to me, she asks which one of these things she should ditch for her own sanity.

Brie and Lindsay live in Boston, so I see them more. Lindsay scrapes by working for a feminist blog, while Brie keeps them afloat working in admissions at Boston University. Every year I eagerly await her email with the rundown of her least favorite applicant essays. An email that always has the subject line HARD PASS.

Alex and I have been together now for five years. When he's not teaching, he's painting in a studio that costs way too much money, but it's an expense we'd never think of cutting. Every evening when he comes home I fall into him and remind him he's my favorite. He always responds by squeezing me tight and never being the first to let go. The first time I took him back to Waterbury to meet my parents, I was terrified. I hadn't brought anyone home since Cam. For dinner, Mom made vegetarian shepherd's pie and Alex asked her for the recipe, then he proceeded to ask her her thoughts on the midterm elections. She answered at length and my dad and I just sat back with goofy grins on our faces. He and my dad passionately debated National League versus American League rules and clinked beer bottles over several shared views. We've talked about getting married, but the cost of a wedding never seems as important as the cost of his studio, the cost of all my printer paper and ink.

My parents weren't the only people Alex met when he came to visit Waterbury that first time. The second night we were in town, we went to Brad's. It was his only night off from the new restaurant where he was a line cook. He'd just learned how to make gnocchi and Alex and I were his guinea pigs. The year between graduating Denman and going to Wisconsin, Brad and I became good friends. I met him at the Low Down for a beer and we stayed until after midnight because we couldn't stop laughing about Mrs. Morgan's wide panties and the way the gym teacher always scratched his balls whenever he blew his whistle. Brad's partner, Brandy, joined us there, too. He'd finally ditched Callie for good, or maybe she'd ditched him. I've never been very clear on that, but he took it as a chance to start again, to do better, and it seemed like he was really trying. We texted while I was in Madison and he didn't believe me when I told him my new boyfriend was covered in tattoos and worked in a grocery store.

Shut up Nerdelli. He'll be a professor in five years.

When Alex got his job at the college, Brad was the first person I told.

On our final day of Alex's first trip to Waterbury, he met Ethan. Not intentionally. We'd gone to Dunkin' to get some coffees for the long drive back to Wisconsin. We were coming out the door with two giant iced coffees just as Ethan was on his way in. Ethan and I locked eyes in the doorway. Neither one of us moved. I, for one, didn't feel I could. Alex watched us, confused.

The last time I'd seen Ethan was at Alison's funeral. We'd stayed on opposite sides of the room the whole time and never made eye contact.

"Hey. How's it going?" he said, looking at Alex, not me, probably sizing up whether this guy was going to punch him. It was summer, so Alex's skinny, tattooed limbs were on full display under his stripey T-shirt and cutoff shorts. Ethan, then in law school, looked just as muscular as he had years before. I don't think Alex could have taken him and I loved him for that.

"Yeah, fine," I said.

Alex reached out his hand. "Hey, I'm Alex."

"Hey," Ethan said, obviously self-conscious about stating his own name, figuring his reputation had preceded him. "Nice to meet you," he said and pushed past us to the counter.

When we got out to the parking lot, Alex looked at me, puzzled.

"Sorry," I said, overwhelmed by what had just happened and suddenly overcome with a rage that hadn't gripped me in years. "I just need to go back in there for a second. Wait here."

Back inside, I raced up to the counter and grabbed Ethan's arm, pulling him toward me. I knew Alex would be watching. I knew it wouldn't take him long to figure it out.

"What you did," I said. "It really wasn't okay."

Ethan just stared at me, clearly freaked.

"Just tell me you understand that," I said. "Tell me you understand that what you did was wrong."

"I understand," he said, looking down at my hand gripping his biceps. Then, regarding me, he said, "You didn't deserve that."

"No one deserves that!" I said, and that's when it first came to me, the thing that's come to be my strongest belief about this world: *No one deserves anything.* I let go of his arm and I left.

Last year, when my first short story collection came out, I got a surprise in the mail. A manila envelope with the return address, *Petrucci, Allerton Heights.* It had been sent to my agent, who sent it to me. In my little galley kitchen, I stared at it for a full minute before I opened it. Inside was a note from Alison's parents and a short story.

Rachel—

We found this the other day while cleaning out some boxes.
We're finally taking the plunge and moving to Florida.

We both knew just who should have it. She'd have been so proud of you.

Sincerely,
Patricia and Bill

. . .

A week before our trip to the pond, Mrs. Morgan had one final short story assignment for us in English class. It was meant to be inspired by our takeaways from *Where the Red Fern Grows,* the final book in a long year of dog protagonists. I don't mean to ruin the ending, but I'm pretty confident any reader would see it coming a mile off anyway: The main character, this kid, Billy, was gifted two hunting dogs by his grandfather and they become his best friends and go on lots of hunting adventures. The dogs save his life at one point, but of course, they die, because that's what dogs always do in books. Billy is distraught until he finds a red fern growing on the gravesite of the dogs that gives him hope. That day in class, we'd discuss what the red fern symbolized. Once armed with that symbolism, we were to write our own story.

It was David Bullock, in the back of the room, who answered first. When Mrs. Morgan called on him, we all turned around in our seats. He said without his usual sarcasm, "Hope." He liked the book, he continued, because he related to the main character's love of his dogs. His own had died that spring, he said earnestly. Mrs. Morgan's eyes glistened at this. Back in the fall, Alison would have gravitated to this kind of discussion, but hope was a feeling that, for her, had long since flown the coop. She was biting at her cuticles. I watched her wipe a bloody finger on her jeans. Ethan watched, too, and then we looked at each other.

"Yes, hope. That's nearly what I'm looking for, but not quite. Any other thoughts?"

The word *faith* occurred to me, and I thought about raising my hand, then immediately thought again, because no eighth grader at Waterbury Junior High would ever utter that word. Well, Alison would, but she was too busy gnawing on her own thumb.

The room went quiet, until I heard a sucking sound. We all turned around again. Alison's finger was freshly out of her mouth. "Rebirth," she said nonchalantly, without even raising her hand.

Everyone stared at her.

She shifted herself upright. "When Billy sees the red fern growing at his dogs' grave, he believes an angel planted it. He understands that his dogs served a higher purpose. They weren't just hunting dogs. They taught him discipline, strength, and faith. They couldn't live forever, but they lived on inside of him."

Now David Bullock burst out laughing, apparently happy to mock Alison's sincerity only minutes after his own. Several other students joined him.

When Mrs. Morgan shot David a look, they all stopped.

"Go on, Alison."

She continued, her voice bored at having to explain this to a bunch of idiots. "The red fern shows that while the dogs are gone from his life, they live on in spirit, guiding Billy as he becomes a man." She went back to slumping in her chair, and we all thought she was done, until she added, "Bad things happen for a reason. You have to believe that if you ever hope to move on or grow."

The room was silent. We all knew what she was talking about. We must have been wondering just how much personal growth and strength Alison was going to have, given the cruelty she'd endured over the years. All because of us. How many silver linings could one person get?

We spent the final week of class writing our stories. Whenever I was stuck, I'd turn around to look at Alison. She wrote feverishly, stopping only to shake out her hand. I asked Ethan what his story was about, but he told me only that it was about soccer. I can't really remember what mine was about, some bullshit about two kids who get lost in the woods and come out the other end understanding each other better. On the last day of class, Mrs. Morgan asked if anyone wanted to read their story out loud. Nobody raised their hand. For weeks, I wondered what Alison had written. Then, like so many things, the question floated from my mind, never to return.

. . .

Reader, I wept like a baby, right there on the linoleum floor with Alison's story in my hands. It hit me like a ton of bricks just how much I missed her; how unfair it was that our relationship had been cut short. Where was her novel? The one that would have inevitably come out with a bigger budget than my book, more fans, and a stint on the *New York Times* bestseller list? The one that would have made me seethe with envy? Where were her interviews, the book clubs, her appearance on the *Today* show? She'd have had it all the first time around. I felt it so deeply in my bones. I wanted it so badly. For her and for me. She was my rival, and until that moment, it had never occurred to me to love her for that.

I've only ever known myself in relation to Alison. Seven years after her death, nothing has changed. I hope it never does.

The Other Unicorns

By Alison Petrucci

The centaur never warned her it wouldn't last forever, never explained how the other unicorns would get jealous. It hadn't occurred to her until too late. After all, the other unicorns were happy, once again top of the food chain. For months after she grew her horn, Guinevere speared buffalo, wolves, and even a woolly mammoth to feed the others. With the renewed sustenance, they grew stronger. Their own horns went from dull and brittle to sharp diamonds once they'd been nourished. Now they could spear their own food. But then they became ungrateful. They told Guinevere they didn't need her anymore. They told her she'd done enough, that she could rest on her laurels. But she didn't want to be sidelined and she didn't want to rest. Her horn was still the sharpest and the brightest, so bright, in fact, that it blinded her prey before she impaled it. She wanted to keep hunting. She wanted to belong.

Outcast once again, she spent her afternoons by the stream, where the swamps used to be. Since the centaur's visit, the water was flowing again; the fish and frogs had returned. Guinevere hoped the centaur would also return to give her more guidance, but he never did. Lounging there by the stream, she wondered if he was ever truly real. None of the other unicorns had ever seen him. Had it not been for her horn, they would never have believed her story in the first place. They rarely came to the stream, the other unicorns.

They mostly drank from the pond they'd seized from a
pack of gazelles.

When Guinevere returned home from the stream that
evening, the other unicorns were in the forest circling
around the day's kill: ten leopards.

"This is more food than we need," she said.

"I wanted them all," the largest unicorn said, his
fur a shiny white, his mane a lustrous yellow. "The
dominant species can take what they want."

Guinevere shook her head. "This can't be. If we kill
all our prey now, there will be no food in the future."

"Nonsense!" the yellow-maned unicorn shouted.
"Besides, if we ever go hungry again, we can just cast
you out into the swamps. Maybe you'll run into another
centaur!"

All the other unicorns laughed. The idea of a
magical centaur was ridiculous. They'd forgotten all
she did for them.

"You'll see," she said. "By winter there'll be
nothing left to eat."

They scoffed at her before returning their ravenous
eyes to their lunch.

Guinevere left them, found a shady spot under a
tree, and started to nibble at the grass. She found she
preferred it. She didn't want to eat the meat slain by
the other unicorns. Or maybe she was just telling
herself that because she feared they'd never offer
her any. But the grass sustained her. She didn't need
anything else.

That night, she fell asleep under the tree, her head
and horn tucked under her hoof to block out the morning

light. When she woke, she lifted her head and found her horn was still resting between her hoofs. She stood up quickly. How could this be? Did it fall off? She felt no pain. It lay there on the ground, lifeless. She pushed it with her hoof. The sharpest, brightest horn, now a useless shard.

In the distance, she could hear the other unicorns snickering.

"You did this!" she shouted, though she didn't know how.

Their laughter grew stronger.

The yellow-haired unicorn stepped forward from the rest of the pack. "You always thought your horn was better than ours," he said. "We prefer you with no horn," he said. "We prefer you broken."

There was nothing Guinevere could do, nothing she could say, so she turned to leave. She didn't know where to go. She'd never been more than a few miles away from the forest. All she knew was that she wanted to be as far away as possible, that she never, ever wanted to see those unicorns again. Maybe she never wanted to see *any* unicorn ever again. If she didn't belong, she'd get used to being alone. She thought this way for days and weeks as she walked through the forest, over mountains, along beaches, across tundras, until one day she found herself in a prairie. In the vast fields in front of her she saw creatures that looked an awful lot like her, but without horns.

She approached the animals cautiously. If they were anything like unicorns, they wouldn't be friendly.

"Excuse me?" she asked when she was close enough to one who was a rusty brown color with a dark brown mane.

The creature regarded her curiously before saying, "You're pink."

Guinevere looked down at her own legs. "Yes, I suppose I am."

"I have never seen a pink horse before."

"What's a horse?" she inquired.

"I am!" the horse said proudly. "And so are you."

"I am?"

"You look like one to me."

"I thought I was a unicorn."

"And I thought unicorns were a myth. Where's your horn?"

Guinevere told the horse her story.

"Do you want to be a unicorn?" the horse asked.

"No," she said. "I'd be happy to eat the grass in this field, just like you."

"You want to be a pink horse?"

"Yes," she confirmed. "Is there enough grass for me, too?"

The horse looked all around. "Looks like plenty to me. Dig in."

She didn't miss being the Faithful Unicorn; the title was easy to give up. She was still faithful, of course, but now she had faith in herself. That was all she needed, that and some grass to eat and long afternoons running through the prairies with all the other horses, not for any particular reason other than to feel the wind in their manes. Alive.

ACKNOWLEDGMENTS

First, a quick note on truth and facts. I hope that in this book you will find a lot of truth: the truth of what it's like to be a young woman when other young women are being assaulted and killed, the truth of what it's like to try to grapple with this kind of injustice alongside your own fear and then package it all as "news"; the truth of what it's like to be bullied and to become a bully, as well as less universal truths, like the experience of being from a small town in central Maine. But *Until Alison* is a work of fiction. Though my relationship to central Maine, college journalism, and the tragic murder of a classmate might suggest otherwise, this book is very short on facts. Rachel Nardelli is not me and Alison Petrucci is not Dawn, my murdered classmate. Any other characters who might feel familiar to you, well, that's school, isn't it? Also, if you think I was an undergrad in 2016, bless you. You're my new favorite person.

There are so many people who helped me get this book over the finish line. I'll start with my awesome agent, Nicole Aragi, who was patient with this book in moments when I definitely wasn't.

I've been fortunate to have two editors on *Until Alison*: Sally Kim and Tarini Sipahimalani. Both have read countless drafts and helped shape the path of this novel in ways I'd never have discovered on my own. Sally, you deserve all the credit for the first line.

ACKNOWLEDGMENTS

"Nobody deserves anything," is something Sally said to me after she read the first draft. We both agreed this idea was at the heart of the novel. Tarini anchored this novel to the newsroom, and it's so much the better for that. A billion thank-yous to both of you.

Thank you to Ivan Held for being this book's cheerleader and for loving just how "Maine" it is. I do apologize for getting Tom Petty stuck in your head, though rest assured, Celine Dion's been stuck in mine for years.

I have to give a shout-out to the 2004 staff of *The Colby Echo*. This book wouldn't exist without you. In particular, Kaitlin, Liz, and Maura, who were right there with me when suddenly it seemed we were real journalists and I, personally, felt completely unprepared. And a big shout-out to my wonderful friend and *Echo* colleague, Steven Weinberg, who has encouraged this book since I told him I was writing it. Some of my favorite memories of the newsroom are you and I laughing at God knows what.

I write always with music, so music permeates everything I write. A shout-out to all the musicians who are referenced in the book, but in particular to R.E.M.'s Michael Stipe. My tastes may have changed a lot since junior high, but you've always been right there with me.

A lifetime of thanks to Jennifer Finney Boylan. It's late nights listening to you and my dad talk that taught me heartbreak and humor are never far apart. May everyone have someone in their life who teaches them this kind of perspective. Thank you for letting this smart-ass kid hang out with you.

And to my brother-in-law, Steve, who had to reteach me algebra.

Thank you to everyone at Aragi and Putnam: Kelsey Day, Alexis Welby, Ashley McClay, and Katie Grinch; everyone in publicity, marketing, design, and copyediting. Thank you for knowing all the things I don't and taking the time to explain them to me.

ACKNOWLEDGMENTS

Thank you to Emily, my sister, for the enduring support and endless publishing world knowledge. Thank you for being my primary audience and laughing at my jokes.

Thank you to my parents, to whom this book is dedicated. Two of the kindest and most supportive people on this earth. They are this book's moral compass and mine.

And Tom. In the words of my musical hero, Michael Stipe, "You Are the Everything."

Lastly, not a thank-you, just a final acknowledgment to Dawn Rossignol. Dawn—I never got to know you, but I'll never forget you.

Photograph of the author © Tom Butler

KATE RUSSO is the author of *Super Host*. She grew up in Maine but now divides her time between there and the United Kingdom. Also an artist, she exhibits in both the US and UK.

katerusso.com
RussoKate